D'Artagnan

by

Alexandre Dumas

British Library Cataloguing-in-Publication Data
A catalogue record for this book is available from the
British Library

Contents

PREFACE

This story augments and incorporates without alteration a fragmentary manuscript whose handwriting has been identified as that of Alexandre Dumas, and as such authenticated by Victor Lemasle, the well known expert of Paris. So far as can be learned, it has remained unpublished hitherto.

No romantic tale can be attached to this manuscript, though one is tempted to weave a fantastic and plausible prologue after the fashion of Rider Haggard. The Thounenin will, whose existence in a French collection of old documents possibly suggested the story to the author, has been secured and is in the possession of the publisher. This sheet of old vellum, stamped with the arms of Lorraine and signed by Leonard, hereditary grand tabellion of the province, is in itself a curiosity.

In here presenting a complete story, the writer has no apologies to offer. Nothing can be learned about this tale from the life or literary remains of Dumas. The child about whom it centers will be recognized as the Vicomte de Bragelonne, hero of the later novels of the series, whose parentage is very plainly set forth by Dumas in "Twenty Years After." The publisher, who is the owner of the manuscript in question, is of course fully informed as to what portion of this novel is from the pen of Dumas, and what from the typewriter of

H. Bedford-Jones. Ann Arbor, April 1, 1928

CHAPTER 1

INTRODUCING A QUEEN, A SOLDIER, AND A ROGUE

On the second Thursday in July, 1630, the ancient city of Lyon had become the second capital of France. Louis XIII and Cardinal de Richelieu, who had been with the army in Savoy, were returned to Grenoble; the court and the two queens had come to Lyon. Paris was empty as the grave, and between Lyon and Grenoble fluctuated all court business, since Marie de Medici, the queen-mother, acted as regent while Louis XIII was on campaign.

On the south side of the Place des Terreaux, overlooking the Saone to the left and the Rhone to the right, stood the vast convent of the Dames Benedictines. This massive building, of which today only the directory remains, rang loud with voices and glittered bravely with gay costumes and weapons. Musketeers guarded the high gates, coaches thundered in the paved courtyard, and at the river-bank below the fair green gardens waited gilded barges; in truth, at this moment two queens of France were residing within its walls.

In an upper room, beside a tiny fire that burned in the wall-hearth to dispel the chill of morning, sat a woman who read a letter in some agitation. Despite the tapestry adorning the walls, and the handsome curtains of the bed, the room bore an air of severity and plainness which spoke of the conventual surroundings.

The woman who sat in this room was about thirty; that is to say, at the height of womanly perfection; the velvety softness of her skin, her powdered chestnut hair, and her beautiful hands, combined to make her appear much younger. Pride mingled with a gentle sadness in her features; a certain lofty majesty in her mien was tempered by kindliness and sweetness. Her eyes were quite brilliant, yet now a cloudy phantom of terror was gathering in their liquid depths, as she read the disturbing phrases of this letter:

"Though it grieves me to trouble you, yet you must be placed on guard. Knowing this goes direct to your hand, I write plainly and trust you to destroy it at once.

"In 1624, six years ago, one Francois Thounenin was a cure at Dompt; he there made his will. In the following year he was transferred to Aubain, near Versailles, by the influence of my family, of which he was a relation. Two years ago he died in this same village of Aubain. Before dying, being on a visit to Dompt,he made a codicil to his will; it was incorporated with the original document deposited at Nancy. This addition, made in the fear of death, concerned a certain child. We knew nothing of the codicil naturally. Thounenin died soon after it was made, and learning of this, we arranged for the child.

"This will has been taken from the archives. The fact was learned at once, pursuit was begun and I have every reason to believe that the document will be recovered and destroyed. That it concern you were impossible; yet I fear, my dear friend, lest it be made to concern you! I am closely watched, my friends are suspect, it is difficult for me to do anything.

"If possible, send me a messenger whom you can trust. I may have no other chance to write you by a sure hand, yet it is imperative that you be kept informed of danger or -- of security. Adieu! Destroy this.

Marie."

The woman who wrote this letter was Marie de Rohan, Duchesse de Chevreuse, the most able and determined of Richelieu's enemies. The woman who read it was Anne of Austria, Queen of France, the most beautiful and helpless of Richelieu's victims. When she had read the letter, the queen let it fall upon the flames in the fireplace; in another moment it had become a black ash lifting upward on the draught. Her head falling on her hand, the queen fell into agitated reverie.

"Good God, what can this mean -- what is it about -- what will they attempt next against me or my friends?" murmured Anne of Austria. Her beautiful eyes were suffused with tears. "And what can I do -- whom can I send -- in what person can I trust, when I am allowed to see no one in private except by express permission?"

At this instant a tap at the door roused her, caused her to efface all trace of emotion. Into the room came Dona Estafania, the only one of her Spanish attendants now remaining at her side. She curtseyed to the queen from the doorway.

"Your Majesty, the courier is here for the despatches. Madame the Queen-mother requests that if yours are ready, they be sent instantly."

"They are lying on my secretary," said the queen. Guessing from the formal address that the messenger was waiting, she added: "This courier -- he is at hand?"

"Yes, madame," said Dona Estafania. "He is M. d'Artagnan, a gentleman of the Musketeers --"

"Ah!" murmured the queen. "Wait --"

At the mention of this name, a swift pallor leaped in her cheeks and then was gone in a suffused red half concealed by her rouge. Perhaps she remembered this name; perhaps other days came before her eyes in this moment; perhaps the memory of dead Buckingham pierced her sharply.

"He is alone?" she asked quickly, impulsive

"Yes madame."

"Ask him to enter. Get the letters. Close the door. You may remain."

Next instant d'Artagnan, booted and spurred knelt above the queen's hand and touched it with his lips. Smiling she looked down at his eager face, brimming with devotion.

"Artagnan -- you depart for Grenoble?

"With despatches for His Majesty, madame."

"Mine are ready -- give them to me, Dona Estafania, if you please."

From her lady she took the sealed letters and handed them to d'Artagnan, who bowed and placed them in his pocket.

"Monsieur," said the queen, her voice a trifle unsteady, "would you serve me?"

D'Artagnan looked at her in astonishment.

"With my life, madame!" he exclaimed, eagerly.

"I believe you," she said. "Indeed, I think that I have some reason to believe you. I am accused of forgetting many things, M. d'Artagnan -- but there are many things I only seem to forget." Once more a slight pallor came into her face. "M. de Bassompierre has declared openly that he serves the king, his master -- and holds it to be the duty of a gentleman to recognize such service as superior to any other."

D'Artagnan bowed, and his eyes flashed a little.

"Madame," he responded vibrantly, "thank God I am M. d'Artagnan, and not M. de Bassompierre! A Marshal of France serves the king. A simple gentleman serves a lady. If Your Majesty has the least need of service -- impart it to me, I implore you! It is the greatest happiness of my life to lay my service at your feet, holding you second only to God Himself!"

Truth shone in the eyes of the young man, sincerity rang in his voice.

"Ah, M. d'Artagnan!" exclaimed the queen softly. "If only you were in the place of M. de Bassompierre!"

"Then were I unfortunate, madame, since he is with the army and not here."

The queen caught a warning gesture from Dona Estafania. Time was short.

"Good." From her finger she took a ring and extended it. "Take this to Dampierre, give it into the hand of Madame de Chevreuse, tell her I sent you. That is all. She will give you a verbal message for me, I think. Go when you can, as you can obtain leave; return when you can. I am powerless to help you -- if I tried, you would fall under suspicion --"

D'Artagnan came to his knee, kissed the fingers she proffered him, and rose.

"Madame," he said simply, "my life is yours, my honor is yours, my devotion is yours! For the trust you confide in me, I thank you."

The next moment, he was gone. The Queen relaxed in her chair, trembling a little, looking at her one faithful woman with frightened eyes.

"Ah !" she murmured. "I acted too impulsively, perhaps -- I have done wrong --"

"You have not done wrong to trust that young man, madame," said Dona Estafania. "His uniform answers for his courage; his face answers for his devotion. Be at ease. He will go to Dampierre."

The queen bowed her head.

D'Artagnan, whose horse was waiting saddled in the courtyard, had no time to see Athos, who was at the Musketeers' quarters. The letters from Anne of Austria and Marie de Medici, the queen-mother, were of imperative haste, admitted of not a moment's delay -- their importance might be judged from the fact that they were confided to an officer of the guards instead of to the post courier. D'Artagnan, therefore, had no choice but to mount and ride for Grenoble, where the king and the cardinal were stopping. It was now past noon; he must reach Grenoble before the following midnight.

In five minutes he was leaving the convent in the Place des Terreaux; in ten minutes he was passing the gates of Lyon.

As he rode, it seemed to him that the very few moments in the chamber of the queen must have been a dream -- but no! He wore a ring to prove them real, and glanced at it. The ring was a large sapphire surrounded by brilliants; obviously, it was no ring for a cavalier to be wearing. Beneath his shirt, d'Artagnan wore a scapulary which his mother had confided to him upon her deathbed; as he rode, he loosened the chain of this scapulary, threaded the ring upon it, and replaced it. As he had said, the service of the queen came indeed next to the service of God.

"Well, I have leave due me -- I can ask for it, take Athos, depart for Dampierre!" he thought with eagerness. "How things work out, eh? Excellent! And to think that I have seen her, have twice kissed her hand, have looked into her eyes -- to think that she remembered me, after all! That she had not forgotten! Ah, damned cardinal that you are, to persecute this angel from heaven!"

He rode on, blind and deaf to all around him, lost in an ecstasy of blissful reverie.

France was at war with the Empire -- with Spain, Italy, Savoy, with all the countries that comprised the empire of the Hapsburgs. Richelieu and the king, who had been together with the army and had conquered all Savoy, were returned to noble; the two queens had brought the court to Lyon, and Louis XIII besought his mother to come to Grenoble, hoping thus to patch up the bitter enmity between her and Richelieu. Marie Medici refused, and this refusal was being taken to Grenoble by d'Artagnan.

Since he was not riding his own horses, he changed at every post-house and spurred hard; because of the rains, the roads were in places almost impassable, and despite all his effforts, d'Artagnan could not make great speed. His consolation was that another in his place would have made no speed whatever.

When darkness fell on the following day, he was still six leagues from Grenoble, had been unable to get a fresh horse at the last station, and was in despair.

"Die, then," he muttered, seeing a long rise ahead, and put in his spurs. "Die if you must, but reach Grenoble ere midnight!"

Thin fantastic moonlight touched and glimmered on the dark Lizere river to the right, fille the trees to the left with strange shadows, broke clear and white on the sharp dust of the high ahead. The road pitched upward here, then broke down through a long descending ravine flanked by dark tree-masses.

At the crest of the rise, d'Artagnan drew rein; next instant, a cry of dismay came to his lips. The quivering gasp breaking from the horse, the animal's terrible shudder, told him the truth -- the poor beast was dying on its feet.

Abruptly, the sharp crack of a pistolet burst from the darkness ahead. This was followed by the fuller roar of an arquebus, and the loud cry of a man in mortal agony.

The cavalier reached for a pistolet and would have reined in, but the dying horse was now plunging forward, bit in his teeth, breath whistling, hooves thundering down the declivity and re-echoing from the trees. Sharp cries of alarm sounded ahead, men called one to another, then came the clatter of hastily departing riders.

"Robbers, pardieu!" muttered d'Artagnan, peering forward. "And they must have caught someone just ahead of me --"

His horse quivered, uttered one strange and awful cry, then came to an abrupt halt with feet braced wide apart, head hanging to the very road, its whole body trembling. The poor beast was dying.

D'Artagnan dismounted. He perceived that his approach had frightened the robbers from their victim. Ahead of him in the open moonlight a man's figure was outstretched; he still gripped in one hand the reins of his horse, standing over him. The horse turned its head and gazed questioningly at the approaching d'Artagnan.

The man on the ground was senseless. D'Artagnan hastened to him, disengaged the reins from his hand, raised his head. The unfortunate traveller had been shot through the body; his clothes were drenched with blood, and be was dying. The moon-light brought out the details of his face, and his rescuer could not repress a gesture of repugnance; this face was brutal, treacherous, with heavy black brows meeting above the eyes.

"A lackey in his master's clothes," muttered d'Artagnan. "Or a rascal --"

As though the sound of human speech had penetrated his brain, the dying man opened his eyes and stared vacantly upward. His lips moved in faint words.

"I have discovered everything -- everything! Bassompierr -- du Vallon -- that false priest d'Herblay -- the evidence! The document was sent to London for safety -- it will reach Paris in a week -- we have them all! And above them all, she -- she herself --"

The voice failed and died. At these names, d'Artagnan started violently. His face changed. One would have said that sudden terror had come into his very soul.

"Du Vallon -- Porthos!" he muttered. "And d'Herblay -- Aramis! Ah,ah -- what is this, then? Is it possible? Am I dreaming?

Abruptly, the dying man clutched at his sleeve, tried to come erect. Now his voice rang out in anguished tones, clear and loud with the unmistakeable accent of death.

"Pere Joseph!" he cried out. "I can report everything -- Betstein is the guardian of the child! A false birth certificate was forged by the priest Thounenin -- the child is in the abbey of the Benedictines at St. Saforin. The prior knows the ring -- I had the copy made! I have a letter from d'Herblay -- he was wounded, du Vallon was killed -- took papers -- His Eminence must know -- send Montforge to Paris -- to Paris --"

The man coughed terribly, groaned, then relaxed from

the spasm. Perfect consciousness came to him. He fastened wild eyes upon the face above.

"Where am I?" he muttered. "Who are you?"

"I am M. d'Artagnan, lieutenant of --"

"Ah, Jesus!" groaned the man, and shuddered as death tore out his soul.

D'Artagnan rose. In one hand he held a plain gold seal-ring, incised with a device unknown to him. In the other hand he held two letters and a small packet of papers, sealed heavily. He looked at the seal in the moonlight; it was the seal Aramis had habitually used.

Aramis -- Porthos! Bewildered, dazed, doubting his own senses, d'Artagnan looked at the two letters. One he could not read, but he could recognize the tiny, perfect, beautiful script of Aramis. The other was a heavy scrawl, its words standing out clearly enough in the rays of the moon; the short message covered a whole sheet of paper, so black and pregnant was the writing:

"M. l'Abbe' d'Herblay; Write me no more. See me no more. Think of me no more. To you, I am dead for ever. Marie Michon."

"What the devil!" exclaimed d'Artagnan. "Marie Michon -- that's the lady-love of Aramis, then! Chevreuse, no less. Oh, fiend take it all -- what I have uncovered here?"

He became pale as death, recalling what the dying man had said. Porthos dead, -- Aramis wounded! Athos had received a letter from Aramis only a month previously; Aramis was then bound on a journey to Lorraine for reasons unstated. Porthos had left the service, had married, was somewhere in the provinces.

With a swift motion, d'Artagnan tore the letter of Marie Michon into tiny fragments and cast them on the breeze. The packet he stowed carefully away -- he must destroy this sacred packet, still under the seal of Aramis. The first letter he studied again but could not read in the pale moon-light, and this he pocketed also. The ring, he slipped on his finger.

"Singular!" he reflected with agitation. "What secret did this miserable spy carry to the grave? Bassompierre, the greatest noble in France, lover of a thousand women -- my poor stupid, honest Porthos -- my crafty, shrewd, intriguing Aramis? And she -- she herself -- what did the rascal mean by those words?"

A terrible conjecture flashed across his mind. The dead man was obviously one of the spies of the silent Capuchin who was Richelieu's secretary, who had organized his system of espionage, without whose advice Richelieu seldom acted -- his Gray Eminence, Pere Joseph le Clerc, Sieur du Tremblay.

"She herself!" D'Artagnan repeated the words as though stupefied by their import. "Above them all -- she herself!" His tone, more than his words -- what had he discovered, then? To what woman did he refer? Who is the child? Who is Betstein?" He passed a hand across his brow; it came away wet with cold perspiration. "Well, at least he spoke the truth -- he has now discovered everything in life and death itself!"

He turned, glanced around, went to his own horse. The poor beast stood in the same fashion, feet wide apart, head low, dying on foot. D'Artagnan took from the saddlebags the despatches he carried, thrust one of the pistols through his sash, then went to the horse of the dead spy.

"An excellent animal!" he observed. "Evidently, this is one of the dispensations of providence the clerics so often mention. That rascal fell among other rascals at the exact moment my horse gave out; he obligingly told me his mind and went his way to the greatest of all discoveries. I step into his stirrups -- and my letters reach the king by midnight, after all! Decidedly Providence is tonight acting much more gracefully toward Louis XIII than toward his minister of war, the amiable Richelieu!"

D'Artagnan mounted. But, finding himself in the seat of a much taller person, it was necessary to adjust the stirrups.

"Now," he said reflectively, as he worked at the leathers, "if the good Athos were in my place, he might think it his duty to carry word of all this to his Gray Eminence -- hm! It would be most polite of me, no doubt -- but what the devil can be in this letter from Aramis? It's not like our clever Aramis to confide his neck to a letter! Why is the name of Porthos linked with that of Bassompierre? Most mysterious of all, who is Betstein, and whose child does he guard in conjunction with a Benedictine prior? Undoubtedly, M. de Richelieu might answer all these questions but I prefer to seek elsewhere."

Again recurred to his mind those significant words: "above them all, she -- she herself!" It was as though he spoke of the highest of women -- but no, that were leaping too far at a venture! Besides, there were two queens in France. More likely some intrigue of Bassompierre was concerned. The marshal had just emerged from a scandalous three-year-suit before the high court of Rouen, and his intrigues with great ladies had resulted in more than one pledge of affection. At this thought, d'Artagnan brightened.

"Vivadiou! I'm making much out of little." He glanced down at the dead man, crossed himself, and gathered up his reins with a sigh. "If only you had uttered a few words more, my good rascal! However, I give you thanks -- your secret is safe with me. Away now -- to Grenoble!"

And driving in his spurs, he was gone in a whirl of moonlit dust.

CHAPTER II

PROVING THAT NEITHER KING NOR MINISTER RULED FRANCE

In the summer of 1630, all France was bubbling with war, treason and civil strife.

True, La Rochelle was fallen, the Protestants were crushed, England was brought to terms -- this was yesterday. Today, Richelieu was leading the army in Savoy to victories against the Empire; yet he was standing on a precipice, and at his back all the winds of France were gathering to blow him over the verge.

He was just discovering the fact, as he was just learning that the deadliest enemies of France were within her frontiers.

Louis XIII, son to Henry of Navarre, was nominal ruler of France. Marie de Medici, widow of Henry of Navarre, could not forget that her husband had actually ruled France. Armand du Plessis, the virtual ruler of France, intended that France should rule Europe. Here were three sides of a triangle -- extremely unequal sides.

Louis was a king at once cruel, jealous, and ambitious to be known to posterity as "The Just." He feared the personal power of Richelieu the man, trusted the statecraft of Richelieu the Cardinal, and did not hesitate to place his armies in the band of Richelieu the Minister. The king was afraid of his mother, detested his brother the Duc d'Orleans, distrusted the great nobles about him, and was wise enough to let responsibility rest on worthier shoulders. And the queen-mother also hated Richelieu furiously and vindictively. She hated him for having stripped her of power and destroyed her influence over the king; she hated him for carrying war into her beloved Italy; she hated him because he did well what she had done so badly; she hated him because he was Richelieu and she was Marie de Medici. And most of all she could not forget that in the beginning it was she herself who had raised him from obscurity. So around the queen-mother gathered all the festering rancor of enmity, supported by the princes of the blood and the nobles of France.

Richelieu, on the third side, began to realize his insecurity. He had subdued the queen-mother, humiliated the queen, Anne of Austria, crushed the Vendomes, stamped out the Huguenots, and driven Chevreuse into exile. He was the victor, but he was not the master. The storm of envy, hatred and malice was checked, but it was secretly gathering force against him.

The sole strength of Richelieu was that none guessed his strength. The princes had lands and wealth and rank; the great nobles bad positions of power; the Duc d'Orleans, heir to the throne, had immunity; Richeiieu had only a man, a simple Capuchin friar. It was keenly significant that this Pere Joseph was confidential secretary to the cardinal, while his brother, M. Charles du Tremblay, commanded the Bastille.

This friar was the only man in France who wanted nothing, who refused everything, who could be given neither reward nor place because he accepted none. He served Richelieu; this was his sole honor, dignity and ambition. Nothing was done in France without his approval, and everything that he advised was brought to pass. The minister depended on the friar's diplomacy, the cardinal depended on the friar's sagacity, the general depended on the friar's knowledge of men and armies; the cardinal who wore the red robe depended on the friar who wore the gray robe.

In the quarters occupied by Richelieu at Grenoble, these two men were alone together. This Pere Joseph who had caused the siege of La Rochelle, who had written a commentary on Machiavelli, and who was the mainstay of his master, was large, well-built, and marked by smallpox. Once his hair had been flaming red; learning that the king had an aversion for this color, he became white before his thirtieth year. His eyes were small, brilliant, filled with hidden fires.

Richelieu, far more imposing in appearance, was at this time at the height of his physical powers. He was handsome, and knew the worth of this quality to the full; he was proud, and used pride as a mask when need was; above all, he was sagacious -- and his sagacity was best proven by the fact that his relations with his secretary were never ambiguous, never strained, never open to misunderstanding from either side. Just now his aristocratic features were thoughtful; the penetrating gaze he bent upon Pere Joseph was disturbed and even melancholy.

"My friend and father," he said, "I believe that affairs are too threatening for me to remain away from Paris. The queen has not provided an heir to the throne; intrigues are rife, the king insists on joining the army. I shall plead ill-health, give the command to Crequy or Bassompierre, and return to the capital."

Pere Joseph was used to these sudden decisions.

"Excellent, Your Eminence, excellent!" he returned in his dry, phlegmatic voice. "The king's confessor writes that you should take this action. It would be your best possible course. Unfortunately, it would not particularly advance the interests of France."

"Do the interests of France then demand that I should be deposed from the ministry?"

Pere Joseph, who had been writing at a secretary, pushed away the papers from before him and folded his lean, powerful hands on the desk, and regarded the cardinal.

"Your Eminence has been too much occupied in the field, perhaps," he said smoothly, "to take thought to other matters. Have I your permission to expound them?"

"Proceed, preacher!" Smiling, Richelieu settled himself in his chair.

"Then consider." The voice of the Capuchin came as from a machine, unemotional, steady, inflexible. "In making war upon the House of Austria, as we now do, Your Eminence picked up the threads of policy dropped when Henri IV died; very good! Personally, I consider that the welfare of France demands that you retain your present position. I argue from this base."

Richelieu inclined his head slightly, as though to signify

that this base was entirely acceptable to him. The Capuchin went on.

"Those who would depose you -- the two queens, and certain great houses -- are more bitter enemies of France than her external foes; because, like the Duc de Rohan, they set personal affairs before the good of their country. It becomes plain, Monseigneur, that France must no longer be a house divided against itself."

"Provided these enemies of Prance can hurt her."

"They can. With Your Eminence leading the army, one serious reverse would be the signal for them to strike."

"Granted," said Richelieu, "if there were danger of such a reverse."

"Within two months it will happen."

The Cardinal gave his secretary a look of startled astonishment.

"Casale is under siege by the Imperial forces," continued Pere Joseph. "Our relief army is insufficient; the city must infallibly be taken. This will be a serious blow to France, and a more serious blow to Your Eminence. A certain policy has occurred to me," and he touched his pile of papers, "toward which end I have drafted a scheme for your approval."

"Tell it to me," said Richelieu. "The ear is less liable to deceit than the eye."

"Very well. In the first place, something occurs next month which everyone in France has forgotten. The Imperial Diet will meet at Ratisbon."

"That I know," and Richelieu frowned slightly, intently.

"What of it?

"By law, the Emperor is strictly forbidden to make peace except with the approval of the Diet."

"Peace? Who has talked of making peace?" exclaimed Richelieu.

"I trust Your Eminence will find it worthy of consideration. I have every reason to believe the Emperor would find an immediate peace with France highly acceptable -- if the matter were rightly presented at Ratisbon. Everything depends on the presentation."

"It would," said Richelieu drily. "The Diet would refuse."

"Your pardon -- the Diet could be made to accept," said Pere Joseph. "On the other hand, I find that Gustavus Adolphus, who is the deadliest foe of Austria --"

Richelieu started. "The arch-heretic! The arch-enemy of Holy Church!"

"And the arch-general of all Europe," added the Capuchin. "He might welcome a treaty of alliance with France, provided it were rightly presented -- as before. In other words, France makes peace with the House of Austria on the one hand, and on the other, an alliance with the bitterest foe of the House of Austria."

"And gains -- what?" demanded Richelieu. He knew well that the four secretaries of Pere Joseph were closely in touch with the entire political and religious affairs not only of Europe, but of the whole world.

"Time to order her internal affairs, Monseigneur. A humiliating reverse in the field is avoided. By the end of summer, the Minister is in Paris again -- and none too soon for the welfare of France. His Majesty insists on being with the army. The army is notoriously unhealthy, even now it is being decimated by fever and sickness."

"Ah!" Richelieu's brow knotted. "Ah! If the King should die --"

"God forbid!" exclaimed the Capuchin piously. "If the King should die, then Monsieur his brother would rule France."

Richelieu stared at him in a singular manner. The Duc d'Orleans on the throne, meant the Cardinal de Richelieu in the Bastille.

"And all these possibilities," said the minister slowly, "might be averted --"

"By proper attention to the sitting of the Diet at Ratisbon."

"The King would never consent."

"Let His Majesty command the victorious campaign in Savoy, and he will consent to anything. Besides, the influence of the queen, Anne of Austria, will here come to our help."

Richelieu remained thoughtful for a space. He began to perceive the value of this advice, though he knew that any treaty with Austria must be galling in its terms. Peace with the Emperor would mean external peace for France --

"Such a peace could not endure," he muttered.

"Monseigneur, we ask only that it endure until spring."

"True."

"Also, no one in France would believe that peace could be

obtained. And it could only be obtained by the right man."

"True again. We have the right man -- Bassompierre. He has served as ambassador to Spain and England," murmured the cardinal reflectively. "He is wealthy, popular, of the highest attainments. He is beloved on all sides --"

"Greatly beloved," corrected the other drily, and Richelieu smiled. Bassompierre had been the rival of Henry IV more than once; and if the Duchesse de Chevreuse had seduced princes, Bassompierre had seduced queens.

"True, Bassompierre is attached to the queen-mother," said Richelieu slowly. "And --"

"He is the second captain in France, Your Eminence being the first."

"But he is not ambitious. He would perform this duty admirably."

"Most admirably, Monseigneur, since he has been secretly married to the Princesse de Conti."

"What!"

Richelieu started out of his chair, stared at Pere Joseph with incredulous eyes.

"The sister of Guise? Impossible! Secretly married?"

"To the princess who bore him a son some years ago."

The minister lowered himself into his chair again, almost with a gasp, as he perceived the gulf opening before him. Bassompierre, marshal of France, who laughed at dukedoms and was content to be Colonel General of the Swiss Guards, content to be the greatest gambler, lover and spendthrift in France -- if this man were no longer content, then beware!

King's favorite, devoted to the two queens, yet fully trusted by Richelieu, the Marshal de Bassompierre was the first and most powerful gentleman of France, ever holding aloof from intrigue and plot. Now that he was secretly married to the sister of the Duc de Guise, all was changed. He was instantly suspect. The princes had won him over to their side.

Bassompierre," went on Pe~re Joseph, "has in his house six caskets of letters, and the keys of these caskets never leave him. This, Monseigneur, is significant. He is a Lorrainer by birth. His influence is extraordinary. True, he has never been ambitious, and therefore has never been feared. But now --"

"But now!" The red minister roused himself. "I see. Who, then, can go to Ratisbon? Who posesses the acumen to fool the German princes, play with them, wind them around his finger?"

"That is for Your Eminence to say, if the proposal meets with your approval."

Richelieu gave him a sharp look. "Peace is imperative?"

"At any cost, Monseigneur."

"Very well. You shall go."

Pere Joseph assumed intense surprise. "Monseigneur, you jest! In my simple robe, to present myself among princes, electors, ambassadors, illustrious men? No, no! I am too humble a person for such a duty."

It was characteristic of Richelieu that he would hear this man to the end, would weigh his advice and judgment, would accept his findings -- and then exercise his own eagle swoop of authority and thought.

The revelation of Bassompierre's marriage to the Princesse de Conti had startled him, alarmed him, roused him. That Bassompierre had been her lover, that she had borne him a son, meant nothing; that he was now allied to the House of Guise meant everything. With a flash, Riche]ieu perceived how urgent was the danger enveloping him.

Everything else must be abandoned; he must lay aside his statecraft, and bend every effort to meet the threat from inside.

He knew only too well that the envoy to Ratisbon must be a consummate juggler, or all was lost. The German princes, who dreamed of crushing France, would not readily consent; Louis XIII, who dreamed of being another Henri IV, would not readily consent. Richelieu could handle the business at home -- but the man handling it at Ratisbon must be another Richelieu abroad.

"Enough!" he exclaimed. "My friend, you go to Ratisbon. Bulart de Leon, now Ambassador to Switzerland, will go as envoy; you'll be associated with him, and the work will be placed in your hands. Let Bulart de Leon glitter among the princes -- let the written treaty come from your pen and brain. You are the man."

"As Your Excellency desires," said the Capuchin humbly.

His eyes glowed with a flame at thought of the intrigue to pass between his hands at Ratisbon. This man, who could read the very heart and thought of other men around him, could have asked nothing greater than the chance to hoodwink all the princes of Germany.

"And the treaty with Gustavus Adolphus?"

"Is in your hands as well," said Richelieu impatiently. "Come! This means that you'll be at Ratisbon for weeks, perhaps months; you must depart at once, and I'll secure full authority for you.

Fortunately, Bulart de Leon is now at Lyon with the court. We must send for him. But -- but --"

The minister's voice died away, his energetic eye became thoughtful; his long, slender fingers tapped on his chair-arm. He had always apprehended that in any approaching crisis, which would certainly come sometime, from some unexpected angle, with hidden enemies exerting every intrigue against him, he would be cut off from the man who had arrested the Marshal d'Ornano, humbled the Duc d'Orleans, discovered the conspiracy of Chalais, and who was openly accused of having caused the murder of Buckingham. How could he dispense with this man, at this moment?

When Richelieu was roused, his decisions were swift.

"My friend," and his eye flashed once more, "everything hinges on Ratisbon; it is in your hands. You'll be given full powers to sign for France. As for matters here at home -- well! The one thing is settled. Let us now proceed to other things. Your advice?"

"Is simplicity itself." The brilliant eyes of the friar, alight with exultation, once more became narrowed, thoughtful, penetrating. His steady and inflexible voice showed no emotion; he might have been expounding theological points which admitted of no dispute. "Only one person can dismiss ministers -- the king."

"Granted."

"Therefore, the king must not dismiss you. If necessary, you must dismiss yourself."

"Understood."

"He must realize clearly that his power depends upon you."

"He does."

"You must become friendly with the queen-mother."

"Impossible. Marie de Medici will hate me to the death."

"You must love your enemies. She is great, because another queen is allied with her -- the Queen of France. The Austrian and the Italian are together against you"

A hint of pain shot through the eyes of Richelieu. He had humiliated the Queen of France, he had humbled Anne of Austria -- but he loved the woman.

"Marie de Medici is the central point of enmity against me," he said slowly. "She would like to see Gaston d'Orleans on the throne. While they live -- "

"Gaston is a greedy fool," said Pere Joseph. "He yields to bribes."

"Marie de Medici yields to nothing."

"What does not yield, can be broken," said Pere Joseph, and now the cardinal looked at him attentively, expectantly. "Louis does not love his mother, but he fears her. He does not love his queen, but he listens to her. Your safety demands two things; first, that the queen-mother and the queen be separated. Second, that the king be left without these insidious voices, always whispering against you. It is possible to exile Marie de Medici. But with Anne of Austria --"

Richelieu lifted his head, and his glance was stern.

"What do you dare suggest?" he demanded in a sharp, angry voice. "When one speaks of the Queen of France --"

"One speaks of a woman, Monseigneur," said the other, and added: "who hates you."

There was a little silence. Richelieu was struggling with himself, but these last words stung him deeply. He knew that behind all this advice was something definite.

"A woman who hates," he said gloomily, "cannot be reconciled."

"She can be deprived of all power to injure, now or later."

"Fh?" The cardinal started slightly, and his gaze rested on the Capuchin for a moment. Then he made a slight gesture as of assent. Another man would have hesitated, but Pere Joseph obeyed the tacit command.

"By chance, Your Eminence, my attention was drawn to the royal abbey of Benedictines at St. Saforin," he said in his inexorable voice. "The prior of this abbey is one Dom Lawrence, of the Luynes family, an excellent man, most discreet. When M. de Bassompierre was Ambassador to England, Dom Lawrence accompanied him as chaplain. This, if you will recall, was before the taking of La Rochelle, while the Duke of Buckingham still lived."

At this name, Richelieu's face slowly drained of its color. Before him seemed to rise the phantom of dead Buckingham, that handsome, proud, reckless man, who doomed to disaster everyone and everything he touched. The minister made an impulsive gesture, as though exorcising this spectre. The terrible look he bent upon Pere Joseph would have made a prince tremble, for a prince would have had much to lose. Pere Joseph, who had nothing to lose, received it calmly.

"Be careful, my friend," said the minister in a low voice. "I do not choose to hear idle conjectures."

"Monseigneur," returned the Capuchin imperturbably, "I have only facts to offer. When one speaks the truth alone, the care belongs to God. If you desire me to be silent -- "

"Speak," said Richelieu.

Pere Joseph laid his hand upon anumber of written reports, enclosed in a vellum cover.

"I utter only the truth, here written, Your Eminence; I leave conjectures to you alone!: Imprimis, Dom Lawrence is prior of St. Saforin, at which place is a school for the children of the provincial nobility. In this school is a boy of about four years. This boy was left with the prior last year by a lackey, whose master also left a sum of money for his care, and who promised to send from time to time to ask after him. Any communication regarding the boy is to be sent to M. Betstein, in care of a jeweler in Rue Gros, at Paris."

A smile touched the lips of the cardinal.

"One must admit," he said ironically, "that M. de Bassompierre provides well for the gages of devotion -- "

"I have not said that M. de Bassompierre was providing for anyone," said the Capuchin. "I am stating only facts, Monseigneur; and now I must remind you of another fact for some time overlooked. On the night of October 8, 1626, while M. de Bassompierre was in London as ambassador, he paid a secret visit to York House, where the Duke of Buckingham then lived. He went unaccompanied, without lights, and remained for a long time closeted with the duke."

Richelieu was silent for some moments, as though searching the meaning behind these words.

"Your catalogue of facts, my dear Pete Joseph, seems very unconnected," he said.

The Capuchin bowed his head in assent. "Undoubtedly, Your Eminence. Let us return to the boy. His name is inscribed on the abbey rolls as Raoul d'Aram. His family is unknown. I found there were certain marks on the clothing he wore when he came to St. Saforin. By means of these marks, commonly placed on garments by the makers, we found that the boy came from Aubain, a village near the royal forest of Verrieres, on the southern road to Versailles."

"You appear to have extraordinary interest in this boy," said the minister drily.

"The interest, Monseigneur, would appear to have extraordinary justification."

"Expound."

"At Aubain the name of d'Aram was unknown," continued the Capuchin. "I found, however, that such a boy had been in care of the curate of Aubain, who died a year ago. His housekeeper, who had taken charge of the boy, died about the same time. The boy was then taken to St. Saforin. The curate was a distant relative of Mme. de Chevreuse -- a man named Thounenin, of Dompt."

"Ah!" The gaze of the Cardinal at once became alert, attentive. He had no more bitter enemy than Marie de Rohan, Duchesse de Chevreuse, now exiled to her estates.

"Your Eminence may recall," pursued the Capuchin, slowly choosing his words, "that some four years ago Her Majesty the Queen was very ill of a fever at the Chateau of Versailles."

"I recall the fact perfectly." Richelieu was now all attention. "She caught this fever from Chevreuse, whose life was despaired of, but whom it pleased God to spare.

"For further mischief," added the Capuchin. "Good. I have only one more fact to present rather. I allow you to present it to yourself, and if there are any conjectures to be drawn, I leave them to you. I beg you to recall the precise date of the secret interview which took place in the gardens of Amiens between Her Majesty and the Duke of Buckingham. That is all, Monseigneur."

The pallor of Richelieu's thin features became accentuated. For a moment he sat absolutely motionless, then a deep and angry rush of color swept into his face. Step by step he had followed the exposition of fact -- and now that he had the clue, he was speechless. He rose from his chair, paced up and down the room with quick and nervous tread, then swung on his secretary.

"Monsieur, this is absolutely incredible!" he exclaimed. "It is an impossibility!"

"I am not aware to what Your Eminence refers," came the

cool response. "However, I assure you that when a man -- or woman -- is well served, nothing is incredible or impossible."

Richelieu made a brusque, impatient gesture.

"This is important -- no rhetoric, if you please!" The harsh and bitter ring in his words told how deeply he was stirred. "I remember now -- Madame de Chevreuse was the devoted nurse of Her Majesty at the time! She herself, barely recovered from illnes -- ah! If this be true -- if this be true --"

He stood silent, staring at the tapestried wall, his long fingers intertwined in a grip that whitened the knuckles. His face was tortured by a thousand emotions. Suddenly he turned.

"Look you," he said crisply. "The intimation that this is the child of Her Majesty -- it is blasphemy! Worse, it is impossible. The child could not have been carried unobserved -- it could not have been born unobserved! It could not have been disposed of --"

Upon his agitated words struck the inexorable voice of the Capuchin, like a bell of steel.

"Your Eminence, consider. You have surmised a certain conclusion from my facts. It is not at all impossible. Chevreuse is a very able woman. Surely she could contrive what any fish-merchant's daughter could contrive?"

"Bah! The Queen is the center of a thousand eyes --"

"For which Chevreuse could manufacture thousand blindfolds. Besides, this cure received the child from her own hands; his silence was bought. On his deathbed he added a codicil to his will which stated these facts."

"What!" The cardinal bent a sharp, astounded gaze upon him. "Does such a will exist?"

"It does; so, at least, I have been informed. The will was abstracted from the archives; the loss was discovered -- it was sent to England for safety. It is now on the way here -- is possibly in Paris at this moment. Provided Your Eminence is sufficiently interested to hear the steps I have taken, I may place all the threads of this affair in your hands -- "

Richelieu resumed his chair with a nod of assent. The slightly satirical accent of Pere Joseph delighted him; this secretary was by no means humble except in public, for Pere Joseph knew his worth and stood firmly upon it. Richelieu liked this sort of man -- in private.

"There is a woman named Helene de Sirle, daughter of a gentleman killed at La Rochelle; a most able woman, devoted to Your Eminence. You may have heard of her?"

The Cardinal's brows lifted slightly. "I have heard something of such a person. What was it -- she lives alone -- hm! I have forgotten."

To Pere Joseph, it was perhaps obvious that His Eminence had forgotten nothing.

"Who lives alone in a small chateau in the Parc du Montmorenci outside Passy -- quite so. She has means. She has relatives in Lorraine. She is never in the public eye, yet she has an extensive acquaintance."

"Indeed!" said Richelieu, veiling the bright flash of his eye. "Such a woman should be of use, upon occasion.

"She is," said Pere Joseph drily. "We dare not employ the

usual channels in regard to that document; it is to be delivered to her upon reaching Paris. Further, she has undertaken to gain information about the child at St. Saforin."

"For what purpose, and from whom?" demanded Richelieu.

"In the event that we desire to take possession of the child. From a gentleman who has twice visited St. Saforin and spoken with the child, who is suspected of being in constant correspondence with Chevreuse, and who is known to be a friend of Bassompierre. One Abbe d'Herblay, at one time, I believe, a Musketeer."

"Ah!" said Richelieu. "D'Herblay -- one of the Inseparables, they were termed! I remember the man. When will you have more definite information?"

"A messenger from Mlle. de Sirle should have arrived today; he will certainly arrive tonight," said Pere Joseph. "He will bear full details verbally, and any documentary evidence that has been procured."

Richelieu nodded thoughtfully. "After all, it is not impossible," he said. "Bassompierre and Buckingham were warm friends. He, acting for Buckingham; Chevreuse, acting for her -- hm! No, you are right; where one is well served, anything is possible. Ah -- someone is arriving below -- "

"Our messenger, no doubt."

From the courtyard rose the sounds of a rider being admitted, greeted, welcomed. The minister struck a bell, and a lackey entered.

"Find out who has just arrived. Bring him here."

In two minutes the lackey returned.

"Your Eminence, M. d'Artagnan, Lieutenant of Musketeers, has just arrived with despatches from the court at Lyon. He will be brought here immediately."

The lackey withdrew. Richelieu waited, a slight frown upon his brow. A knock, and d'Artagnan entered, saluted, stood at attention.

"Ah, M. d'Artagnan! We are happy to have you with us again!" said the Cardinal affably.

The musketeer bowed. "Your Eminence does me too much honor. It is I who am proud to find myself again near the person of Your Eminence."

"I think, Pere Joseph," and Richelieu turned, "you desired to ask M.d'Artagnan something?"

"Ah, yes! Perhaps, monsieur, on your way from Lyon you encountered a gentleman named M. Connetans?"

"I have never heard the name," said d'Artagnan, and I encountered no one upon the road except a dead man, some leagues from here."

"A dead man?" The Capuchin was suddenly agitated. "Describe him, if you please -- "

"Gladly, monsieur. He was unknown to me, and had not long before been attacked and shot by robbers, evidently. His horse was close by, mine was dying. I took his animal and came on -- "

"His description?" interrupted the Capuchin anxiously.

"A tall man, since I had to shorten his stirrups. He had a rather brutal face marked by very black brows meeting above his eyes. I could do nothing for him, and did not delay."

Pere Joseph seemed overcome, and Richelieu intervened.

"Thank you, monsieur," he said, with the graciousness he could so well summon at command.

"You are, I believe, attached to duty with the court?"

"Yes, Your Eminence. My company has the honor of acting as Her Majesty's guards at Lyon."

"Then I shall see you again, I trust. We will not detain you further -- good night, monsieur!"

D'Artagnan departed. The Capuchin lifted a suddenly tortured face.

"My man -- waylaid by robbers -- ah, destiny is unkind!" he exclaimed.

The cardinal affectionately laid his hand on Pere Joseph's shoulder. "You complain of destiny? I shall make destiny complain of me, I promise you!"

"Then, Monseigneur, you find my facts worthy your interest?"

"All facts are worthy of interest," said the cardinal. "And they may even make conjectures worthy of interest, my friend and father! By the way, you did not chance to notice the gold ring upon the hand of M. d'Artagnan -- graven with the arms of-"

"I noticed nothing," confessed Pere Joseph. "I was agitated, Monseigneur. The ring -- whose arms, did you say?"

Richelieu told him. The two men looked one at another for a long, silent moment.

CHAPTER III

MENTION THE DEVIL, AND HE APPEARS

His despatches delivered, d'Artagnan found himself taken in charge by Comte de Moreau, a gentleman of the king's household. Moreau carried d'Artagnan to his own quarters, bedded him on a couch in his own room, wakened him in the morning, and insisted on accompanying him to a nearby tavern for the morning draught. At any other time this pressing hospitality would have delighted our lieutenant of musketeers, but at the moment he found it devilish inopportune -- he had a letter in his pocket which he was burning to read, and could find no opportunity of perusing it in private.

He did, however, deposit the sealed packet upon the fire in their quarters, and watched it go up in flames. Whatever might be in that packet, was evidently the secret of Aramis alone; the letter was a different matter.

"His Majesty and the Cardinal are quartered in the Hotel des Lesdigue'res," said Moreau, when they had dispelled the remnants of slumber with good wine of the countryside. "If you wish to attend the king's levee -- "

"Not I," said d'Artagnan. "With all the thanks in the world, my friend, I beg to decline the honor. I've had nothing but risings and beddings for a month past; dressings and undressings, paintings and powderings -- plague take it! I hoped our company would go with the army; instead, we dance attendance on two queens and court officials."

Moreau laughed. "You're in good company at all events -- how Bassompierre would envy you! And seriously, you're in luck. Fever is widespread in the army, and before the summer's over we'll hear more of it. Then you'll not come?"

"Not for a bit," said d'Artagnan. "I'll show myself later. Don't let me detain you if duty calls, I beg of you!"

Moreau departed. At this instant a group of officers entered, and d'Artagnan sighed in vexation as they came to the next table, close by. He ordered another bottle of wine, resolving to out-drink them; his uniform made him conspicuous in the streets, and he strongly desired the privacy of the tavern in order to read the letter in his pocket -- the letter from which he hoped to get some explanation of the strange and tragic words of the dying man.

Then, as he waited, he grew interested in the talk at the next table. One of the officers had come from Lyon to join the king; the other three had come in the suite of the Cardinal from the army, and gossip was rife from both directions.

Listening, d'Artagnan, who never despised current knowledge, learned a large number of things. Bassompierre was expected to arrive here any hour, any day. The marshal was extremely annoyed because he shared the command of the army with Schomberg and Crequy, and had complained hotly to the king, but without result.

Everywhere intrigue was raising its head, against everyone in sight, and was openly discussed. Chiefly it arose from Marie de Medici, who took the part of Savoy. She was furious because Richelieu had conquered practically the entire dukedom, and now it was said she intended to prevent the king from rejoining the army.

"Bah!" exclaimed one of the Cardinalists. "The Italian woman hopes that Casale will fall, then she'll blame Richelieu and stir up trouble. Ten to one she'll flatter Bassompierre and try to disaffect him!"

"Well, if she has a pretty maid of honor to do the flattering, she may succeed!" observed another, and there was a laugh. "What's this about the queen-mother coming here, eh?"

"Rumor," and another shrugged. "I hear that His Majesty has sent for her, hoping she'll come and patch up matters with His Eminence. Not likely, with Marillac at Lyon! That rascal hates everything red -- "

"Your pardon, gentlemen," spoke up the king's officer with dignity. "M. de Marillac is the Keeper of the Seals and a high official of France. I do not care to sit and hear him thus miscalled; what is more to the point, he is a relative of my family."

"Your pardon, M. Constant -- we did not know that," came the response in chorus, for everyone was in too good humor to stand on punctilio. One of the officers lifted his flagon. "A health to all the royal family, ministers, officials and what not in France! And damnation to the enemy Austrian!"

"Which Austrian?" cried another, laughing. "The enemy in France or the enemy in Austria?"

The mustaches of d'Artagnan began to quiver.

"Whichever you like!" returned the officer. "Peste, gentlemen -- where's the difference?"

"Difference enough, Montforge!" came the laughing response. "Confidant of our good Pere Joseph, conducting private campaigns in Paris while we're conducting public ones with the army --, faith, you may not know there's a difference, but we do! Ill talk, my friend, ill talk! I don't believe half this gossip about Imperialist intrigue going on court --

"The devil you don't!" exclaimed Montforge.

He was a large and powerful man, very handsomely dressed and armed. "I'll wager M. Constant here can bear me out -- he's fresh from Lyon! Eh, my friend? Isn't it true that the Austrian in France is more to be feared than all the Austrians in Italy and the Empire put together?"

"I'm afraid I don't quite get the point, gentlemen," said the king's officer, with an air of embarrassment. "There are no Austrians in France."

D'Artagnan's eyes were very bright and gleaming now.

Peste!" said Montforge, with a guffaw. "Come, come, talk's free on campaign! You know well enough that the Austrian in the Louvre fights against us -- "

A sudden deluge of wine stopped his words, choked his voice, filled his eyes and face and dribbled down over his fine apparel. With an amazed and angry oath, he leaped to his feet and wiped his eyes.

D'Artagnan bowed profoundly.

"My compliments, gentlemen, my compliments!" he exclaimed gravely. "Upon my word, this is a most unfortunate occurrence! You see, gentlemen, I was sound asleep, and thinking that I heard someone traduce Her Gracious Majesty -- "

"Devil take you!" roared out Montforge, "Enough of this pleasantry! You confounded little rogue of a Gascon, is this some jest?"

D'Artagnan twirled his mustache and inspected the cavalier critically.

"Just what I was asking, indeed! Do you know, monsieur, I begin to believe that it was?"

In the eyes of the Gascon, in the steady, implacable gaze, Montforge read the truth. He became deadly pale, and bowed slightly.

"Very well, monsieur. I perceive that you belong to the Musketeers; you will, therefore, have no compunction in rendering me satisfaction?"

"With all my heart, monsieur!" replied d'Artagnan. "I am M. d'Artagnan, lieutenant in the company of M. Rambure's. May I have the honor of knowing with whom I speak?"

He perceived instantly that his name had created an impression.

"This is M. le Comte de Montforge," said another officer, and introduced the group. "You have friends here,monsieur?"

"Undoubtedly," said d'Artagnan, "but since I arrived only last night, I'm somewhat at a loss whither to direct you. I -- I -- I -- "

A species of stupefaction descended upon him. His voice failed. He staggered back a step and remained staring, his jaw fallen.

Into the inn room had just entered a man of large build. His boots, cloak, garb, all bespoke recent arrival -- he was covered with dust from head to foot. He flung hat and cloak upon a settle, raising a cloud of dust, and showed that he bore his left arm in a sling. "Wine!" he cried out, in a voice that reverberated under the rafters and rang back from the copper kettles about the fireplace. "Wine! Food! Name of a name of a name -- must I die of thirst and hunger and fatigue because you lazy dogs of scullions can't -- for the love of the good God! Am I dreaming or -- or -- "

His eyes had fallen on the group about the tables -- the group, who in turn were gazing at him, following the petrified stare of d'Artagnan, who thought he was looking at a ghost. The large man's mouth flew open and stayed open. His eyes protruded. Then, just as d'Artagnan moved to cross himself, he took two enormous strides across the room and swept an arm about the musketeer.

"D'Artagnan!"

"Porthos!"

For the moment, all else was forgotten -- the scene around, the group of officers, the furious and livid Montforge -- in this genuinely amazing meeting.

Porthos, living or dead, was the last person d'Artagnan expected to see here in Grenoble. In the previous year M. du Vallon had left the service, marrying the 800,000 livres of

Madame Coquenard, and had disappeared from sight. And here he was, dust covered, huge, tears on his cheeks at sight of d'Artagnan -- not a ghost at all, but indisputably alive.

Tears were likewise on the cheeks of d'Artagnan, though not from the same cause. The one-armed hug of Porthos came near to crushing in his ribs.

"While this," observed Comte de Montforge mockingly, "is extremely touching, it is aside from the matter under discussion."

Porthos released d'Artagnan and turned. His naturally haughty countenance took on a look of ineffable scorn.

"And who," he inquired, "is this insect passing commentaries upon us?"

"This, my friend," said d'Artagnan, "is M. le Comte de Montforge, who also dislikes my fashion of passing commentaries,and who is about to do me the honor of teaching me his own manner with the sword-point. Gentlemen, I am happy to present my friend, M. du Vallon, late of the company of M. de Treville. If you will arrange the meeting with him, I shall be very glad, as I am eager to have speech with him before presenting myself to His Majesty. Time presses.

However bewildered he might have been, Porthos was quick to comprehend the situation, and with his most magnificent bow, assumed the duties of second.

"At your most humble service, gentlemen!" he exclaimed. "I am sorry to say that my left arm is disabled by the knife of a scoundrel rascal, but - " "This is between me and M.

de Montforge alone," interposed d'Artagnan, and sat down again to his wine.

"The devil!" he ejaculated to himself. "Am I going to have a chance to read this letter or not? Still, if I do it now, it will lend me the appearance of being entirely at my ease --"

He glanced around. Porthos had joined the companions of Montforge and was talking with them. Montforge was drinking and eyeing the winestains on his magnificent doublet. Removing the letter from his pocket, d'Artagnan looked at the superscription. He read, in the very fine, beautiful writing of Aramis:

"Mlle. Helene de Sirle, Parc de Montmorenci."

"Hm! Parc de Montmorenci -- that might be anywhere," reflected d'Artagnan, "but it must be the one at Passy. Therefore, Aramis is at Paris. Vivadiou! Something learned."

He turned over and unfolded the letter. Before he had glanced at the writing, a heavy step interrupted him, and he looked up as -- Porthos approached.

"Ha! At once, all together, to a spot nearby. Agreed?"

"Agreed," said d'Artagnan, and sighed as he pocketed the letter. "Decidedly," he said to himself, "if this devilish interference proceeds much farther, I shall have to kill someone!"

The six men left the tavern in company and in silence. A hundred yards away was the College of the Recolets. Behind the rear wall of this enclosure was the Rue du Dauphine, and across the street was the charming little park and garden where Marie de Medici had been triumphally received on her way from Italy to marriage with Henry IV. At this hour of the morning, the park was entirely deserted, and few were passing along the streets.

"Admirably conceived, this spot!" exclaimed Porthos grandly. "In the city yet not of it eh, my dear d'Artagnan? A pretty spot for foot-work -- what excellent clipped grass!"

The party halted. D'Artagnan turned to the count.

"My dear M. de Montforge," he said, "it were a pity if any misapprehension of my own should cause vexation. It may be that you had no intention of casting aspersions upon a lady whom I am very honored in serving -- "

"A truce to politeness, monsieur!" exclaimed Montforge angrily. "What you heard, you heard. What you did, you did. The devil fly away with apologies! En garde!"

"En garde, messieurs," echoed Porthos.

"One moment, gentlemen!" interposed M. Constant, the king's officer, looking a trifle nervously from d'Artagnan to Montforge. "I must say that if this difficulty could be composed, it were much the better course, in view of the edict against duelling. M. de Montforge's remarks -- "

"Have nothing to do with it!" snapped that gentleman, angrily. "M. d'Artagnan emptied his winecup in my face -- there's the crux of the whole thing!"

"Good! Excellent! Via crucis, via crucis!" boomed Porthos, who was proud of his scanty Latin. "En garde, messieurs -- "

The two swords crossed. The two men parried, feinted, tested each the other.

In this moment, a singular prescience seized upon the

soul of d'Artagnan. Perhaps the astounding meeting with Porthos had set a spark to his imagination; perhaps his agile mind was somewhat disturbed at finding Montforge an absolute master of his weapon, whether in French or Italian style. He did not know Montforge, had never heard the man mentioned among the skilled blades of the court; and this was singular in the extreme.

Over the crossed steel he saw two blazing black eyes, intrepid as his own, proud as his own, confident as his own; in them he read a determined enmity. Ere this, he had looked into eyes afire with the intention of killing; he knew as he stood there that Montforge meant to kill him. Across his mind flashed the memory of other men; of Jussac, of Count de Wardes -- above all, of Rochefort the implacable.

Another Rochefort here -- from some unguessed source it came to him that he had here entered upon something deeper than he knew, something that must go farther than he wished, unless he killed the man before him. "Kill this man -- kill him swiftly!" The mental warning fairly screamed at the ears of his soul.

D'Artagnan fought with his back to the street. He was entirely absorbed in his adversary; he saw nothing save those savage black eyes, he felt nothing save the pressure of blade against blade, he heard nothing save the sharp click and slither of the crossed steel. Still wet with morning dew, the grass underfoot sent up a sharply sweet fragrance as it was crushed by their stamping boots.

Angered by those flaming eyes, d'Artagnan suddenly

abandoned the defensive and began to exert himself. He worked into a shrewd and merciless attack, so agile, so vibrant with energy, as to be irresistible. He saw a look of intense astonishment and dismay sweep into the face of Montforge, saw his enemy give back --saw him slip suddenly in the grass and go all asprawl, his blade flying afar. With an effort, d'Artagnan checked himself midway of a lunge, and drew back.

"When you are ready, monsieur," he said calmly, sure of himself now.

Montforge came to one knee, then paused, staring. No one had moved to pick up his rapier, nor did he reach out for it. D'Artagnan glanced surprisedly at the others -- saw Porthos agape, the image of consternation, saw the others apparently paralyzed, saw they were not looking at him or at Montforge, but at a point behind him, on which every eye seemed fixed with a species of stupefied fascination.

"The devil!" exclaimed d'Artagnan, and turned.

"Not in person, at all events," said a man who had approached behind him -- a man who had turned into the park from the street, and who was accompanied by two gentlemen.

This man was Richelieu.

"Well, gentlemen," said the cardinal, sweeping an icy eye over the group, "I confess that you have conspired to present me with a surprise this fine morning. Montforge -- d'Artagnan -- Constant "

His gaze rested on Porthos for an instant as though he

half recognized the large man.

Porthos bowed.

"M. du Vallon, Your Eminence, late of the company of M.Treville."

"Ah!" said the Cardinal. "I remember you.'

Porthos paled at these ominous words. Montforge rose, in some agitation, and drew out a handkerchief, with which he wiped perspiration from his brow.

"Your Eminence," he said, "I beg that you will absolve these gentlemen; any blame connected with this scene rests upon me alone, for I challenged M. d'Artagnan."

"Ah!" said d'Artagnan to himself, throwing Montforge a glance of admiration. "I could love this man -- if he did not hate me!"

"Yes?" said Richelieu drily. "Each of you, no doubt,imagined that the other was an enemy of France -- eh, gentlemen?"

D'Artagnan bowed. "Exactly, Monseigneur."

"Your Eminence has discerned the truth," said Montforge, his dark face slightly pale. None knew better than he that Richelieu was most to be feared when he jested.

There was an instant of silence, while the cardinal looked from one to the other. Then he spoke, slowly, gravely, as though the affair were to be held in abeyance, not forgotten.

"Justice, gentlemen, is said to be blind. It is my desire that you two gentlemen shake hands and end this matter."

Blank astonishment greeted these words. "So!" thought d'Artagnan, with the rapidity of light.

"Our honest cardinal has something to be gained by not hanging us!" Sheathing his rapier, which he was still holding, he turned and held out his hand to Montforge.

"Come, monsieur!" he said with a smile. "This gentleman is our superior in rank, since he is minister of war. He is our superior in intelligence, since he is a cardinal. And certainly he is our superior in wisdom, since he gives us very practical advice which had occurred to neither of us! Upon my word, monsieur, I think we should grant his desire!"

"With all my heart," said Montforge, and shook hands heartily. But the look he gave d'Artagnan belied his words.

"Excellently done, gentlemen!" said Richelieu. "M. de Montforge, I desire your company in my cabinet within ten minutes, if you please. M. d'Artagnan, may I inquire whether you return to Lyon?"

"I do not know, Your Eminence," said d'Artagnan. "I have not yet presented myself to His Majesty."

"Then, if you will have the kindness to present yourself to me in an hour's time," returned the cardinal, "I should be very happy to have the honor of a little conversation with you."

D'Artagnan bowed profoundly.

When the cardinal had departed Montforge approached d'Artagnan, who was adjusting his uniform cloak, and regarded him intently.

"Monsieur, I trust we shall have the pleasure of a future meeting?"

D'Artagnan's smile, which could add so much charm to his features, leaped out straightway.

"By all means, monsieur -- let us leave it to the finger of destiny! I only trust you will not suffer for your very frank avowal of blame."

Montforge shrugged, as though it were of no moment. "Very well," he said, and bowed. "We shall, then, meet again."

D'Artagnan noted that this was uttered as a statement of fact predetermined.

"Where to?" asked Porthos, as they came to the street together.

"To the tavern, pardieu!" said d'Artagnan. "We're an hour together, at all events. Well, old friend, I see that the red minister remembers you, eh?"

"Yes, devil take him!" said Porthos, twirling his mustache complacently. "He remembers that little scene on the road outside La Rochelle, eh? Come you're with the king here? I thought your company was at Lyon with the court?"

D'Artagnan whistled to himself. "You did, eh? And who put that thought into your head, I wonder? Cautiously, here -- cautiously!" he reflected to himself. Aloud, he replied; "It is, it is -- I arrived here last night with despatches. When I've seen His Eminence, I'll probably know my future plans. But have you repented matrimony! You must be going to join the army, since you're here -- and whence comes your wound?"

"From the devil," said Porthos seriously. "By the way, here's your handkerchief. You must have dropped it when His Eminence appeared. I retrieved it."

"Handkerchief? I haven't one to my name," said d'Artagnan. He took the bit of cambric which Porthos handed him, and stared at it, while the giant clapped him on the back.

"Ha! Up to the old tricks of Aramis, are you! I know a lady's kerchief when I see it, comrade! And deuce take me but it's got a monogram! Here, give me a look -- "

"Go to the devil," said d'Artagnan, and laughed as they turned in at the tavern entrance. He thrust the kerchief swiftly away, for he had perceived one thing, and remembered another.

He remembered that Montforge had wiped his face with a handkerchief. And on this bit of cambric he perceived the monogram "H de S." -- the initials of Helene de Sine. Montforge had dropped this handkerchief, therefore -- therefore a hundred conjectures! He thrust them all out of his bewildered brain and bent his thought on the more important thing: the letter in his pocket, as yet unread.

Porthos, finding himself thick and grimy with dust, departed to the pump. He was bursting to talk, but disgust at his own condition was stronger, so he left d'Artagnan to order the wine. Alone for the moment, the musketeer drew the letter from his pocket and unfolded it, and now there was none to interfere. He read.

"Dear Mademoiselle: The bearer of this letter is a friend to be trusted. I have received terrible news, and I am ill. Meantime, my friend will serve you as would I myself, had I the honor to be at your side. d'Herblay."

"So!" D'Artagnan pocketed the letter, with some dismay. "Nothing learned. Who is the friend of Aramis from whom that rascal took this letter? Ah -- the ring! I'd be fool to present myself before the cardinal-Vivadiou! But I was wearing that ring last night -- ah, well, he would not have observed it."

None the less, as he put the ring in his pocket, his face was a little pale at remembering how he had appeared before the cardinal and Pere Joseph on his arrival -- he had certainly worn the ring, like a fool! An uneasy conscience whispered that the conversation desired by Richelieu might be on the subject of the dead spy. Now Porthos came stamping in, seized a flagon, and emptied it at a draught. When he sat down, the bench groaned beneath him.

"Ah! Ah! Embrace me, d'Artagnan!" he exclaimed gustily. "This is good, this is like old times -- wine and sword of a morning, and a hard night's ride behind! Why the devil have you degenerated into a post courier? You, a lieutenant, bearing despatches?"

"A courier to the king, with letters from the two queens.

"That explains it. Our noble Athos -- where is he?"

"In Lyon. He talks of leaving the service, drinks his Spanish wine as usual, and has the devil's own luck at dice. If you knew our company was with the court in Lyon, why didn't you drop in to see us?"

This confused Porthos, who seized a bottle and emptied another flagon. D'Artagan began to watch him closely, though without seeming to do so.

"I wasn't in Lyon ten minutes," said the giant, and bellowed at the host for more wine and food. "Listen, comrade! Last week I came to Paris. Madame du Vallon is thinking of buying a property in Picardy; she went to look it over. I came to Paris to handle a certain business for her. There -- what, think you, happened to me? Guess!"

"Certainly not a love-affair, to the husband of eight hundred thousand livres!" and d'Artagnan laughed. He was all on the alert now -- he had a conviction that Porthos was not entirely confiding in him. This rendered him curious, precautious to tell what he himself knew.

"Something different -- I was robbed," declared Porthos, reddening with anger. "Robbed! Three men set upon me, got a noose about my neck, strangled me. I pounded one on the head and felt his skull go smash; I kicked a second, and he was dead the next minute. But the third -- ah, The third! The abominable rascal! The black-browed scoundrel! What do you think he did? He sat on my back and used a knife on me, tried to murder me! True, it only tore the flesh of my arrn, but between the loss of blood and the strangulation, I became unconscious. He robbed me and fled."

"Not to Grenoble, surely?" exclaim d'Artagnan.

"Exactly! You have guessed it. Listen! By good luck I saw him leaving Paris that same night. I called for a horse, followed him. I have money, you understand! I rode after him like a madman; the horse died under me. I got another horse. Mile by mile, inch by inch, I gained upon him. I entered Lyon not five minutes after him -- upon my word, it is the truth! Instead of stopping there, the unspeakable devil changed horses and had gone when I got to the posthouse.

My horse was played out, there was not a fresh animal to be had. I took a tired one, and the brute went bad on me halfway here -- has been limping in since midnight. The man's here ahead of me -- you must help me find him, trace him!"

"With all my heart," said d'Artagnan. "Who was he?"

"I don't know. He was a tall man with the face of a rogue. He had heavy black brows that met above his nose -- eh? What? You've seen him?"

D'Artagnan started.

"Black brows that met -- diantre! Did he ride a piebald horse? Did he have a cloak of dark blue or black slashed with silver?"

Porthos leaped from his seat. "You know him? Come! Take me to him, this moment! Up!"

"He is dead," said d'Artagnan. "Sit down, sit down, comrade -- your man's dead! You should have seen him lying in the road as you came, for I must have been just ahead of you. He died in my arms --"

"Pardieu! I saw nothing of him!" cried the amazed Porthos, and then sank back on the bench with an expression of utter dismay and consternation. "Mon Dieu, I am ruined, ruined! Now what shall I ever say to Aramis?"

CHAPTER IV

A MARSHAL ARRIVES, A LIEUTENANT DEPARTS

"So you have seen Aramis?" asked d'Artagnan quickly.

Porthos swallowed hard, and turned a wild gaze upon the Gascon.

"I am a fool," he said thickly. "I have said too much. I promised --"

"I think, my dear Porthos," said d'Artagnan coolly, "that you and I have been somewhat in company in other days, and I have never heard you complain of having trusted me too much. Ma foi! If you have no confidence in me --"

Porthos began to swear horribly.

"For the love of the saints give me time, give me time!" he cried out in despair. "My dear comrade, you don't understand! Listen to me. I met Aramis in Paris. He was in terrible straits; he had been flung into the depths of despair, he spoke of killing himself -- Aramis! Can you fancy such a thing? He was gloomy as the foul fiend! I don't know exactly what had caused it."

"I think you do," said d'Artagnan -- to himself. Aloud: "Yes?"

"Well," and here Porthos began to flounder, "Aramis gave me a packet of money to deliver -- a sum he had collected for some lady, I know not what it was. I promised to take it to her. He made me swear not to breathe his name -- "

D'Artagnan laughed. He saw that the giant was genuinely overwhelmed at being unable to confide in him, and he was melted instantly.

"So the robbers took the money, eh?" he asked.

"Anything else?"

"No -- it was some gold in rouleaux," said Porthos, but reddened a trifle as he spoke. "The devil of it is that I don't know the exact amount. They sprang upon me just after I left poor Aramis."

"He was not wounded when you left him?"

"He? Wounded?" Porthos stared. "Not in the least, except in spirit."

With an air as though he were glad to escape further questioning for the moment, Porthos applied himself to the food and wine that was set before them.

D'Artagnan whistled to himself -- he began to see a good many things. Aramis had received a letter from his Marie Michon, which had stricken him. He sent Porthos to Mlle. de Sine, whoever this might be; not with money, but with a letter. Porthos was attacked, robbed, left for dead; Aramis was then attacked, wounded, robbed, and the black-browed spy set forth for Grenoble.

But now -- Porthos was still lying about it! Very well, then -- he would not get his letter back very readily. In what net of intrigue had Aramis enmeshed this huge man with a child's heart? D'Artagnan felt a twinge of anger at the thought. It was all very well for Aramis to indulge his own bent for intrigue, but it was not right for him to ensnare poor simple, honest Porthos.

"Tell me what you know of this man-you say he died on the road, in your arms?" said Porthos. "Tell me, I conjure you! Did you get my rouleaux of gold from him?"

"I did not look to see if he had any," said d'Artagnan drily, and with truth. Since Porthos stubbornly concealed all mention of the letter, the less said the better. Aramis, he reflected, has drawn our big comrade into some conspiracy; since Porthos is the worst possible conspirator, let him now remain out of it for his own good!

D'Artagnan told of finding the dead man in the road, taking the fresher horse, and coming on to Grenoble -- exactly as he had told Richelieu. Upon hearing this tale, Porthos was plunged into the depths of despair. He himself had seen nothing of the dead man or of d'Artagnan's horse, and the inference was plain.

"The robbers returned to their prey after you had passed," he said gloomily. "They plundered the man, flung him into the river, and took your horse away. Ah, miserable wretches! If I had you under my hands, I'd wring your cursed necks! My friend, I am ruined."

"Why?" asked d'Artagnan.

"Because the lady was to confide a mission to me in place of Aramis," said the other. "I swore that I would take the money to her, accept an errand from her -- and now! I am ruined."

"On the contrary,' said d'Artagnan, you are saved."

"Saved?" Porthos stared at him, "In what way? How do you mean?"

"Eat, drink, fortify yourself, my friend," and d'Artagnan gestured toward the file of scullions bringing further dishes and platters. "Talk when alone."

The magnificent bellows of Porthos had set everyone to running, and now were produced capons, a brace of ducks, the excellent sausages for which Grenoble was renowned, pastries, venison; dish followed dish, bottle pursued bottle, and in between details of the service d'Artagnan expounded details drawn largely from his own fertile imagination.

"You need not hesitate over confiding in me, my friend," he said confidentially. "Perhaps I know more of the whole affair than you suppose -- more, perhaps, than you yourself know! Picture our Aramis, now, engaged in helping a great man, a friend of his -- a Marshal of France, now with the army -- you comprehend?"

"Ah, ah!" cried Porthos in amazement. "You know about that? Then Aramis wrote you, eh? He said I must be most particular not to mention the name of Bassompierre --"

"Then don't mention it," said d'Artagnan, twirling his mustache complacently. "Aramis receives a letter from his lady-love; it throws him into consternation, into despair! Everything pales before this. Nothing matters. He is disheartened, talks of suicide, entering a monastery, taking the vows and writing a thesis for ordination --"

"Upon my soul, his very words!" exclaimed the staring Porthos, but for all his amazement he did not forget to attack the fortifications now before him.

"Well, then -- Aramis encounters you. He knows your valor, your disregard of odds -- he has reason to know them! And he also knows your modesty, your hesitancy at undertaking anything of dubious nature, your reluctance to push yourself forward is it not?"

Porthos deftly removed half the breast of a duck, placed it in his mouth, and nodded complacently. Being anything but modest, he loved to picture himself possessed of this virtue.

"Would Aramis mention these qualities?" pursued d'Artagnan. "No! He feared lest you beg him to select a braver, abler man. Instead, he merely asked you to do him a small favor -- deliver a sum of money to a lady, and accept a commission from her. He parts from you. A few moments afterward, you are set upon, brought to earth like a Hercules assailed by base foes -- and you are robbed. Why? Because you had been spied upon. It was suspected that he had given you this money. In fact, no sooner had you parted than he in turn was assaulted, attacked, badly wounded, and plundered also. You comprehend?"

The eyes of Porthos opened tremendously, but, his mouth being filled with duck-breast, he could only nod amazed comprehension.

"You killed two of the rascals," pursued d'Artagnan. "The third escaped, went to attack Aramis, thinking you were dead. He presently took to the road. He had the best of horses waiting everywhere for him, he was known wherever he went --"

"Who -- who the devil told you all this?" blurted out Porthos, stupefied.

"I reconstruct, my friend. Now, this man was not fleeing from you, as you think -- on the contrary, he was hastening to reach another man, riding like mad to bring this other man the money he stole from you, the papers he stole from Aramis you comprehend? They were vitally important. He stayed not to eat nor sleep, but rode, leaped from horse to horse, spurred from hill to hill, never looked behind! At Lyon he inquired the road to Grenoble, climbed into the fresh saddle, and was gone. Why? Because he was bringing his loot to a man here,"

"Eh?" Porthos, who had just drunk an entire bottle of wine at a draught, set down his flagon an stared afresh. "A man -- here? Bringing them -- pardieu! I never thought of that! Who told you so?"

"The man to whom he was bringing them," said d'Artagnan placidly. "Last night when I arrived he asked after such a courier, whom he was expecting hourly. He described the man, I recognized the dead man in the road -- "

The veins swelled in the forehead of Porthos. His nostrils distended, a flood of color rushed into his face. He brought down one fist on the board and the impact smashed half the crockery.

"His name!" he thundered. "Who is this man? I'll attend to him! His name, instantly!"

"Armand, Cardinal de Richelieu."

This name froze Porthos into stone. He did not move,

his eyes remained fastened upon d'Artagnan; but the color slowly drained out of his face.

"Ah! Ah!" he said slowly. "But that is impossible! That -- that would mean -- would mean --"

"Exactly," said d'Artagnan. "That would mean your assassin was a spy who no doubt supposed you to be engaged in some intrigue against the Cardinal."

"I see it all," said Porthos, and his head fell in dejection. "I am lost."

"How so?"

Porthos paused, gulped at his wine. Still he lacked the imagination to confess everything and obtain a spiritual absolution from his friend.

"The money," he said, wiping his lips. "Without it, I could not reach the lady -- it was my ambassadorial letters. Now I cannot place myself at her service in the stead of Aramis. And you heard what the Cardinal said to me, my dear d'Artagnan? The tone of voice in which he spoke? Yes, his spies must have been on my trail. He remembers me, indeed! Leave me, d'Artagnan; leave me, for I am a lost man. I may be arrested any moment, taken to a royal chateau -- Mont St. Michel, the Bastille, Vincennes!"

The gloom, terror, utter despondency of Porthos drew a slight smile from d'Artagnan.

"My dear Porthos," he said, calmly tasting his wine, "did you ever know me to deceive you, to feed you with false hopes, to desert you?"

"You are the soul of honor and of friendship," said

Porthos unhappily.

"Did you ever know me to break a promise to you?"

"The thought is inconceivable."

"Good. Then I bid you hope. I promise you that in this matter you are no longer alone. I must go to the Cardinal at once. Well! I shall ask for leave, which is overdue me, both for myself and for Athos. Your assassin is dead, your gold is gone, instead, you gain two friends. Aramis is wounded in Paris -- that man told me so before he died in my arms. He uttered your name -- dead -- and that of Aramis -- wounded. You see? At Paris, I swear to you upon the faith of a gentleman that we shall gain access to the lady, we shall convince her that we are to be trusted, we shall make good for you all you have lost. Do you believe me?"

Having the means of access to the lady now inside his pocket, d'Artagnan could very well make this promise.

Porthos lifted his head, stared incredulously at him.

"D'Artagnan! You would do this -- for me?"

"All for one, one for all!" exclaimed d'Artagnan. "You would do as much for me. Agreed?"

Porthos sprang to his feet, seized d'Artagnan in a warm embrace, and tears started from his eyes.

"My friend, my friend!" he cried out with emotion. "Ask of me what you will -- I am yours! What you will -- anything -- "

D'Artagnan freed himself from that dangerous embrace.

"Then I ask that you remain here until I return from my conversation with His Eminence," he said coolly. "If leave is granted me, we may have to depart at once. You need sleep?"

"I need nothing, since I have found you," exclaimed Porthos. "That is to say, I need everything -- but I can do without anything. Go with God, my friend -- I await you!"

D'Artagnan caught up his cloak and departed in some haste for the palace.

He was at once uneasy and at rest mentally. He was at rest on the subject of Aramis, for he was confident that he had pieced the truth together. He was uneasy on the subject of Richelieu, for now it seemed certain that the Cardinal would desire further details regarding the dead man in the road. He cursed his own imprudence for having borne that ring on his finger the previous night; whatever the ring was, whatever it meant, he should have exercised discretion.

"What a devilish imbroglio!" he reflected, as he made his way to the Hotel des Lesdigue'res.

"Aramis is wounded. Porthos receives a letter from him, to Helene de Sine, whoever she is; he is robbed of it. I take it, and the papers of Aramis, from a dead man. Comte de Montforge, evidently a Cardinalist agent, loses a handkerchief which bears the initials of this same lady. Richelieu, instead of clapping a penalty on us for duelling, sweetly commands us to be friends -- and summons us to his cabinet! Decidedly, this affair is going take some very careful stepping."

As he came to the entrance of the palace, horseman came dashing out of the courtyard and passed d'Artagnan with a wave of the hand. It was Montforge, booted and spurred.

When the musketeer was ushered into the presence of

Richelieu, he found Pere Joseph present as on the previous night. And at the very first moment, a cold shiver passed over d'Artagnan, for he thought he saw both men glance at his left hand where he had worn the ring. However, the Cardinal seemed anything but angry, greeted him affably took his arm and walked with him to the window that overlooked the courtyard.

"Look, M. d'Artagnan, and tell me what you see."

D'Artagnan looked down. "Your Eminence, I see guards on duty, I see a very handsome jennet being groomed by the stables. I see a superb horse being saddled -- ah, what an animal! A horse fit for a king, indeed!"

He fell silent in admiration. Richelieu pressed his arm and turned.

"That animal belongs to you, M. d'Artagnan. Come, I wish to ask you something. Do you by any chance recall how you happened to receive a commission as lieutenant?"

D'Artagnan felt fate upon him. "Certainly, Monseigneur; from your own hands -- a kindness for which I have never ceased to be grateful."

"In ten minutes I go to the king," said Richelieu. "I am going to ask him something else for you.

"For me, Your Eminence?" stammered d'Artagnan. Richelieu regarded him with a smile, and did not fail to read the caution behind his amazement.

"Of course, with your permission only. If -- "

His voice died. He flung a glance through the window and now stood silent, looking down at the courtyard; the affability of his features was instantly changed to alert tenseness. A sound of voices rose to the room -- shouts, greetings, cheers, the resounding hollow smash of pike-butts grounded on the stones. D'Artagnan, looking, saw a file of dusty guards drawing up in line, while a number of handsomely dressed cavaliers rode into the courtyard, headed by a slightly stout gentleman with a large nose, a gay smile, and magnificent armor. He was saluted on all sides with respect and hearty cordiality, and the Cardinal's guards presented arms.

"Pere Joseph -- here!" exclaimed Richelieu. The gray secretary was already approaching the window, and now laughed shortly as he glanced out.

"So Bassompierre arrives! Monseigneur, you need not hasten to your audience."

Richelieu drew back, made a gesture. "Leave me with M. d'Artagnan, if you please."

When they were alone, the Cardinal turned from the window and looked at d'Artagnan.

"Monsieur, I suppose you wonder whether I go to ask the king for a lettre de cachet or a captaincy on your behalf? Come, confess! We have met before today."

"I am entirely at the service of Your Eminence," said d'Artagnan, with a composure he was far from feeling. "If I have done nothing to merit a cell, certainly I have done nothing to merit a captaincy."

Richelieu regarded him steadily for a moment.

"No evasions, monsieur. We are alone. Shall we be frank?"

"If Your Eminence pleases, most gladly."

"With your permission, I shall ask the king to grant you an indefinite leave, in order that you may perform certain services for me. Do you wish to accept?"

D'Artagnan bowed, partly in order to hide the relief in his face.

"I am honored by the choice, for in serving Your Eminence, I serve the king --"

"A truce to compliments," interrupted Richelieu brusquely. "I know you of old, M. d'Artagnan. I desire a man who is attached to His Majesty, a gentleman of finesse, of discretion -- I might almost say that I desire the service of an enemy rather than of a friend."

"Then I cannot have the pleasure of serving you, Monseigneur," said d'Artagnan. "I am not your enemy. Even had I the wish, I could not aspire to such a height."

The eye of the Cardinal was penetrating. "You are aware, perhaps, that Madame de Chevreuse is exiled from Paris to her estates at Dampierre. You are aware, I imagine, of a good deal that cannot be put into words -- that princes are ambitious, that mortal life is frail, that those who are great and wealthy and respected today, may be in chains tomorrow.

D'Artagnan trembled inwardly-more at the half-mocking tone of Richelieu than at these words.

"Gossip runs to that effect, Your Eminence," he returned cautiously.

"A despatch now awaiting His Majesty's signature goes to the Keeper of the Seals at Lyon," pursued Richelieu. He was in a dangerous humor this morning, as d'Artagnan perceived; this man who ruled France could not always rule himself -- he had even been known to strike Cavoie, the captain of his guards, as he had been known to take the Chancellor of France by the throat. "From Lyon you will seek Madame de Chevreuse at Dampierre, to whom you will deliver a verbal message. You will then return to Paris and deliver a letter for me. After which, you will be free -- that is to say, if you accept.

D'Artagnan bowed. He did not miss the indescribable tone in which those singular final words were uttered, nor the piercing regard of the Cardinal.

"I am most happy to serve Your Eminence," he said quietly.

"I must warn you, monsieur," said Richelieu slowly, "that in delivering this message to Madame de Chevreuse, you will find it a dangerous matter."

A disdainful smile touched the lips of d'Artagnan.

"The danger, Monseigneur, is for those who oppose me.

"Ah, Gascon!" Richelieu broke into a short laugh. "Yet there is greater danger in the delivery of the letter -- it goes to a lady so beautiful that all who know her fall in love with her at once!"

This touched d'Artagnan's all but mortal hurt and spurred him to audacity.

"From such risk, Monseigneur, you and I are alike immune; you, by reason of the cloth, and I, by reason of a loss I have not forgotten."

The Cardinal was silent for a moment. Perhaps he, too,

had not forgotten Constance de Bonacieux; perhaps he had not forgotten Milady, who, as his agent, had poisoned the unhappy Constance and torn d'Artagnan's heart asunder. After a moment be lifted his head, moved to his secretary, sat down before it and wrote a few lines. Sanding them, he folded and sealed the letter, and addressed it. Then he extended it to d'Artagnan.

"The letter; a personal matter for which I give you thanks."

"I am honored, Monseigneur. And the verbal message?"

The Cardinal spoke reflectively, with a certain air of savage and cruel assurance.

"You may say that you had it from my lips, but couch it in these terms: 'His Majesty has learned all and is taking the child under his own protection. Be very quiet during the next six months. If you indulge your liking for letters and visitors you are lost.' That is all. Repeat the message, monsieur, if you please."

D'Artagnan repeated it, word for word, but he could not keep a note of astonishment from his voice. Richelieu, watching him narrowly, smiled as though gratified by the effect of his words.

"You think, perhaps, I am sending a warning? No, monsieur; I am sending a threat."

This was true. Richelieu never sent warnings his purposes were guessed only after they were accomplished.

"Pardon, Your Eminence," said d'Artagnan. "I do not think regarding such matters. They pass directly from ears to lips, without reaching my brain; and they are then forgotten."

"Very well, monsieur. When can you start?"

"The moment I receive my despatches."

"They will be ready in five minutes. Wait below. The horse standing there is a present for you -- a token of my gratitude for your kindness. You ride alone?"

"With a friend, Monseigneur -- a M. du Vallon, formerly of the Musketeers, whom I encountered this morning."

"Ah, yes -- Porthos, is it not?" Richelieu smiled, and this smile struck terror into d'Artagnan, so singular was its quality. "You will, perhaps -- want to have a word with M. de Bassompierre, who has just arrived from the army?"

"I, Monseigneur?" D'Artagnan looked surprised. "Not at all. I am not one of M. de Bassompierre's gentlemen -- I know him very slightly, indeed."

"Indeed!" echoed Richelieu. "Very well; that is all, monsieur."

D'Artagnan bowed and departed. When he found himself outside the room, he was trembling, as though he had just emerged from some terrible danger.

Scarcely was he gone, when Pere Joseph entered the room and addressed the Cardinal.

"Monseigneur, His Majesty awaits you -- he is being barbered now."

"Good. And Bassompierre?"

"Is, I think, going to Paris at once."

"So? My friend and father," and Richelieu tapped his arm affectionately. "I have accomplished two things within a very few minutes. First, Chevreuse is eliminated from whatever may happen within the next few months."

"Then Your Eminence has accomplished a miracle."

"Second, that dangerous young man who wore a ring yesterday and does not wear it today, will cause no further trouble."

"So?" The Capuchin looked doubtful. "He is a better man than Montforge. He may -- escape."

"In which case he will fall into a pit from which there is no escape. See to it that he is provided with a purse when the papers are sent him."

Pere Joseph looked astonished at this unwonted liberality, for at this period Richelieu was niggardly with money. He had twice received Marion de l'Orme, the most famous hetera of Paris; he received her most magnificently on each occasion; after the second time, he sent her a purse by his lackey Bournais. She opened it, found a hundred pistoles, threw them into the street, and told the story to everyone.

Going directly to the courtyard, d'Artagnan paused to peep at the letter given him: all his curiosity had been keenly aroused. He glanced at the superscription. This letter was addressed to Helene de Sirle, at the Parc du Montmorenci.

With a bewildered air, d'Artagnan went to the horse that a groom was holding, and mounted with scarcely a glance at the superb animal. He sat waiting, a thousand conjectures flashing across his mind. One thing was clear -- his mission ended with the delivery of this letter.

"Therefore," he reflected, "once my errand's done I'm free to help Porthos. And the Cardinal sends me to the same point, to the same person, as the Queen! Now, if I had Athos to advise me in this -- ah, fool that I am!"

It had just occurred to him that since Athos was at Lyon, there was nothing to prevent him from taking Athos with him. And at this admirable inspiration, d'Artagnan could scarce control his eagerness to be off, pick up Porthos, and depart.

Abruptly, as he sat there, a terrible memory rose before him. The words of the dying man recurred to him with sinister emphasis:

"Above them all, she -- she herself!"

She herself! A child in the abbey of St. Saforin, guarded by an unknown Betstein; Aramis and Bassompierre and a plot -- what was it all? How did a child enter into it? Was this the same child mentioned in Richelieu's message? Sudden relief came at the thought. "Ah!" he murmured, wiping a trickle of sweat from his eyes. "Then it's a question of Chevreuse, not of the Queen -- excellent And here, I see, are my despatches --"

A secretary approached him, handed him a packet of letters and a purse.

D'Artagnan turned his horse and twirled his mustache as the magnificent animal bore him from the courtyard and past the guards saluting at the gates. He returned their salute, and two minutes later was on his way to rejoin Porthos.

CHAPTER V

FOUR LETTERS ARE SENT, ONE ARRIVES

At the moment d'Artagnan and Porthos left Grenoble, the affairs of France were in divers hands and conditions. The Imperialists had captured Mantua by assault and Casale was under siege; on the other hand, the army had swept all before it in Savoy and Piedmont, hence the queen-mother was more than ever furious against Richelieu. Both the king and the cardinal had left the army for the best of reasons -- the plague. Louis XIII, never a robust man, had come to Grenoble and paused there, with illness creeping upon him. He had intended to rejoin the army, but it began to look as though he would rejoin the court instead.

The queens were at Lyon, and Paris ruled itself. Bassompierre arrived at Grenoble more in guise of a triumphing Caesar than a grumbling general.

He found the king at his levee, and was received most joyfully by Louis, who was at the moment in the hands of his hairdresser.

"Ha! Our beloved marshal foregoes the pomps of war to rejoin us!" exclaimed the king, as Bassompierre knelt to kiss his hand. "Come, Francois, tell me something! I hear that when you entered Madrid as our ambassador, you rode a mule. Is that true?"

"Faith, sire, entirely true!" and Bassompierre chuckled.

He was extremely handsome, and was wearing superb armor, expressly donned for the occasion. His hearty, genial laugh, his air of breezy frankness, swept into the room like a freshening breath of morning, "A mule of the finest Andaluzian strain, sent me by the Emperor; a mule to make a bishop weep with envy -- "

Well, well," interrupted Louis, "I never thought to see the day when an ass was mounted upon a mule!"

Those around broke into laughter. Bassompierre swept the king a low bow.

"True, very true," he rejoined. "But all things are possible to those anointed of the Lord! Upon that occasion I was, naturally, representing Your Majesty."

The superb audacity of this reply delighted the king, who burst into laughter that ended the business of his hairdresser.

"Francois, you have a tongue in a thousand -- I love you for it," he cried gaily. "They say you would sooner lose a friend than a good jest, Francois! Be careful you do not lose a friend in me!"

"God forbid, Your Majesty!" said Bassompierre devoutly. "For then I should have to seek a friend in His Eminence."

"Impossible, Betstein, impossible!" Louis laughed heartily, and according to his custom used the German form of Bassompierre's name, as a token of familiarity. "Our good cardinal has no maids of honor at his court."

"In such case," said the audacious Lorrainer, "let us both return to Lyon, sire, and be at our ease!"

Louis chuckled at this thrust. It was no secret that the king was madly but virtuously enamored of Mlle. de Hautefort, maid of honor to the queen. Leaning back in his chair, Louis resigned himself again to the hands of his hairdresser. He was handsome, in his thinly cruel fashion, but his temper was extremely uneven; he rose to a certain largeness of spirit only with Bassompierre.

This man, who alone could jest with the king on even terms, moved among the gentlemen present, his impressive personality dominating them all, even his enemies. Of these he had not a few. The polished and imposing presence, the very force of character which so contributed to his success as courtier or gambler, lover or ambassador, assured him the solid testimonial of envious foes.

One of these gentlemen, who fancied the raillery of the king betokened a change in the marshal's fortunes, thought the occasion opportune to intrude a suave hint of intrigue. He turned to Bassompierre.

"So, monsieur, we are to judge that you have joined the party of Guise?"

"Eh?" said Bassompierre, astonished, "I? And why should you think that, monsieur?"

The other shrugged. "Why not, indeed, after the tender manner in which you embrace his sister, the Princesse de Conti?"

"Ho!" Bassompierre inflated his cheeks in hearty laughter. "Nonsense, my dear monsieur, nonsense! I assure you that I have embraced your wife with far greater warmth -- and I do not love you any the more because of it!"

The king broke into a roar of mirth in which all his gentlemen joined, and in the midst of this mirth, the cardinal was announced. Richelieu entered, saluted profoundly, kissed the king's hand, and greeted Bassompiere very warmly. Now, as it chanced, Louis remembered d'Artagnan and asked where he was.

"He has just departed, sire," said the cardinal. "He received your letters for the court, and was next moment in the saddle."

"Ah! A pity I missed him!" said Bassompierre. "I like that young man. He is impetuous, he is afraid of nothing, he is a good officer. Above all, he is faithful."

"You admire faithful men more than faithful women, eh?" jested the king.

"Faith, sire, it's all one to me!" Bassompierre's laughing brown eyes twinkled, and he twirled the waxed points of his mustache. Then, meeting the eye of Richelieu, he sensed a coming attack, and fell silent with disconcerted surprise. How he had offended the minister, he could not conceive.

"M. le Marechal wears armor," said the cardinal smoothly. "Surely, sire, he does not fear the weapons of enemies here?"

An ominous hint. Bassompierre was too old a courtier to show his astonishment, however; the king, rising from the chair, took his arm affectionately.

"Eh, Betstein? Surely you have no such fear in our presence?"

"Alas, sire -- I have great fear of assassination," admitted Bassompierre, who was no man to refuse a challenge from the cardinal or any other. At the word, there was a stir. The king's hand fell, his face changed. Those around stood frozen, and Richelieu's eye held a satiric gleam of triumph. With that word, Bassompierre had wrecked his future -- all felt this to be certain.

"Assassination!" echoed Louis. "In our presence? Explain yourself, monsieur!"

Bassompierre bowed.

"Sire, His Eminence is, as usual, entirely right. Regard this corselet -- expressly made for me, never worn until this morning! You will observe, sire, the remarkable gold inlay, the supreme lightness yet excellence of the steel!"

"It is indeed magnificent," said the king coldly. "I doubt whether its like is in our own armory. But, Francois, if you seem to doubt our ability to protect -- "

It was coming. Another instant, and Bassompierre would be dismissed, sent to his estates, ruined! He intervened, coolly.

"Pardon, sir -- you misapprehend. Assassination is indeed my greatest fear; but not for myself. I wore this corselet in the hope that you would deign to accept it from me, wear it, and so set at rest all the fears that have weighed upon me! This bit of steel is too beauteous for me -- only the son of Henri Quatre could wear it fittingly!"

And with a gesture, Bassompierre unbuckled the corselet.

The king was astonished, delighted, charmed as a boy with a new toy. The cardinal bit his lip with vexation. Although slightly large for Louis XIII, the corselet proved a fairly good fit, and the king insisted on wearing it immediately.

He discovered that it became him admirably, and was put into excellent humor. So, when Bassompierre requested permission to go to Paris it was granted instantly.

"As you like, Betstein, as you like," said the king. "But, I order you -- tell us her name!"

"Her name, sire, is Chaillot," said Bassompiere, giving the title of the magnificent estate he had recently purchased. "I go to build my home, hoping that some day I may have the honor to entertain Your Majesty there."

"See that you build your house upon the rock, my dear marshal," said Richelieu drily. Bassonpierre smiled at him.

"Monseigneur, it shall be built upon a stone!" he said, playing on his own name.

"When one builds a house," said the cardinal reflectively, "the next step is to bring home the bride. You are not, by any chance, thinking of marriage?"

In these words, Bassompierre perceived that his secret marriage had become known to the cardinal. He passed off the question with a jest, but ten minutes afterward he took his leave of the king and retired.

"If I remain here? I am a lost man!" he said to his secretary. "The horses, swiftly -- let us ride for Paris!"

He little dreamed that because he did not remain here he was, indeed, a lost man. These things lay in the future.

When Bassompierre and his princely suite were half a league out of Grenoble, there came riding after them a gentleman of the king's household, a distant relative of the marshal. Catching up with them, he drew Bassompierre to one side the road.

"News for you, monsieur," he said. "Do you know an officer of Musketeers named d'Artagnan?"

"I know of him, at least," said Bassompierre curiously. "Why?"

"He precedes you to Paris."

"That is no news."

"He carries a letter."

"I carry fifty. Did you spur after us to tell me this?"

"To tell you, monsieur, that I was standing in the courtyard when he drew out this letter and looked at the superscription, which was written in the hand of Richelieu."

"Ah!" murmured Bassompierre. "And did it concern me?"

"That, monsieur, I leave to you. I saw the writing; the letter was addressed to a certain Mlle. de Sirle."

Bassompierre became pale as death.

"Impossible!" he ejaculated. "Richelieu never heard of her!"

"On the contrary, monsieur, Richelieu met her at the hotel of the Duc de Montmorenci, and is said to have visited her since then."

The pallor of the marshal became a deep and angry flush.

"So! But it is impossible. The Cardinal -- " He checked himself abruptly, smiled, and held out his hand with a swift change of manner. "My thanks, my thanks! It was good of you to think this matter might concern me, but I assure you it does not. I am sorry you have lost your time and trouble, my friend."

"I have not lost it, monsieur, since I have gained your thanks," said the other, and so turned about and rode back to Grenoble.

Bassompierre continued his way but with this difference -- he now rode at headlong speed.

D'Artagnan and Porthos gained Lyon without pause. Upon reaching the artillery barracks where the Musketeers were quartered, Porthos dismounted, staggered, and was only saved from falling by d'Artagnan.

"My friend," he confessed, "I have been in the saddle four days and nights. I need sleep. I need salves and ointment. For the love of heaven, show me a bed and leave me!"

D'Artagnan took him to his own quarters, then delivered his despatches,learned that Athos was on duty, and sought out M. Rambure's, the captain of his company, whom he found at table.

"Monsieur," he said with his simple directness, "As you know, I bore letters to His Majesty at Grenoble. There I had the honor of seeing the Cardinal."

"Peste!" exclaimed Rambures, facetiously. "And you're not in the Bastille, my dear fellow?"

"On the contrary, I'm on my way to Paris at the request of His Eminence, who promised me leave, advised me to make haste, and authorized me do what I liked. Therefore, with your permission, I should like my friend M. Athos to ride with me."

"Gladly, M. d'Artagnan, gladly. But come! To Paris -- for the cardinal? Just between ourselves, when did M. du Plessis obtain the services of His Majesty's guards?"

"By convincing the guards, monsieur, that they were acting in His Majesty's interests."

Rambure's broke into laughter. "Good, good! Put in the application -- I'll attend to it. Take our good Athos and go when you desire. Sit down and help me finish this bottle of wine; the guard will be changed in ten minutes, and you can then gobble Athos and run. What news from the army?"

D'Artagnan made himself comfortable.

"None that I know of -- I got into Grenoble late, and left early in the morning. By the way, Rambure's, do you happen to know a gentleman of the cardinal's household named Montforge?"

The captain, who was a Gascon like two-thirds of the guards, frowned.

"Hm -- yes, I've heard the name! Of course he's the man who killed Aubain, Guise's fencing master, last year. Isn't he some relative of Mme. de Chavigny? You know, the complaisant lady who bore His Eminence a son -- tut, what scandal!" Rambure's laughed. "Here's long life to you, and wishing I were going to Paris in your company!"

D'Artagnan knew already that Montforge was an excellent blade; he knew already that the man was a favorite of Richelieu; so, having learned nothing, he presently departed to find Athos, and came upon him just going off duty. Athos embraced him warmly, as though he had been absent four months instead of four days.

"Ha, my son -- back already? What news?"

"Every sort imaginable," said d'Artagnan. "Come over to that auberge and settle down to talk it out in comfort -- "

"Unfortunately," said Athos, "I have been assigned to escort their majesties, who go riding in the park in half an hour."

"Bah!" D'Artagnan beckoned to another gentleman of the Musketeers, who was approaching. "You are on leave, my dear Athos -- you ride to Paris with me. M. de Bret will take your place and be glad to do it."

This proving true, the two friends repaired to the auberge across the street.

"To Paris?" said Athos, and then shrugged. "Good! As well one place as another."

Such was the philosophy of the Comte de la Fere at this period.

Since that terrible night on the banks of the Lys, when d'Artagnan, Lord de Winter, and the Three Musketeers had witnessed the execution of Milady, Athos had once more sunk into the depths of his own negligence toward life. He had no ambition. He lived for nothing. He drank huge quantities of his favorite Spanish wine, spoke little, appeared drowned in a dark and mysterious sadness. Yet neither wine nor melancholy affected this man outwardly -- this man who, so far as others were concerned, lived as a perfect model of chivalry and honor. His voice retained its soft liquid quality, his features retained their indefinable air of nobility, of sweetness, his wrist retained its marvelous flexibility; all this despite his more frequent turning to the material side of life -- to tavern debauches where he uttered scarce a word, to steady drinking until Grimaud took his arm and led him home. It seemed as though Athos had resolved to drown all that lay behind and ahead of him.

As the two friends turned in at the tavern, a man suddenly appeared in front of them and blocked the way. This man was Grimaud, the lackey of Athos.

Athos motioned him aside, but Grimaud did not budge.

"Well?" asked Athos. In reply, Grimaud drew a letter from his pocket and presented it. This letter was addressed to the Comte de la Fere.

"Who brought this?" demanded Athos in astonishment. Grimaud, trained to silence, shrugged to indicate his ignorance. D'Artagnan, who knew that Athos never wrote or received a letter, was astonished.

"Bah!" said Athos. "Your news first, d'Artagnan. Come!"

They entered the auberge and settled themselves in a corner. When the wine was brought and they were alone, d'Artagnan took the ring and letter from his pocket. He handed the ring to Athos, whose amazing knowledge of heraldry had ere this astonished him.

"Do you know whose arms these are!"

Athos smiled slightly. "Certainly. They belong to the man who would have been married to the daughter of the old Constable de Montmorenci, had he not neglected the etiquette of paying a visit to the Duc de Bouillon, nephew of the Constable. In consequence, she was married to Conde -- "

"I am not a historian," interrupted d'Artagnan. "Whose are these arms?"

Athos drank deeply. "They belong to the man who refused to be made Duc d'Aumale."

"His name?"

"He has two."

"Devil take you!" said d'Artagnan impatiently. Athos, seeing that he was in earnest, at once lost his jesting manner.

"Pardon, my son -- yet you astonished me by your ignorance! This man is captain of the Chateau de Monceaux; a knight of the Ordre du St. Esprit; he refused a bribe of 100,000 crowns; he played tennis with Wallenstein before Emperor Maximilian; he outdrank the canons of Saverne; he won a wager of a thousand crowns from Henri IV; he was given the honor of having fifty guards; he refused the Duchy of Beaupreau; he was made Marshal of France --"

"Ah! ah!" exclaimed d'Artagnan in stupefied astonishment. "You cannot mean Schomberg -- "

"Certainly not. I mean Bassompierre -- whose name originally was Betstein, the same name in Germanized form."

D'Artagnan was overcome with stupefaction. Betstein!

"Read this," he said, and handed the letter of Aramis to his friend. Athos glanced at it, and pushed it away a little with his hand.

"I have a letter of my own, not yet read," he said. "A gentleman does not read the letters of others, my son.

"A soldier reads the correspondence of the enemy," said d'Artagnan.

"True," said Athos, and picked up the letter. A slight pallor came into his face, and his eyes darted a fiery glance at d'Artagnan. "A letter -- to a lady -- and in the hands of Aramis! And you say -- an enemy --

"Read it," said d'Artagnan calmly. "It contains no secrets."

Athos met his gaze steadily for a moment, found it serene and unclouded, nodded slightly, and opened the letter.

"I have read it," he said.

"Good. Now -- can you conceive to whom it refers? To what bearer?"

The singularly imperturbable eyes of Athos rested on him, and then that sweet and expressive smile touched the lips of the older man.

"Ah, my son! I know the suppressed eagerness burning in you! Were it not impossible, I would say that the bearer of this letter -- this friend of Aramis -- must be also a friend of ours. Porthos. But that is impossible."

D'Artagnan was seized with wonder at this evidence of insight.

"Athos -- you are divine!" he exclaimed. "Porthos is at this moment asleep on my bed. Come -- here is the whole story."

And he poured out all that had happened since he had left Lyon for Grenoble.

Athos listened, tapping with his long and beautiful fingers on the letter he had received but had not opened. He showed no astonishment at what he heard -- only a miracle could make Athos lift an eyebrow. But, when d'Artagnan repeated the words uttered by the dying spy of Richelieu, the gaze of Athos became singularly penetrating, alert, alive. The names of Porthos and of Aramis still had power for him. When the tale came to the meeting with Porthos, his gaze showed interest. When it came to the interrupted duel, it revealed satisfaction.

"Ah, my son, I am proud of you!" he said quietly, and those words thrilled d'Artagnan above all praise from Richelieu or Louis himself. "I have heard of this Montforge -- a man of noble blood and ignoble speech and deed. Continue."

D'Artagnan finished his recital, and the eye of Athos began to sparkle. D'Artagnan showed Richelieu's letter to Helene de Sirle, and was about to repeat the verbal message to Chevreuse, when Athos checked him.

"Tut, tut -- that message is sacred!"

"But I have no secrets from you, my friend."

"That is not your secret."

"True." D'Artagnan reflected. "Richelieu said the message was not a warning, but a threat, and was extremely dangerous to me as the bearer."

A disdainful smile touched the lips of Athos.

"Undoubtedly. Chevreuse is the most dangerous woman in France, as Richelieu knows to his cost; she stops at nothing, stoops to anything!"

"Well, leave that aside. What do you think of the other matter?"

"I think Bassompierre is facing destruction," and Athos drank an entire goblet of Malaga as though it were a duty.

"No, no -- I mean the business of the child! That's why I wanted to repeat the message -- it has a vital connection."

"So?" Athos looked thoughtful. "You think Porthos knows all about it?"

"I have not asked him. Theories are wasted time."

"Exactly my opinion. Let's dismiss the whole affair for the moment -- ride to Paris, then to Dampierre -- or to Dampierre first. We can go by way of Bourg-la-Reine and circle back to Paris. Once there, we deliver your letter to Mlle. de Sirle and Porthos delivers his."

"Or we for him. I promised to gain him admission to her presence."

"You must give him the letter."

"And confess that I kept silent about it?"

"Not at all. Give it to Grimaud." Athos turned and crooked his finger. As though by magic, Grimaud came forward and stood before the table. Athos handed him the letter.

"M. Porthos."

Grimaud had not heard of Porthos in above a year's time, but said nothing.

The horses, immediately after supper tonight," said Athos, Grimaud gave d'Artagnan an inquiring look.

"No, I have a new mount," said d'Artagnan. "Go to my room first."

"Ah!" Grimaud started. "Then M. Por--"

"Silence, you villain!" commanded Athos.

Demanding pardon with a profound bow, Grimaud

departed on his errand. D'Artagnan laughed; he understood perfectly. Grimaud would put the letter in the pocket of Porthos, who would discover it upon wakening.

"So we have money, horses, freedom, and we ride upon business for the queen and the Cardinal -- excellent!" said Athos, taking all this as a matter of course. "Aramis is wounded; you destroyed the packet taken from him -- better still! That spy said he had had this ring with Bassompierre's arms made -- I wonder why? Bah! No use wondering. Ride and discover."

"Have you forgotten your own letter?" asked d'Artagnan.

With a careless shrug, Athos picked up the letter, found the seal illegible, and tore open the folded paper. It was a very stout paper, a sort of parchment; the letter had been sent on from the Hotel of the Musketeers at Paris.

Reading the letter, Athos did not change his expression, but the color slowly drained out of his face and was replaced by a mortal pallor. He lifted his eyes, looked at d'Artagnan, and spoke with visible effort.

"Do you -- do you remember a man -- an Englishman -- " his voice failed. D'Artagnan, startled, leaned over the table.

"You do not mean -- Lord de Winter?"

Athos inclined his head and pushed forward the letter. D'Artagnan, stupefied, turned it about and read:

"M. Athos: Lest one letter fail, I send four, to you and to your three friends. I shall be in Paris, at the Hotel of the Marquis de St. Luc, Place Royale, on July 30th. WINTER."

D'Artagnan looked at the letter, then looked at Athos,

then at the letter again, with a puzzled frown. Something was lacking here -- he did not know what. On that fateful night beside the River Lys two years ago, when Milady was executed, a fifth man had stood beside the four friends. She, who had been the mistress of d'Artagnan and the wife of Athos, had also been the sister-in-law of Lord de Winter; this woman was dead, but she had left frightful memories behind.

"What does he mean?" Athos passed a hand across his pallid brow. "I do not want to see him. Why should he write the four of us --"

"Ah, ah!" exclaimed d'Artagnan, and lifted his voice. "Host! A lighted candle -- name of the devil, be quick about it!" He looked at Athos, his eyes sparkling. "My friend, 1 have just thought of something -- this signature is well below the body of the letter -- "

The inn-keeper brought a lighted candle and departed. When he was gone, d'Artagnan held the letter above the flame. Words appeared, written in the thick paper with secret ink and momentarily shown by the heat:

"He is dead; she remains. Come, if you would save her!"

D'Artagnan lifted his head and regarded Athos, who had read the writing.

"He -- ah! That means Buckingham. And she -- then it's a question of the queen -- "

"Silence, foolish tongue!" exclaimed Athos severely. "Of course, of course! This Englishman is faithful and a gentleman. But St. Luc is brother-in-law to Bassompierre! I do not understand this at all -- "

"Therefore dismiss conjecture, accept your own medicine, and don't waste time!" D'Artagnan held the paper in the flame and watched it burn. "One letter out of four arrived. This is the twenty-fifth of July. We must ride to Dampierre first; that's understood. If we're to be in Paris on the thirtieth --"

"We must leave this evening," said Athos. "Except that Porthos needs sleep, we should leave now, this moment!"

D'Artagnan rose. "Good. Pray wait for me at my quarters -- make yourself at home there, my dear Athos. I may not return until late."

"Oh!" Athos looked at him with a touch of sadness. "That pretty little lady in Rue de Grenoble, eh? Well, well, I do not repeat my warnings."

D'Artagnan flushed slightly. It was true that Athos had warned him, though for no particular reason; if he had ignored the warning, he had not forgotten it.

"One romance begins, another is ended," he said lightly. "Do not reproach me; the lady has treated me well and I cannot leave her like a bumpkin without saying farewell. And, since her husband is the equerry of the Duc de Lesdigueres, and with the army -- "

"All is safe," concluded Athos satirically. "Go with God or the devil, my friend! I have nothing to live for except your friendship, so come back safe."

And Athos drained another flagon of Malaga at one draught.

CHAPTER VI

IN WHICH ATHOS UTTERS PREDICTIONS

For above a year d'Artagnan had remained faithful to the memory of his devoted Constance, who had been poisoned by Milady; but when one is young and ardent, wounds heal swiftly. It must be confessed that Sophie de Bruler was an excellent agent of healing. Her little house in the Rue de Grenoble was discreet, charming, even rich; her husband in earlier years had fought in Hungary against the Turks and had brought home two wagon-loads of booty. Sophie herself was, like other young wives of elderly warriors, inconsolable in the absence of her lord, and did not rebuff the attempts at consolation which d'Artagnan made. In person she was small, with the most brilliant brown eyes in the world, and her graceful, supple figure was the envy of half the ladies of Lyon. If our hero had in some wise consoled her for the absence of her knightly husband, then she had offered him no little consolation for his own deeper and more bitter loss. D'Artagnan was not in love with her, but he made love as though he were, and at moments he almost deceived himself in this regard.

Although his coming was unexpected, he did not hesitate on this account. The house being on a corner, there was a garden gate opening on the side street; to this gate, d'Artagnan possessed the key.

Letting himself in at this gate, he found the garden empty. The afternoon was late, but darkness was still an hour or two away. Knowing that the little bell attached to the gate gave warning of each arrival, he eyed the windows as he crossed the garden, hoping to catch sight of the fair Sophie. No one appeared, however.

He knocked at the door, which was instantly opened to him by the femme-de-chambre.

"Come in, monsieur," she said. "Madame saw your approach and sent me to tell you that she would not keep you a moment. She is engaged with her notary. Will you enter the little salon!"

Giving her his hat and cloak, d'Artagnan stepped into the tiny reception salon near the entrance -- a very handsome little room hung with yellow satin and containing a superb Titian which M. de Bruler had removed from a Hungarian altar.

"Peste! Madame is devoted to her notary!" thought d'Artagnan. "This is the third time in two weeks she has been engaged with him."

However, since Sophie was managing the affairs of her absent husband, she had some excuse for her attachment to business.

D'Artagnan, indeed, had not waited five minutes when the femme-de-chambre appeared and said her mistress would receive him.

"She has been suffering all day from a migraine and is in her chamber," she said. "If monsieur will follow -- "

D'Artagnan pressed a coin into her hand.

"You need not show me the way," he said eagerly. "I know it already, my good woman -- "

And he sprang for the stairway.

Sophie de Bruler, wearing a charming negligee of sky-blue silk encrusted with silver stars, reclined on a chaise-longue near a table on which were documents, ink, quills and sand-sifter. The walls of the room were covered by that magnificent set of tapestries designed by Rubens and representing the rape of Lucrece and the fall of the Tarquins, for which M. de Bruler had refused 40,000 crowns.

The room was in disorder, as was invariably the case. The curtains of the tall carven bed in one corner were drawn. On the tables was heaped a medley of bottles and boxes and toilet articles -- pomades, mirrors, perfumes, powders; clothes were everywhere, flung about carelessly. The one quality lacking to Madame de Bruler was neatness.

D'Artagnan parted the curtains, stood on the threshold an instant; then, with the rapidity of light, was across the room and kneeling beside his mistress. He pressed his lips to hers, she returned the embrace warmly, yielding to his ardor with a passionate abandon that enchanted him. Then, suddenly, she drew away, looked into his eyes, smiled.

"Ah, in what a state you find me!" she exclaimed. "This terrible room -- always in confusion, always at sixes and sevens! I am ashamed, my dear d'Artagnan -- "

"Let love assoil your shame, then," he returned quickly. "I ride to Paris and beyond, my fair one -- a long journey, a long errand! I may not return. Before leaving, I stole an hour or two to see you, to mingle my tears with yours, to protest my devotion -- "

"Ah, horror!" she exclaimed. "You -- leaving? Impossible! Cruel that you are, to greet me with such words! Here, sit beside me, tell me you are only jesting -- "

"Alas, would that I were!" responded d'Artagnan, obeying her command. "Are we alone?"

"Absolutely, my treasure!" she replied, touching his hair with caressing fingers. "Georgette has orders not to disturb us until supper is served. Ah, my hero -- surely you were jesting?"

D'Artagnan drew her to him. "Jesting? No, unfortunately! So come -- let us forget tomorrow in today!"

"Gladly -- if you trust me a little!" she returned, with a warm response to his kisses.

"Eh? Trust you -- my source of all happiness?" D'Artagnan was astonished, and broke into his quick, kindling smile. "With my life!"

"Then why do you go to Paris -- after you swore to me you would be here all summer? The court is not leaving."

"Ah!" he exclaimed. "I go because I am ordered, not because I desire it."

"On duty or on errands of love?"

D'Artagnan laughed. "On errands of state, believe me! Love and duty I leave here."

"Liar!" she said, her brown eyes very merry and bright. "You go to see a lady, I wager!"

"Oh! That is true," said d'Artagnan, disconcerted. "But I also go to see another lady, and I have never seen either of them in my life, so -- "

"So," she mocked him, "you'll see them and forget me straightway!"

"No, I swear it!" cried d'Artagnan impulsively.

"My sweet love, not for any lady save the queen whom I serve, would I forget you! And to tell the truth, I think my main errand is to be with a man, an Englishman -- "

He checked himself abruptly. It seemed to him that the tapestry to one side had waved a little, as though a draught of air were in the room; this trifling matter had the effect of halting the indiscreet disclosure he had been about to make in self defense.

"An Englishman!" exclaimed Sophie, opening her eyes wide. "Not truly! A monster!"

"No," and d'Artagnan laughed. "A nobleman. And besides, I shall not go alone. I shall have with me -- "

Something checked him again -- some instinct, some inner warning. He drew the yielding lips of Sophie to his, held her in a passionate embrace. And, as he released her from this embrace, he saw the tapestry move for the second time.

The blood in the veins of d'Artagnan turned to ice. He scarce realized that Sophie had drawn him down beside her, that she was covering his face with kisses.

"So you do love me!" she cried softly. "Foolish woman that I am, I thought your mission was concerned with the will of Francois Thounenin of Dompt, of whom a kinsman in Lorraine wrote me! Swear to me that you would not imperil yourself in that affair!"

With an effort, d'Artagnan collected himself.

"Thounenin of Dompt!" he repeated, astonished. "Upon my honor, I have never heard the name -- I know nothing about it!"

Sophie thought him merely amazed at her knowledge. A shallow woman, absolutely unfitted for the part she was playing, she could not see that to this man such an oath meant the exact truth. With an air of making a vast impression, she reached out and took a small paper from the table nearby.

"See, where I copied it from my kinsman's letter!" she exclaimed. "The will drawn up by Thounenin before Leonard, hereditary grand tabellion to the Duchy of Lorraine, on May 29, 1624 -- the will which is now being so much talked about -- "

D'Artagnan, to whom all this talk meant nothing, was staring at the paper, thunderstruck. He did not regard the words written there, but the paper itself. It was an Italian paper, made with an intricate and heavy watermark -- the identical paper used by Richelieu in writing Helene de Sirle. This sheet, therefore, must have come from the very desk of the cardinal at Grenoble.

"My angel, your kinsman is singularly well informed," said d'Artagnan, without the least evidence of his surprise.

"So he should be, my love, since he is one of the Duke's gentlemen! I was worried lest you become involved in the business and draw down the anger of the great Cardinal -- "

"Be assured," said the young man. "What beautiful paper this is -- Italian, I think?"

Sophie shrugged. "I do not know. It was one of a few sheets my notary left."

She drew d'Artagnan's lips to hers. Under cover of a long embrace, he deftly contrived to fold the fragment of paper in his fingers; then, slipping it into his cuff, he pressed the perfumed curls of Sophie against his shoulder and covered her eyes with impassioned kisses. Looking up as he did so, he again perceived a slight movement in the tapestry -- and beneath its edge, at the floor, caught a glint as of a sword-point there.

"Athos did well to warn me!" thought d'Artagnan.

Having no inclination for the role of Samson, he glanced swiftly about -- not neglecting, however, the beautiful woman who was sighing in his arms and stirring as with passionate abandon.

The only weapon in sight was a long Turkish poniard, inlaid with gold and gems. It hung by the window, barely a foot from the suspicious point in the tapestry. Since the chamber had, so far as he knew, only the one door, and escape from the window was impossible because of its height above the ground, d'Artagnan realized that he must act swiftly and shrewdly if he were to escape. He no longer doubted that Sophie was acting as a spy, or had a spy concealed behind her hangings. This paper had been given her, doubtless in order that she should question him about the will of Thounenin;

she bad blundered in putting it into his hands. So this was why she had been so curious about his errand!

"My angel, I am about to show my confidence in you," said D'Artagnan, caressing the silken locks that fell about his breast and watching the tapestry narrowly as he spoke. "True, I can have no secrets from you! Know, then, that I have been given an important mission by His Eminence the Cardinal."

"Ah!" The lovely arms of Sophie tightened about him. "By Richelieu himself?"

"Himself," repeated d'Artagnan. "A conspiracy has been discovered at Paris -- a conspiracy to kill the king, place the Duc d'Orleans on the throne, and arrest the cardinal. Well, then! I go to seize the leaders of this conspiracy. It is the way of our great cardinal, my angel, to strike when least expected -- to foresee the blow aimed at him and launch a stroke which will paralyze it. An excellent fashion, I assure you, and one which I myself endeavor to imitate whenever possible -- as for example -- "

While speaking, he had gently loosened the clinging arms that enfolded him. Now, with one sudden and agile spring, he gained the window, grasped the Turkish poniard, ripped it from its hangings, and unsheathing it, thrust it with all his strength at the tapestry.

Swift as he was, his blow was evaded.

The tapestry was flung aside, a man there leaped back from the blow, a sword glittered and drove at the heart of d'Artagnan. One piercing shriek burst from Sophie -- but d'Artagnan had no time to look at her. He had missed his blow, but with the dagger he caught and parried the sword-stroke aimed at him -- and he recognized the man facing him.

It was the Comte de Montforge.

"Ah, villain!" cried d'Artagnan furiously. "Assassin that you are -- "

Montforge laughed, pressed in upon him. Having only the poniard, d'Artagnan could scarce hope to defend himself for long against the rapier that sought his throat; he darted backward, holding the longer steel in play. A table overturned with a crash. Montforge struck against a chair, was momentarily flung off balance -- and like a panther, d'Artagnan leaped in upon him and struck him full above the heart.

The poniard shattered. Montforge was unharmed.

"Mail!" cried d'Artagnan. "Coward as well as villain -- "

He hurled the hilt of the poniard into the eyes of Montforge, gained the door with one leap, and slammed it behind him as he darted for the stairs.

He encountered none of the domestics. Burning with mortification, with fury, with shame, he caught up his sword, bared it, turned and ran back up the stairs to encounter Montforge on an equal basis. When he burst into the room again, however, Montforge was not there. Sophie lay upon the couch, in a faint; a turned-back corner of the tapestry disclosed another door, now locked, by which Montforge had evidently departed.

D'Artagnan, raging, retraced his steps, took up baldric,

hat and cloak, and in another moment was out in the Rue de Grenoble. Darkness was falling, there were no passers-by, the street was empty. Then, recalling the side street by which he himself had entered, d'Artagnan ran to the corner.

"Ah!" he cried out. "Scoundrel -- wait!"

At the little garden gate, Montforge was just mounting into the saddle of a horse. He gave d'Artagnan one glance, flung a mocking laugh at him, and thrust in his spurs. He was darting away before d'Artagnan could reach him, another laugh trailing back. With a furious curse, d'Artagnan put up his sword and bent his steps toward his own quarters.

"The devil!" he exclaimed, torn between bewilderment and chagrin. "Here's our precious notary, then -- ah! Athos, you were right, as always!"

When he came to his own quarters, Grimaud was before the door.

"The horses are ready?" asked d'Artagnan. Grimaud made a sign of assent, and d'Artagnan went into the room.

Porthos was sitting on the edge of the bed, eyes still heavy with sleep. Athos sat beside the window, flinging dice idly with one hand against the other. At sight of d'Artagnan, Porthos uttered a sharp exclamation.

"Ah, my friend! Imagine! I am a fool -- I was never robbed at all! I came to myself, found my -- my belongings, my rouleaux of gold, inside the lining of my cloak --"

"Wait!" Athos rose. He had perceived the disordered attire, the changed aspect, of d'Artagnan; now, as the latter dropped his cloak, Athos pointed to a slit in his sleeve. "What has happened? Then my warning was not futile, after all?"

"My dear Athos," said d'Artagnan gloomily, "your warning saved my life. So you have found your money, Porthos? Good. Listen, my friends!" He broke off momentarily. He had only told Porthos of his mission to Dampierre, not of the letter to Mlle. de Sirle. "First, I must tell you that, besides my errand to Dampierre, M. de Richelieu confided a second mission to me. This was to deliver a letter to a certain Mlle. de Sirle at Paris -- "

"Eh? What's that?" Porthos opened his eyes wide. "Why, it was to her that -- that -- "

"That Aramis sent you? Excellent. We shall kill two birds with one stone. Now listen attentively, my Porthos! And you, Athos -- you shall hear how well founded was your warning -- "

He told them everything that had happened at the house of Sophie de Bruler.

Porthos, not comprehending the half of it all, uttered ejaculations of fury and wonder; Athos, who understood everything perfectly, said nothing until d'Artagnan had finished. Then he held out his hand.

"The paper -- you saved it?"

"Here it is." D'Artagnan gave him the folded paper.

"Your letter to Mlle. de Sirle?"

From the inner pocket of his tunic, d'Artagnan took the Cardinal's letter. Athos glanced at it, then returned it.

"Very simple, my friend. This notation is in the hand of Richelieu himself. Montforge had it from him; was probably showing it to Sophie, instructing her what to ask you about, when you arrived. You comprehend? Richelieu suspected you knew something about it, and took this means to find out more. Undoubtedly he suspects you learned something from the dead man in the road."

D'Artagnan felt the sweat start on his forehead. That accursed ring, bearing the chevrons of Bassompierre! It was on his hand now -- no harm in wearing it, since the damage was done. Montforge had come to Lyon and had persuaded Sophie to make him talk if possible.

"Then -- then why should he send me to Dampierre on an errand of confidence?"

"Perhaps he desired to make your errand dangerous."

D'Artagnan wiped his brow, as he remembered that interview with Richelieu -- the strange air and narrow looks of the Cardinal. And that message about the child -- yes, yes! Richelieu had been testing him, had been trying to see whether he knew anything!

"Strange about this will of a Lorrainer," said Athos, frowning. "You know nothing about it, D'Artagnan?"

"Nothing, upon my honor."

"But I do!" cried Porthos.

The others turned to him, astonished. The giant lifted his head, groaned, flung out his hands like a man forced to a certain confession despite himself.

"Come, come, I lay bare everything -- peccavi, peccavi, my friends!" he said in a hollow voice, looking at them with strained and bloodshot eyes. "Aramis mentioned this will to me. It was connected with my errand -- I know not how. Nor do I know what it is. He merely mentioned the name. D'Artagnan, my friend, I am a miserable sinner; I lied to you. It was no money that I lost, but a letter to Mlle. de Sirle. I humbly beg your pardon, my friend; you see, I swore secrecy to Aramis, and even though it hurt me, I could not tell you."

D'Artagnan could not keep down a laugh, amazed as he was to find the Thounenin will somehow connected with this affair.

"Porthos, I'll pardon you if you will pardon me," he said. "I told you of finding the dying spy in the road -- well, I took a letter from him -- several letters, in fact. He carried your letter, and others he had taken from Aramis, bearing our friend's seal. These I destroyed. Your letter was unsealed, and I read it. I did not give it to you, because you denied having lost anything except money. However, I had Grimaud place the letter in your cloak. Are we quits?"

"Ah! Ah!" Porthos leaped to his feet and the floor trembled. "Embrace me, my friend! I am a new man -- I am ashamed of myself! There are no secrets now between us -- among us three -- "

"Among us four," corrected Athos gravely. "Listen, my friends! We do not know the position of Aramis in this matter; we do not know in what we are mixing. All we do know is that we are to meet Lord de Winter in Paris on July 30th -- and I suggest that we wait not another moment in Lyon, but take our horses and go."

"Go -- where?" asked Porthos.

"To Dampierre, first. We ride thither with d'Artagnan."

"And why?" queried Porthos, knitting his brow.

"I have an errand there from Richelieu," said d'Artagnan. "And first, I had an errand there for the queen -- a secret errand. Now I can guess something of it -- a dreadful guess! Yes, my friends, we ride for the queen, I promise you!"

"Ah!" the frown of Porthos vanished. "That resolves everything. Once more we are together, then. Once more, as in the old days -- all for one, one for all! Agreed?"

"Agreed." Athos turned to d'Artagnan. "Consider, my son! Who was with you and the Queen?"

"Her Spanish woman," said d'Artagnan. "No one else."

"She gave you an errand to Chevreuse, you say? Then the Spanish woman has been bought over by Richelieu, depend upon it. A courier followed you to Grenoble. What did Richelieu do? He pardoned you for duelling. He presented you with a superb horse. He sent you to Chevreuse with a verbal message -- and to Paris with a letter. You see his intent?"

"Devil take me if I do!" said d'Artagnan. "He was most gracious to me -- and yet all the while I had a premonition of danger -- "

Athos uttered a short, ironic laugh. "We who are about to die, salute! You are doomed."

"Impossible! You cannot mean that he would send me to be killed"

"My son, my son, did Montforge have sword drawn or not? Answer."

"Yes," said d'Artagnan, and reflected. "Athos, you are magnificent -- you always pierce to the truth of things, make them plain as day! Yes, the scoundrel did his best to kill me. But why should Richelieu give me a letter to deliver in Paris, if he meant to kill me en route?"

"Our Cardinal knows you, my son. If one trapfails, he has another ready -- you carry the means of it in your pocket. And in all this affair we shall find, not only Aramis, but the Comte de Montforge, vitally concerned. I predict it! Remember, the handkerchief he dropped; his fury against the queen; his connection with the Cardinal's household; lastly, how he came direct to Sophie de Bruler and all but trapped you! That man is dangerous."

"So." D'Artagnan turned pale. "Well, Athos, I cannot let you go with me."

"Bah!" exclaimed Athos. "Have you observed in me any great attachment to my life? Nonsense! Porthos, here, should not go. He has married a wife -- "

"Name of ten thousand devils!" thundered Porthos, shaking his fist in the air. "You are my friends -- that's enough! I go -- we all go! And if the Cardinal tries to stop us, then so much the worse for the Cardinal!"

"Admirable!" D'Artagnan broke into a laugh.

"In this sentiment, then, let's be off!"

"None too soon," said Athos. "I make another prediction. I predict that, since Montforge undoubtedly knows your errand, he will be ahead of us."

"So much the worse for Montforge," said d'Artagnan in

a low voice.

Twenty minutes later, having paused for a bite and a sup, the three friends were mounting and riding forth, with Grimaud behind them.

CHAPTER VII

MIRACLES ARE SOMETIMES UNWELCOME

SINCE the night when a group of men witnessed the execution of a woman beside the River Lys, one of those men had vanished from human ken.

Aramis resigned from the service, and with him the Chevalier d'Herblay disappeared. A few letters came from him; he was bound, he said, on a journey to Lorraine. Then silence. It was rumored that he had taken orders, had become a Sulpician; Athos, at least, believed this profoundly.

While Athos, Porthos and d'Artagnan were spurring for Orleans, to reach Dampierre more swiftly by avoiding Paris, and while Marechal de Bassompierre was killing horses in the endeavor to reach Paris, peculiar conversations were going on in an upper room of the Croix de Bernay -- that famous tavern so pleasantly situated a short day's ride south of Paris on the Orleans road, where the western highway crossed.

This upper room was large, commodious and comfortable. Upon a couch by the window half-reclined Aramis; under his hand was a species of bed-side table, bearing paper, ink, quills and sand. He was clad only in a loose black gown, which revealed bandages about his chest. His features were pale and sunken; from time to time he paused, as though the effort of writing overtaxed his strength. A crucifix hung on the wall just above his couch.

A knock, and Bazin entered. As once before, Bazin perceived his master wounded both in mind and in body and turned from things of this world to things of the next; the joy of Bazin was, however, tempered by the fact that his master's wound was this time no slight matter.

"Monsieur!" exclaimed Bazin in dismay, on seeing his master's occupation. "Monsieur -- you are not writing, surely! Any exertion has been forbidden -- and here is the chirurgeon below, and the Cure of Bernay with him -- "

"Excellent, my good Bazin, excellent," said Aramis in a faint voice. "Bring them up at once."

He laid aside his quill and sank back on his pillows.

A moment later Bazin ushered the two men into the room. The chirurgeon came to the couch and shook his head as he regarded his patient.

"This is bad, very bad!" he declared, without responding to the greetings of Aramis. "You see, M. le Cure, he has been writing!"

"Exactly," said Aramis, and smiled at the reverend gentleman. "Monsieur, I had an excellent idea last night for the thesis of which we were speaking yesterday -- "

The chirurgeon intervened brusquely. "Your pardon, gentlemen -- I must demand silence. M. le Cure, look at this poor man! Regard his pallor, regard his eye, regard his weakness; you can see for yourself. He is sinking."

"God preserve us!" exclaimed the cure', and crossed himself. "Surely, monsieur, you cannot mean that -- that -- "

"That this excellent young man is doomed," said the chirurgeon firmly. "That, monsieur, is precisely my meaning. In ten minutes the reaction from his efforts will take place and will produce fever. With sunset, this fever will die out. By midnight, he will be in a coma of exhaustion. If he lives until sun-rise, he will die tomorrow afternoon. I have no hesitation in making this prediction to his face -- for he has disobeyed my most particular commands. He has undone all my work."

"In the service of God," added Aramis. "Besides, my friends, there is really nothing to cause you such distraction. If it be the divine will, I am content to die."

"You are too devilishly content," said the blunt man of medicine. "You make no effort to recover. Your will is not at work. I've bled you and bled you -- and what good does it do?"

"It makes me weaker, I can assure you," said Aramis. "As for the wound -- "

"The wound cannot heal when fever comes upon you," said the other. He produced certain vials and called for water, which the anxious Bazin fetched. When he had mixed a potion, he entrusted it to the lackey. "Give your master a spoonful of this every hour," he said, and took up his hat. "Gentlemen, I bid you good day. I shall return toward sunset and change the dressings."

With this he departed, very angry because of his unheeded instructions. On the stairs, Bazin followed and waylayed him.

"Monsieur," begged the poor fellow, with tears in his eyes, "tell me the truth, in the name of God! Do not make me suffer. My master is not -- ah, surely there is some hope for him?"

"My good man, I cannot deceive you," said the physician, not unkindly. "He has been at work there for an hour or more; the results are evident. He cannot live more than a day."

"Jesus!" exclaimed Bazin in horror. "Can nothing help him, nothing save him?"

"Nothing but a miracle," said the other.

"Then I shall pray for the miracle," said Bazin.

With a shrug, the physician went his way.

The cure, meantime, sat beside Aramis and felt his brow.

"True, there is fever," he said, compassionately.

"My dear Abbe' d'Herblay, I am distressed beyond words -- "

"Nonsense!" said Aramis, with a wan smile. "That man was right, my friend. I have no will to live. I have been hurt, wounded, more grievously in spirit than in body. My thoughts are no longer fastened upon things of this earth. Come, let me read you this thesis! I have the idea of confounding the followers of Jansenius, of placing his infamous book, the 'Angustinus', in the light of schismatic heresy. To this effect -- but hand me those sheets, I beg of you -- let me read to you -- "

The cure assisted him to sit up a trifle, handed him the written sheets, and watched him anxiously. With his charming smile, Aramis thanked him, and selected his first sheet.

"Here we have it, my father -- you will note that I say nothing of Jansenius at the opening: in fact I have given the thesis a distinct general title."

In his low, clear voice he began to read:

NEW SCHISMS OF THE WEST

Three great schisms have occurred from the establishment of the Christian religion to our day. The schism which separated the Greek Church from the communion of the Roman Church, and which, begun by Photius in 802, was finished by the Patriarch Cerularius in 1053, is called the Eastern Schism. That which took place after the double election of Urbain VI and Clement VII in 1378, is called the Great Western Schism. Last, the Schism of England, which separated the English from the Roman communion under Ilenry VIII in 1534; from this the Anglican Church took its rise.

Photius was born at Constantinople. He had been ambassador to Persia, and First Secretary of the Emperor Michael, when he was exalted to even greater height -- to the Patriarchate of Constantinople in place of Ignace, recently deposed. Pope Nicholas I was opposed to his intrusion and anathematised him in his councils; on his side, Photius gathered his bishops and anathematised the Pope. The Greek Emperor, Basil the Macedonian, re-established Ignace and Photius did not resume the functions of the Patriarchate until after -- "

M. le Cure' intervened.

"Enough, enough, my dear Abbe'," he said gently though firmly. "I perceive the scholarly trend of this thesis, and can well imagine how you will turn it to present-day value -- I beg of you, read no more! Let me peruse the work at my leisure. Linguam compescere, virtus non minima est -- it is not the least of virtues, to restrain the tongue -- "

"Ah!" exclaimed Aramis. "That reminds me the text I have chosen for this thesis, my dear cure! I really must have your opinion in the matter -- "

There was a knock at the door. To the impatient word of Aramis, in came Bazin, looking extremely agitated, and holding a letter in his hand.

"Well?"

"Monsieur!" implored Bazin, desperate. "I swore that you were not here, that you were ill, that you were dying -- but they had already learned you were here. Two confounded cavaliers -- I mean, two gentlemen -- they asked me to bring you this letter --"

"Very well, give it to me," said Aramis. He sighed and fell back upon the pillows. "What are letters?" he said, after looking at the superscription. "I have nothing to do with the things of this world."

None the less, he tore open the missive, and a little color came into his face as he read it. The letter was one of the four sent by Lord de Winter; in all respects it was a duplicate of that which Athos had received.

"Singular!" murmured Aramis, and looked up.

"Bazin, you say this was brought by hand?"

"One of the gentlemen said he had fetched it from your former lodgings in Paris, monsieur," said Bazin, in terror at this new contact with the oldlife. "He is most anxious to have speech with you."

"Who is he?" said Aramis.

"A stranger, monsieur, masked."

Aramis handed him the letter, with a gesture of resignation.

"Take this, burn it, destroy it, eat it -- what you will. It is nothing to me."

The cure rose. "My dear friend," he said, "let me have these sheets you have written -- let me read this admirable thesis at my leisure! 1 shall make place -- if you have a visitor, then see him by all means. You should not be here, alone and friendless, desperately ill -- "

"I have more than I deserve," said Aramis in a gloomy voice. "What is the world, after all? A place where anger breeds anger, where wrong begets wrong -- litem paret lis, noxa item noxam parit! And have I not brought all my misfortune upon myself by forgetting the first maxim of a devout man -- nemo militans De -- no servant of God should mix in secular affairs? Take the thesis if you like, my friend. Return soon to me. Bazin! Show M. le Cure' out and fetch in this cavalier who seeks me -- "

Bazin had been holding the letter over a candle. His sharp eyes did not fail to sight the hidden writing, and a subdued groan broke from him as he comprehended its import and read the signature of Lord de Winter. He said nothing of this to Aramis, however; the last scrap of the letter curling up, he pinched out the candle and showed the good cure to the door.

"Winter!" murmured Aramis, left alone, and stared out of the window at the trees. "That Englishman! Well, it has nothing to do with me. I am finished -- everything is finished. Let the dead bury their dead. When she -- "

Two tears gathered in his eyes and slowly rolled upon his cheeks.

The door opened. A cavalier entered, turned, calmly pushed Bazin outside, then closed the door and turned the key. He approached the couch. Aramis was astonished to see that he was masked. He had fair hair, a mustache and goatee of the same; his hands were as beautiful and as elegantly tended as those of Aramis himself. Blue eyes glittered through the mask. His garments were of blue velvet, and a magnificent diamond sparkled on his right hand.

"Be seated, monsieur," said Aramis. "I am, as you see, too weak to rise -- "

"You are the Abbe' d'Herblay?" asked the stranger.

"I am. And you?"

"I am the Chevalier Nemo," and white, beautiful teeth showed as the stranger smiled and sat down.

"No One!" repeated Aramis, frowning slightly. "I do not like this, monsieur -- "

"Your pardon; a few questions, monsieur, and I give you

my true name," said the other. His voice seemed touched with emotion. "Your lackey has told me of your condition -- have I your permission to speak frankly?"

The head of Aramis sank back. "What you like, what you like," he said. "I have no secrets. I have no will to live. I have -- nothing."

"My poor -- " began the other, then checked himself. "Two days ago, monsieur, I was in Paris. I was speaking with Mlle. de Sirle."

Aramis started slightly, then essayed a feeble shrug.

"What of it?" he murmured. "She is a beautiful woman, monsieur, and wicked as she is beautiful. Everyone who knows her, loves her instantly; she lives by love, in fact."

"And you, monsieur?"

"I? I am impervious to love," said Aramis with a trace of hauteur. "I have eschewed the vanities of this world. All is vanity, folly, crackling of thorns under a pot!"

"Precisely," said the other. "Monsieur, you are ill -- "

"No," said Aramis. "I am dying."

The visitor was silent for a moment, as though in restraint of some deep emotion.

"Then allow me to mention private matters, for which I promise you entire justification," he rejoined. "You are, I believe, a friend of Mlle. de Sirle."

"Of that woman!" The lip of Aramis curled slightly. "You do not know me, my friend. She is the most dangerous person in Paris."

"As you warned M. de Bassompierre."

Aramis turned, if it were possible, even paler than before.

"How do you know these things?"

"I am coming to that. First tell me -- you sent a friend to render Mlle. de Sirle a certain service?"

Aramis hesitated. "Yes. I could not go myself; I had just received a letter which wrecked my entire life. So I sent a friend, for reasons of my own. Three hours afterward I was wounded and robbed, and was brought here. Are you content?"

His voice had become very weak. His eyes closed.

"And where is your friend?"

"I know not," murmured Aramis. "What matter? Porthos can take care of himself. I sent him -- she would make use of him -- he would tell me everything. Such was my intent. Then -- the letter. Then -- the wound. I came this far from Paris -- and I am dying. What matter?"

"Ah! I understand now," said the visitor. "I should have known that La Sirle could never entangle you. This letter you received -- it was, perhaps, from a lady named Marie?"

Aramis looked up, started slightly, and regarded the stranger fixedly.

"You -- you come from her?"

"No."

Aramis turned his face away.

"No matter," he said. "Nothing matters. I am a dead man, and have no hope in this world; say your say and get you gone, for I feel weakness upon me, and all these things have passed out of my life forever."

Again his eyes closed. It was, indeed, symptomatic of his utter weakness and dejection that he should consent to thus mention names with a stranger. Nothing could have been farther from the usual discreet, even secretive, nature of Aramis, who never let his right hand know what his left hand was about.

Now occurred one of those strange things which never happen for the world to see -- those queerly silent things which pass unknown and unvisualized.

Two tears escaped from beneath the vizard of the stranger, as he looked down upon the changed form of the man upon the couch.

"My poor Aramis!" he said in a new voice -- a low, rich, ringing voice that broke upon the silence like a chord of music. With a swift gesture, the stranger removed his mask, plucked hard at false goatee and mustache, pulled them away -- revealed himself smiling, blue-eyed, soft and dimpled of face as any woman.

Aramis had turned at that voice. One low cry burst from his lips. His eyes widened, and he came to one elbow, staring terribly, the pallor of death in his face.

"You!" he cried in a strangled tone. "You Marie -- "

"I, Marie -- Marie of Tours -- Marie de Rohan -- Marie de Chevreuse -- Marie who loves you -- ah, my poor, poor Aramis! Could you not have guessed that my frightful letter was only a blind for the eyes of others?"

And with a magnificent, impulsive gesture, the speaker was upon her knees and holding the head of Aramis in her arms, against her breast, as she might have held that of a child.

This woman, in whose person were united the most princely names of France, was the sole enemy of Richelieu who could meet him on equal ground, word for word, act for act, genius for genius -- and defy him. Against this woman all the power of the great minister was as naught. He might humble her, he might exile her, he might treat with her as with an equal, but he could never outwit or destroy her.

At this moment, in this room, her effulgent beauty was at its zenith. Those dazzling charms which, five years later, were to seduce an emperor, and after another five years a viceroy, were in this moment at the height of their perfection. Only supreme beauty can indulge in passionate tears and yet remain undimmed. As Marie de Chevreuse knelt beside the couch, her tears of pity warm upon the face of him she believed dying, this most beautiful woman of France had never appeared so resplendent, of such sublime loveliness. Marie de Chevreuse, who could swear like a trooper, could weep like an angel.

Outside in the corridor, listening at the locked door, was Bazin. When he heard this cry and this name burst from the lips of Aramis, he straightened up, he staggered, he put out one hand to the wall for support and with the other he crossed himself rapidly.

Then, with a wild and stricken air, he hastened down the corridor with trembling steps, and presently was in the courtyard. A dust-covered coach stood there, a coach bearing no arms nor insignia. Beside it was the horse of the physician, who had stayed his departure in order to cleanse and bind up the hurt of an hostler kicked by a horse. The chirurgeon was washing his hands when Bazin approached him, and he turned in sharp alarm.

"What?" he exclaimed, startled by the lackey's air. "Your master is not dead already?"

Bazin groaned. "Ah, monsieur, you are a terrible man!" he responded. "You bade me pray for a miracle, and I prayed and -- and -- "

The physician surveyed him in puzzled wonder.

"And what, my good man?"

"And the miracle happened, monsieur!" exclaimed Bazin in a hollow voice.

"The devil! You do not appear to be very happy about it."

The casement of the upper room was flung open. The voice of Aramis floated down.

"Bazin! Name of the devil, where are you? Come and pack! We are leaving at once!"

From the inn-room came the companion of Mme. de Chevreus -- an elderly, shrewd man in the attire of a valet. The host, whose account had evidently just been paid, brought him to the physician.

"Monsieur," said the valet, "will you have the goodness to inform me of the amount of your fee in the case of the sick man above?"

The physician did so, and then followed Bazin up the stairs, jingling the money in his pouch. The door of the upper room was standing open. The stranger, again masked, mustache and goatee again in place, was supporting Aramis and helping him dress. The physician paused at sight of his patient's changed aspect.

"I see you are right," he said to Bazin. "The age of miracles has returned."

Aramis looked at him and laughed. "Monsieur, I grieve to disappoint you! But devil take me if I intend to die today or tomorrow either!"

"Obviously." The physician looked at the sparkling eye, the heightened color, the sudden animation and laughing eagerness of his late patient.

"Well, monsieur, at least take the potion I left for you -- and if your wound reopens, bid your lackey pray once more but don't waste the time of a chirurgeon, for your case will be hopeless. Bon voyage, monsieur."

And, with a bow, he departed.

Bazin, now aiding Aramis into his shirt, murmured a low and despairing word.

"But the thesis, monsieur -- the thesis on the Great Schisms! M. le Cure has those precious sheets and he is departed -- "

"To the devil with him and the thesis!" said Aramis. "Get my things packed and stowed, saddle the horses, ride mine yourself. I go in the coach."

"To Paris, monsieur?" queried the unhappy lackey.

"Name of the devil, no!" and the masked stranger broke into a ringing, merry laugh. "In the other direction, my good

Bazin -- you don't remember me, eh? Very well, then. At least you'll remember the place whither we go! To Dampierre."

Bazin uttered a strangled sound-a combined response and groan. And, furtively, he crossed him self and rolled his eyes to heaven. Monsieur Bazin was a devout man yet he did not congratulate himself on having brought a miracle to pass.

CHAPTER VIII

IN WHICH A GENTLEMAN PROVES TO BE A GOOD WORKMAN

Riding north and west, d'Artagnan and his companions were followed by only one lackey. Porthos had left his plump mousqueton to act as squire for Madame du Vallon. Planchet, the former lackey of d'Artagnan, was now a sergeant in the guards, and within the past week his successor had been trounced and discharged for theft; thus, d'Artagnan was without a lackey. Grimaud, the silent servant of Athos, alone followed the three.

They rode from Lyon to Nevers without a halt, and came into the charming capital of the Nivernais with staggering horses and parched throats. They went to the post-tavern, turned over their horses to the hostlers, and stumbled into the inn-room for dinner before seeking rest for the night. Grimaud, after his custom, remained with the horses to be certain they received proper attention.

"Ah!" Porthos sighed as he lowered himself into a chair, which groaned beneath him. "We are at Nevers. From Nevers we ride on to Melun. From -- "

"Not so fast!" said d'Artagnan, with a cry of joy as bottles and food began to rain upon the table. "From here we ride to Orleans."

"Eh?" Porthos opened his eyes wide. Athos, who cared

nothing about their road, was pouring wine.

"But Orleans is not the road for Paris!"

"We do not go to Paris," said d'Artagnan. "We go to Orleans, thence to Longjumeau. There we head west for Dampierre."

"An excellent program!" Athos lifted his flagon.

"To a safe journey!"

Presently Grimaud entered, came opposite his master, and paused until Athos looked up. Then Grimaud put out a hand as though taking a horse's reins, looked the imaginary animal up and down, and turned his head, speaking to an imaginary person.

"This is the horse, as described."

His gaze came to rest upon d'Artagnan.

Athos dismissed him with a gesture, and looked at his two friends. D'Artagnan was frowning, Porthos was gaping in astonishment.

"You see -- the Cardinal gave you a horse, my dear d'Artagnan!" said Athos quizzically. "A beautiful horse, a horse in a thousand! An hostler takes his bridle, turns and says that this is the horse as described. Voila'! The description is known. Montforge has passed this way ahead of us -- and has left men behind! Beware!"

And having said, he refilled his flagon.

"Well," said d'Artagnan after a moment, "and what do you expect?"

"Naturally, the unexpected," retorted Athos, with a shrug. "Why worry?"

"Good. I'm too weary to care what happens."

None the less, d'Artagnan questioned the grooms and hostlers carefully, inquired after a cavalier of Montforge's description, and learned exactly nothing. The three comrades slept soundly that night, and were off with sunrise.

Despite this disturbing incident, nothing happened to justify the expectations of Athos. The towers of Orleans smiled sunnily upon them of a midday, and they bore straight on to make another five leagues of the northern highway ere night. They considered that if anything happened, it should come at Orleans; thus, once past that city, they took small thought of any peril.

Porthos had discarded his sling, for his wound no longer incommoded him. He had secured a huge horse of Norman strain, which might have served some mail-clad Roland as destrier; this animal had no speed, but bore the weight of Porthos like a feather. With his great figure, his gallant air, his enormous horse, Porthos was the admired of all beholders, and was taken to be a duke at the very least.

Late on a warm summer's afternoon they came into Longjumeau, with the silver thread of the Yvette glistening along the valley below. They avoided the post-tavern here, lest it prove dangerous. Instead, they sought the Pomme d'Or, rode into the courtyard of this hostelry so famous for its wine and fowl, and Porthos at once vanished inside to look over the situation and command a fitting dinner. Athos, who was somewhat particular about his rooms, departed with the host to inspect the proffered chambers.

D'Artagnan approached the horse4rough, which an hostler was filling from the pump, and held his wrists beneath the flow of water to cool his blood, for the day was hot and the highway was thick with dust despite its paving of stone flags. At this instant a coach passed in the street, outside the wide-open courtyard gates. The coach was white with dust, the four horses were flecked with lather, and its pace was rapid. D'Artagnan glanced at it as it rumbled past.

Framed in the window of this coach he glimpsed the face of a man -- a man who was looking straight at him, a face suddenly agape with recognition, a face he knew and that knew him. Then it was gone, rolling away down the street toward the bridge.

In that coach-window had been framed the face of Aramis.

For a moment d'Artagnan remained absolute petrified with astounded incredulity. Pale and haggard the face had been -- yet he recognized it instantly, and knew he himself had been recognized. And no word, no halt! By nature very curious, he was instantly aflame.

He gained the gateway with one leap and stood staring down the street. The coach went on without pause; indeed, the postilion was whipping up the horses as though the occupants had ordered more speed. It whirled on toward the bridge and the city gates. Evidently, Aramis had no intention of stopping.

With an oath, d'Artagnan turned, and ran like a madman toward the horses, which the staring Grimaud and a groom were unsaddling. His own animal was being led to the stables. He disdained the horse of Porthos, and instead caught at that of Athos, as yet saddled and bridled. He tore the reins from the hand of Grimaud, flung himself into the saddle at a bound, and one glance told him that neither Porthos nor Athos were in sight.

"Aramis!" he cried to Grimaud. "I have seen Aramis -- "

His startled horse plunged, leaped, turned at the pull of the bridle and went out of the courtyard like an arrow. D'Artagnan had his sword, and the pistols of Athos were at the saddle; he was bare-headed, and his cloak reposed with his hat.

As he came thus plunging out into the street, the people there scattered with cries of fright and anger. The horse slipped, recovered; d'Artagnan thrust in his spurs and sent the frightened animal hurtling in the wake of the coach, unheeding the shouts of those he barely avoided. Luckily, the street was not blocked ahead, and he had a clear way.

In his haste, in his furious concentration upon the coach ahead, our Musketeer did not perceive two cavaliers who had dismounted in the street outside the Pomme d'Or and were conversing. They, however, did not fail to observe his sudden emergence and his mad gallop toward the bridge.

"It is he!" exclaimed one, and they hurriedly mounted and rode after.

D'Artagnan had no trouble in sighting his quarry, once he gained the bridge and was across the Yvette. The coach had not taken the northern highway for Paris, but that to the west, a road leading to Palaisau and beyond. It had gained on him. He sighted it half a mile away, climbing the higher ground there, dust rolling out behind it in a great cloud.

"The devil!" said d'Artagnan, putting in his spurs. "They're whipping up -- can it be that Aramis does not want me to catch up with him? Bah! There's too much at stake to pause upon his sly whims."

Tired though his animal was, it responded nobly to his urgings. The coach had passed beyond his range of vision long ere he had in turn reached the uplands, but the heavy dust it raised showed that he was gaining. Here on level ground, however, four horses had the advantage over one, already wearied by climbing the rise, and with dismay d'Artagnan perceived his animal to be flagging.

At a bend in the road he caught sight of two figures behind. So thick was his own dust that he could see only that they were riding furiously, gaining on him fast.

"Ha! Grimaud and Athos, no doubt!" he reflected, and then gave his attention to the road ahead. He determined to expend his horse in one last, supreme effort, and if he could not come up with the coach, a bullet would at least drop one of its horses. It was vital that Aramis be halted, that an explanation be obtained, at any and all costs.

To this end, d'Artagnan drew from their holsters the two pistols at his saddle, which were already loaded, and made shift to prime them, as he rode. He had just primed the second pistol when he became aware of a rider close behind him, and turned.

At this instant the man behind him fired a pistol. The bullet tore the hat from the head of d'Artagnan, but did not injure him.

Only then did he perceive his mistake -- this rider, and the other slightly in the rear, were strangers! The second man held a pistol drawn, ready for use. Without hesitation, d'Artagnan raised the weapon in his own hand. As he pressed the trigger, his horse stumbled. His bullet missed the first man, but struck the horse of the second.

"Assassins!" exclaimed d'Artagnan. His horse stumbled again, then pitched forward and fell. Unprepared,.he was flung clear of the saddle and sent rolling in the dust of the road.

Catlike, d'Artagnan was upon his feet almost instantly -- only to pause there in sharp dismay. In the fall, his right shoulder had been struck; for the moment, his arm was next to useless, numbed, paralyzed. The first rider had just dismounted, and, sword out, was running at him. The second, flung by his wounded horse, was on his feet and plucking at his sword.

"Assassins!" cried d'Artagnan, furious. "Do you know you are dealing with a royal officer?"

He had no reply, except a snarling grin. Both men, he perceived, were bretteurs, or bravos of a certain type very common at this period -- veterans of the wars in Italy and Germany, men used to every trick of arms, who would cut a throat for a pistole and do it with all the address of long practice.

With an effort of the will, d'Artagnan's numbed fingers closed on his sword-hilt and bared the blade. It was high time; the first bretteur was already lunging at him. There was now no doubt whatever -- this was no mistake, but deliberate assassination. D'Artagnan knew he was dealing with men who were unscrupulous, pitiless, who would either kill or be killed.

Avoiding that first lunge by a miracle of agility, d'Artagnan engaged the sword of the bretteur with his own rapier, and at the very first pass, perceived his adversary to be a master of the weapon after the somewhat rough style of the army. For a moment he could do no more than hold the defensive. The shock of a rude fall unsettles the nerves and affects those delicate sensitory ganglia whose messages control the brain of a swordsman.

"Flank oblique, Carabin!" cried out the bravo suddenly.

"Understood," replied the second, who had come up, and he fell upon d'Artagnan from the left side.

"Cowards!" cried d'Artagnan, finding himself thus engaged by two men at once.

"No, monsieur -- good workmen," replied Carabin, with a grin.

D'Artagnan fell back a step, the better to hold both swords in play. He was himself again; the dazzling rapidity of his thrusts and parries astonished and angered the two bretteurs, who redoubled their efforts. The sun was setting; in this reddish light their blades took on a copper tinge, and their eyes seemed glowing with infernal fires. Carabin began to work around to the rear of the Musketeer, but the agility of d'Artagnan defeated his purpose. And now the anger of d'Artagnan passed into that furious ecstasy which seized upon him in battle, uplifting him above all thought of peril. The dust raised by their tramping feet, the hoarse breathing of men, the bloodshot eyes and snarling lips, the sweat that streamed from brow and neck, the clink and click of blades, the sharp death glinting there at their throats -- all this swept through the veins of d'Artagnan like wine.

He broke into sudden laughter. Still engaged with the first man, he avoided a lunge from Carabin and then, with the flashing swoop of a falcon, was away and entirely clear of Carabin. In this momentary respite he hurled himself upon the first bretteur with fiery abandon. It was his only chance, as he now saw -- to cope with both at once was impossible. He must kill one of them swiftly, then finish with the other one.

Ten seconds passed before Carabin could work around the Musketeer, returning to the attack.

In this ten seconds, the rapier of d'Artagnan flashed before the eyes of the first bretteur like the white fire of a thunderbolt. The blades crossed, met, clung as though magnetized together. Suddenly, with the rapidity of light, d'Artagnan disengaged -- and dashed the hilt of his sword into the bretteur's face; almost in the same motion, it seemed, he leaped sideways and ran the dazed man through the throat.

The second was upon him with a howl of rage and fury.

"Coward!" roared Carabin, seeing his comrade clutch at his throat and fall. "That was not the act of a gentleman!"

"Certainly not," returned d'Artagnan coolly, as he engaged, parried, riposted. "I am not dealing with gentlemen, but with good workmen. My faith, but I'm a good workman myself, my friend!"

"Work, then," growled Carabin, "for you'll feed the devil's fires tonight!"

And he attacked with a ferocity, a grim determination, that alarmed d'Artagnan. Here was a better swordsman than the first; one, also, who knew every trick of camp and field and put them into play -- his business was not to fence, but to kill.

D'Artagnan, however, had been on more than one campaign; also, the hotel of the Musketeers was not a place where one played with blunted rapiers. Thus, he was not caught asleep when the bretteur produced a poniard in his left hand and, forcing up the rapiers, drove in at him with the shorter weapon -- vainly.

The minutes passed; the sun dropped from sight. Still the two men fought there about the dead bretteur, two horses watching them amazedly, the third dying with slow and shuddering coughs. Twice the point of Carabin touched d'Artagnan, once in the arm, once in the throat -- mere touches, scarce sufficient to draw blood. Trick foiled trick, riposte answered lunge; about them the dust rose in a continual cloud, suffocating them, as their feet stamped the earth, and their breath came in hoarse pantings. D'Artagnan was astonished, and grew more furious every moment -- that a mere bretteur, a bravo, a hireling assassin, should thus withstand a Musketeer, was intolerable!

Abruptly, so swiftly as to be past the eyesight, a thrust went home. Carabin staggered, recovered; the sword fell from his hand; he stood there staring terribly upon d'Artagnan, as blood gushed out across his sweat-stained shirt.

"Ah!" he exclaimed hoarsely. "You have -- you have -- killed me -- "

His knees gave way and he pitched forward, and lay still, for a moment. Then his eyes opened. He came to one elbow, panting, the pallor of death growing in his face.

D'Artagnan stood holding his sword, gulping fresh air into his lungs as the dust-cloud thinned and dissipated on the evening breeze. There was no sound save the cough of the dying horse and the rattling breath of the dying man. Presently d'Artagnan sighed, looked at his rapier, found no blood upon it, and sheathed it.

"Water!" gasped out Carabin. "On -- my saddle -- "

"With all my heart," said d'Artagnan.

He strode to the bretteur's horse and removed a leathern bottle hung at the saddle, which was still half full of liquid. He unstopped it, came back to the dying Carabin, and knelt, holding the bottle to the man's lips. Then Carabin drew back his head.

"You are a swordsman, my friend," he said faintly. "It is a pleasure to be killed by such a man. Your name?"

"D'Artagnan, lieutenant in -- "

"Ah! You are d'Artagnan -- the man who killed Jussac -- then it is no disgrace! My only regret is that I have failed in my errand. More water -- "

D'Artagnan leaned forward, held the leathern bottle again to the man's lips. But this time the hand of Carabin moved -- the hand that still held the poniard. Almost at the same instant, the other had clutched d'Artagnan by the sleeve.

Overbalanced by this clutch, pulled forward, d'Artagnan fell across the legs of Carabin. The poniard missed its stroke -- tore the skin of d'Artagnan's neck, no more.

"Scoundrel!" he exclaimed, trying to wrench from that dying grip. "If -- "

Like a flash, the bretteur uplifted himself. A cry of despair broke from his lips -- he was dying in the very act! With one desperate, superhuman effort, he dashed his clenched hand into the face of d'Artagnan, and fell back dead.

The hilt of the poniard struck d'Artagnan between the eyes. He fell face down, and lay like a man mortally stricken.

Two hours passed.

When d'Artagnan came to himself, it was with a vague and wandering bewilderment. Grotesque dreams had seized upon him, and for a space he thought himself still in dream. He was numb with cold, for he found himself stripped to his shirt; the stars blinked overhead, and in his ears was the sound of rude, harsh voices in dispute.

"Keep the gold, then, and give me the silver," said one voice. "You know very well I dare not have any gold. I'll take the silver and this coat."

"It's a good coat," objected another. "It isn't bloody like the others. And these boots are of fine leather -- "

"Leave them, fool!" broke in a third. "Do you want questions asked of us? These boots are dangerous. Leave them. Give Louis the silver and the coat -- "

"There's a letter or a paper in the pocket," said the first. "Here -- throw it away and leave it. What about this man's shirt?"

A hand pawed the throat of d'Artagnan, and he saw a shape above him, blotting out the stars.

"Something hard under the shirt!" exclaimed the man. "By the saints, this one is still warm -- "

D'Artagnan stirred suddenly, sat up. He comprehended that some peasants had come upon the scene and had looted the bodies. He saw three figures, but when he opened his lips to speak, cries of fright broke from them, and all three fled into the night.

"Fools ! Dolts! Come back!" cried d'Artagnan. "I'll not harm you -- "

Useless; they were gone. He rose, cursed them, tried to pursue them. His feet were bare and he stumbled into a patch of briars. With fresh curses he returned to where the other two bodies gleamed white and naked under the stars. In some dismay he forced himself to grapple with the situation.

His boots lay nearby; except for these and his shirt, he was naked as the two bretteurs. He drew on the boots, then retrieved Richelieu's letter and his own papers, which had been flung to the ground. At one side he found his baldric and sword. The peasants had not dared carry off anything which might cause questions to be asked of them later on. Thus, they had not touched the two horses, which were cropping the grass nearby. They had borne away every scrap of clothing, however.

Except for a bruise, d'Artagnan found himself unhurt. His money was gone; his saddle-bags were emptied. He had, however, his own horse, now rested and recovered, also an extra horse with equipment. The sale of this animal would provide him with clothes and money.

"Alas, where is Athos?" he murmured. "Surely he and Porthos would have followed -- ah! They must have taken the other road, the Paris highway! Well, no matter. We have a rendezvous in Paris with Milord de Winter -- that's understood. Meanwhile, I must press on to Dampierre and find Madame de Chevreuse. And now -- back to Longjumeau, or ahead?"

His hesitation was brief. If he returned to Longjumeau, he would doubtless find his companions gone; and his appearance in such costume would provoke mirth, to say the least. Much better to follow the road westward and get clothes in the first village he reached. So, taking the reins of the dead bretteur's horse, he mounted, grimaced, and started out along the road.

He looked back at the two white things in the starlight. Not they were to blame, he knew well -- but Montforge.

Curiously, he found himself angered; not by what had happened, but by the fact that he had so nearly lost the ring beneath his shirt. He might, he reflected, yet have need of the queen's jewel -- money did not come to one out of the air!

Thus thinking, he came to a crest and, some distance ahead, saw the yellow-gleaming lights of a village.

CHAPTER IX

A NAKED MAN HAS NO CHOICE

The village of Champlan was small. Aside from the church, the only building of any consequence was the inn, to which d'Artagnan directed his horse. A lantern burned above the gates, which were open.

In the courtyard, near a blazing cresset, stood a coach which a groom was washing. At sight of this coach, d'Artagnan drew rein in astonishment -- it was the same vehicle which he had been pursuing that afternoon! So, then, Aramis had halted here!

No sooner did this thought strike into his mind, than a man, the only person in sight except for the groom, turned from the coach and peered at him. This man, who was somewhat elderly, had the appearance of a lackey.

"So, you have come!" he exclaimed, then started in surprise at the aspect of d'Artagnan as the latter came into the circle of light. "Name of the devil! I told the fool to fetch a surgeon -- not to drag him out of his bed!"

D'Artagnan was alert to the situation. A surgeon had been hastily summoned, probably from the next village or town; he recalled the haggard face of Aramis at the coach window, knew Aramis was wounded.

"Ergo," he reflected as he dismounted, "I cease to be a musketeer -- and become a surgeon!"

"Good!" he said to the man. "A wound, I understand? Clothes do not matter. It is true that I was brought out of bed -- so much the better! Where is the patient?"

"Diantre! Clothes matter more than you think, perhaps -- but it's your business, not mine," and the lackey grinned wryly. "You look like a soldier rather than a physician, my friend."

"Undoubtedly Mother Eve made some similar remark to Adam, the first time she saw him clad," returned d'Artagnan crisply. "Well, does the patient die while you talk? Lead on!"

The impatience in his voice checked the lackey, who perceived that he was dealing with a gentleman. D'Artagnan was in a hurry, indeed. Any of the inn-folk would know he was not the expected surgeon. The one groom in sight was a half-witted lout, fortunately, who paid no heed to what was said.

"Come," said the lackey, turning to the stone stairs that ascended the inner wall of the courtyard. "My master is at dinner. His friend has a bad wound, which has been slow in healing, and the jolting of the coach today has hurt him terribly. If the wound has opened, he is a dead man; we have not dared to look, as yet."

"Fear not," said d'Artagnan. "I have a balsam of oil and rosemary which has the miraculous virtue of curing all wounds that do not touch the heart!. I promise you I will cure him."

Then he remembered that he had lost everything, including his vial of that balsam, whose recipe his mother had had from a Bohemian, which he ever carried with him. However, this could not be helped, and since he knew the recipe by heart, he could have more of the balsam prepared for the patient.

The lackey guided d'Artagnan to the upper corridor, upon which an open doorway emitted a blaze of light. In the hallway were grouped scullions and chambermaids, while into the open doorway the host of the inn was himself bearing a platter holding an enormous roast duck, almost a goose in size. Obviously the friend of Aramis was about to sup well.

The door of the room adjoining this was opened by the lackey, and d'Artagnan entered. One glance around showed that he had reached his goal. Upon the bed lay Aramis, senseless, loosely wrapped in a black gown. No one else was in the room, and one poor candle burned dimly beside the bed.

In the wall was a door which opened into the adjoining room. The lackey went to this door, knocked, and opened it at a curt command.

"Monsieur," he said to the unseen friend of Aramis, "the physician is here, but he came literally in his shirt. If you wish to order that he be clothed -- "

"Name of the fiend!" cried out d'Artagnan angrily. "Clothe yourself, lackey, and let your betters alone! Shut the hall door and keep those women outside. I'm here to work, not to parade myself. Vivadiou! Time enough for clothes when there's nothing else to do. Be off! Have my horse looked after. Bring clean cloths and water. Fetch more candles. Lively!"

The lackey scuttled hastily out. A burst of laughter sounded from the adjoining room. Into the communicating doorway strode a laughing cavalier, masked and hatted, who held a candelabrum in one hand.

"Here are lights, M. Aesculapius!" he exclaimed gaily. "And if my friend recovers, I promise you six pistoles; if he dies, six inches of steel!"

"To the devil with your pistoles, your steel, and yourself," snapped d'Artagnan, who was now bending over Aramis and laying bare the bandaged chest. "So! He's in bad shape, but I've seen him in worse. We must have warm water to remove these wrappings -- they're blood-hardened. Well, my friend, at whom are you staring?"

The cavalier in the doorway was inspecting d'Artagnan in some amusement.

"Sword and shirt -- your costume, monsieur, might be bettered!" he said merrily. "Shall I lend you a pair of breeches to go with that sword?"

D'Artagnan was removing his baidric. With it came a portion of his tattered shirt. He surveyed himself ruefully.

"Well, well, monsieur, I shall attend first to my patient, then to myself," he replied, not knowing whether to be angered or amused.

"And so, my Gascon," returned the cavalier, "you have seen this gentleman in worse shape, have you? May I ask where?"

D'Artagnan could have bitten off his tongue. "I said I had seen others in worse shape," he replied. "I see a pair of breeches there on a chair if you'll have the goodness to retire to your dinner and leave me to my work, I'll be obliged."

"With all my heart, most testy physician!" said the other mockingly, swept a low bow, and stepped back into the other room. "And, when your work is finished, perhaps you will do me the honor of joining me."

"Ah!" exclaimed d'Artagn an. "Since I haven't eaten this afternoon, I'll be glad to do so, monsieur."

The other closed the door. D'Artagnan reached for the breeches on the chair, which fitted him passably. As he put them on, there was a tinkIe -- the chain of the scapulary around his neck had parted. Doubtless a link had given way during his exertions that afternoon. The sapphire ring of the queen fell upon the floor.

D'Artagnan picked it up, placed it on the litt1e finger of his right hand, pocketed the scapulary, and buttoned up the breeches, just as the lackey entered with a tray. He motioned to the bedside table.

"Put it there. Now, help me with these bandages. Removing them will hurt him, and that will bring him to his senses. Have the fresh cloths ready."

The bandages were undone. The wound was bathed in warm water, the cloths came away. A low word broke from d'Artagnan at sight of the wound. Then he saw the eyes of Aramis flicker open and stare up at him.

"Vivadiou! It's angry, but has not broken open," he

exclaimed. Then, at the ear of Aramis: "Quiet, comrade! Let your mind be at rest. That sealed packet and that letter from Marie Michon have been destroyed. All is safe. If you hadn't run away from me, you'd have learned it sooner. Quiet, now!"

The stare of Aramis, at these words, passed into a look of wide-eyed incredulity, of stark amazement. However, Aramis had no chance to appease his curiosity or wonder, for he was being deftly bandaged afresh.

"No talking," said d'Artagnan to him, mindful of the lackey. "Set your mind at rest and go to sleep. I'll be here in the morning, and if you'll have the goodness to tell this lackey that I'm a doctor to your taste, all will be well."

Aramis quite understood, and a faint smile touched his lips. He looked at the lackey.

"Tell your master that we stay here for the night, or that I do at all events," he said. "I must speak with this gentleman in the morning."

"Very good, monsieur," said the lackey, and held the water while d'Artagnan rinsed his hands.

"But I do not know where this gentleman can sleep -- we have taken every bed in this tiny country inn!"

"Bah! Your master and I will share a bed," said d'Artagnan carelessly. "Aramis, no more talk! I'm dining with your friend. By the way, since he is masked, do you care to tell me his name? I can allow you two words, at least."

Aramis regarded him with a rather amused uneasiness.

"Alas, my dear d'Artagnan, I regret that the secret is not mine to impart -- "

"Keep it to yourself, then," said d'Artagnan brusquely. The lackey had already taken his departure, apparently in some agitation. "Listen, my friend! Porthos is close by. All goes well. I'm on my way to Dampierre, and we'll talk in the morning. So turn over and sleep!"

"Wait!" exclaimed Aramis. At this moment, however, the door between the two rooms opened, and the cavalier appeared, still masked.

"I hear your voice, M. d'Herblay -- excellent! This is indeed a worthy physician, even if he came in his shirt, and a torn and bloody shirt to boot! Come, my Aesculapius, come and join me, and let our friend here sleep."

D'Artagnan, nothing loath, followed into the adjoining room. The lackey, already there, held a chair for him, at a table bountifully spread.

Once seated, d'Artagnan, who was extremely curious, turned all his attention to his host, but found himself completely baffled. Certainly, here was no one he knew. The cavalier retained his mask and his hat, upon which was a magnificent plume; his garments were of the most beautiful quality, and the lace at his throat and cuffs was superb Mechlin. The voice of the cavalier was a thin contralto of peculiar timbre; and this gentleman, observing the frank curiosity of d'Artagnan, lightly touched his throat.

"Monsieur, you will pardon my singular speech! Some years ago I was wounded in the throat, and my speech has been affected since. To judge from your attire, you came hither from the bed of another patient -- or perhaps from your own bed?"

D'Artagnan, noting the flash of jewels, concluded that he was speaking with some noble.

"You have hit it, monsieur," he replied, with his frank and winning smile. "To be more exact, two patients -- who tried to rob me. Vivadiou! They came close to doing it, too."

"So that explains it!" The cavalier appeared to be vastly amused. D'Artagnan was eating and drinking while he talked. "As to sharing a bed with you, monsieur, I regret to say that I am not in the habit of accepting such proposals. We might indeed share this room, which has two couches -- "

"Better still," rejoined d'Artagnan, his mouth full. "Having recently slept with two dead men, I prefer not to sleep with any man at all for some time to come."

The masked cavalier laughed heartily, showing white and perfect teeth.

"I have never tried that novelty," he observed, "although I understand that the late Queen Margot put the prescription into effect at one time. Now, if we -- "

He paused suddenly. D'Artagnan, in lifting his winecup, had passed his hand near the candles; the sapphire on his finger blazed suddenly. He saw that the cavalier observed it, and quickly turned the bezel inward, but too late.

"Monsieur -- that ring!" exclaimed the other, leaning forward, the color ebbing from his face. "It is most astonishing, but if I mistake not, it is well known to me -- "

"Impossible," said d'Artagnan, in swift alarm. "It was a gift to me from a lady, long ago, and I wear it in memory of her."

At this instant came a knock at the door. The lackey opened, there was a moment of agitated conversation, then the lackey came to the table and bowed to his master, respectfully.

"Monsieur, it seems that another physician has arrived -- there has been some mistake -- "

"Pay him and send him away," said the cavalier, who seemed in some agitation. "Go out, shut the door, leave us alone! Devil take you --" he hurled a volley of oaths at the lackey, who hurriedly went out of the room and shut the door.

D'Artagnan, however, observed that these oaths seemed to come from emotion rather than anger. The masked cavalier turned to him quickly.

"Monsieur," he said, "will you permit me to ask you one question? You are no surgeon, yet you have done your work well. Who you are, I care not. But I should like to ask you whether, on the inner side of that ring, there are not engraved the words 'Dolor hic tibi proderit ohm'?"

"Hm!" said d'Artagnan. "I have not forgotten my Ovid, at all events -- 'this grief will some day avail you,' is it not? Well, monsieur, a very pretty motto there -- "

"Damnation take you, will you answer my question?" snapped the cavalier. D'Artagnan leaned back in his chair, twirled his mustache, and met the angry blue eyes behind the mask.

"Come, come, monsieur!" he said, coolly. "This ring is no

concern of yours, I assure you."

"According to your own statement," said the other, with an effort at self-control, "you are the King of France, monsieur! Having the honor of knowing our good Louis, I find it hard to credit your words."

"Eh? My statement?" exclaimed d'Artagnan in dismay.

"Exactly. The only lady who could have given you that ring is Her Majesty the Queen."

D'Artagnan took the ring from his finger and looked inside it. The words were indeed graven there. He had already pocketed the gold signet-ring, and now he pocketed the sapphire and pushed back his chair.

"Monsieur," he said with a curious deadly severity, "do you insist that I tell you whence comes this ring, and my connection with it?"

"Insist? I demand!" exclaimed the other imperiously. D'Artagnan now knew beyond a doubt that he was dealing with some noble of the court, perhaps with the Duc d'Orleans himself, who had seen that ring on the queen's hand, and who knew it intimately.

"Very well, monsieur, I comply with your request," said d'Artagnan. "And, having told you what is not my secret, I shall then kill you."

Upon these words he stood up and drew his sword. The masked cavalier did not move.

"Speak!" he commanded, evidently disdaining the threat as mere bravado.

"With the greatest of pleasure, monsieur," said d'Artagnan

politely, and selected the exact point of the other's throat for his thrust. "That ring was given me by Her Majesty, to show Madame de Chevreuse as surety that I was Her Majesty's messenger. I regret, monsieur, that I must now keep my word, which is never broken -- "

And with the rapidity of light, before his purpose could be guessed, he thrust his rapier to the point he had selected.

This thunderbolt of a lunge could not be escaped -- but it could be evaded.

The masked cavalier had been playing with a long carving-knife; he whipped it up, half-parried the blow -- the rapier of d'Artagnan, instead of piercing his throat, merely touched his ribs, scarce letting blood, and tore itself clear. From the cavalier broke a singular cry, and he fell sideways in his chair as though dead.

D'Artagnan, poised for a second thrust, stood gaping down at his senseless figure.

"The devil! I cannot very well kill an unconscious man," he murmured. "Still, it must be done. First, let me see with whom I'm dealing. After all, if this is some prince of the blood who is protecting Aramis, I might -- "

He laid his sword on the table, lifted the fainting cavalier, and removed the mask. The face thus exposed was unknown to him. He loosened the cavalier's garments, felt the wound -- and abruptly recoiled. The wound itself was nothing -- it was scarce bleeding, in fact -- but d'Artagnan had placed his hand upon the least expected object in the world.

"So, my Aramis!" he murmured, then checked his

amazement, collected himself.

He swiftly replaced the kerchief he had disarranged, buttoned the tunic again, put the mask again in position, and over the cavalier's brow sprinkled a little water. One glance at the sparkling jewels, the beautiful hands, the dull gold masses of knotted hair, told him all that was necessary to confirm his discovery. Until this moment the cavalier's hat had remained in place; d'Artagnan straightened it, found that it was pinned fast, and chuckled.

The blue eyes opened beneath the mask, and d'Artagnan stepped back a pace. He seized his rapier and placed its point at the throat of his host.

"Not a word!" he commanded. "Monsieur, you see that I am not to be trifled with. Luckily for you, I remembered just in time that you were protecting my friend Aramis. Instead of killing you, I turned the point, gave you a bare scratch, and now I shall be very glad to have a little further speech with you. I am M. d'Artagnan, lieutenant of Musketeers -- your name?"

The cavalier straightened, touched his side, grimaced. His gaze searched the impassive countenance of d'Artagnan, then his lips parted in a smile.

"Thank heaven for your memory, monsieur, tardy as it was!" he exclaimed. "So you are the friend of Aramis, who followed us this afternoon? I guessed as much. I am the Chevalier de Moreau, a relative and intimate of Madame de Chevreuse; in fact, all her business passes through my hands. She is at this moment very ill and can see no one. Thus, monsieur, your message would have to be delivered to me in any case. A few words with Aramis will convince you that I am speaking the truth."

D'Artagnan lowered his sword.

"And the ring, Chevalier -- "

"Was one given the queen by Chevreuse," said the other quietly. "I myself had the stone mounted for Madame."

D'Artagnan sheathed his weapon and bowed. He now knew with whom he was dealing.

"Monsieur, will you accept my apologies?" he said. "If you will permit me to look at the wound I was so unfortunate as to give you, I -- "

"No, no, it is nothing," said the chevalier, and laughed, a trifle maliciously. "But you yourself are wounded, M. d'Artagnan -- at least let me -- "

D'Artagnan blinked, at recollection of earlier passages with the chevalier.

"Bah! Mere scratches, my dear chevalier, not worth attention," he said. "Well, shall we resume our dinner? I believe, in view of what you say, that I may confide my messages to you.

"Absolutely, I assure you," said the chevalier, and drained a glass of wine. "I am forced, in the illness of Mme. de Chevreuse, to handle all her affairs."

"Then," said d'Artagnan, "you may be able to tell me what name was signed to a letter, not long ago received by M. d'Herblay -- a letter which told him never to see the writer again, never to speak with the writer, never to think of the writer?"

The chevalier turned pale. "Monsieur, how do you know of such a letter?"

"It was taken from Aramis when he was attacked and wounded. The man who took it, and other papers, died in my arms. I destroyed these papers, recognizing the seal of Aramis."

"Ah!" A breath, as of intense relief, escaped the chevalier. He rose and held out a hand to d'Artagnan. "Monsieur, you are an honorable man. I salute you."

For a moment d'Artagnan pressed those soft yet strong fingers, and felt a magnetic current pass through his veins. Then, resuming his seat, the chevalier continued.

"The letter was signed by the name of Marie Michon."

"Exactly," said d'Artagnan. "Now," and he poured more wine,"we may come to business. I have two errands to Madame de Chevreuse -- one from a man, one from a woman. Choose!"

"Ladies first, always!" said the chevalier gaily.

"Good." D'Artagnan touched the sapphire on his finger. "Her Majesty gave me this ring to show Madame, asked me to bring whatever message might be given me. That was all."

"Hm!" The chevalier reflected. "I can speak for Madame here, I believe. Tell Her Majesty that the will of Thounenin is being sent to Paris by way of London, but a sure friend is on guard. The moment this will is seized and destroyed, danger ceases. I dare not communicate with her; Marshal de Bassompierre will let her know the outcome."

"For the ears of all the court to hear?" asked d'Artagnan drily.

"In four words which she alone will understand: 'God loves the brave.' Understood?"

D'Artagnan inclined his head. "The message will be delivered, monsieur. May I ask whither you are taking my friend Aramis?"

"To the Chateau of Dampierre. He is in need of care; his recovery will be slow."

"Lucky Aramis!" thought d'Artagnan to himself. "Beloved by one of the greatest ladies of France, the most beautiful woman in Europe -- who would wish swift recovery in such a case?"

The chevalier drew from his finger a large ring ornamented with a small magnificent diamond of the most exquisite quality.

"If you please, M. d'Artagnan, give me the token of Her Majesty, and accept this, instead, as evidence to her that your mission was fulfilled. She will recognize the jewel, since it was a gift from her. And now -- your second errand?"

"Is less agreeable, I fear." D'Artagnan slipped the ring on his finger, but not without a sigh. The Queen's jewel had been to him more than a jewel merely. "His Eminence Cardinal de Richelieu sent me to Dampierre with a verbal message."

The other stiffened perceptibly, fastened a sharp and alert gaze upon d'Artagnan.

"A verbal message? From his own lips?"

D'Artagnan assented. "It is not impossible," he said, "that

His Eminence had learned of the mission confided to me in secret by Her Majesty. In fact, I have every reason to believe that I was not expected to reach Dampierre alive. However -- 'me voici!'"

"And the message?" The chevalier leaned forward in breathless suspense.

"It is this, from the lips of His Eminence: 'His Majesty has learned all and is taking the child under his own protection. Be very quiet during the next six months. If you indulge your liking for letters and visitors -- you are lost.' That is all."

The effect upon his listener was extraordinary. Across the face of the chevalier spread a deadly pallor; his lips parted in a gasp, and then he uttered a cry of mortal anguish -- a low piercing cry, as though these words had stricken him to the very heart. His head fell forward -- he had fainted, for the second time.

"The devil!" D'Artagnan rose, hearing a knock at the door. He opened, found the lackey there, and beckoned. "Look to your master -- he has fainted. No harm done. I'll see to my patient."

He knew that the lackey was, of course, in the secret of his master.

Passing into the next room, where the candle still burned dimly, d'Artagnan closed the door, then looked down at Aramis. To his gratification, the latter was sleeping soundly and peacefully, with a half-smile which lent his features an almost angelic expression.

"Ah, my dear Aramis, one can forgive a duchess for

loving you!" murmured d'Artagnan to himself. "You have your faults, yes, but to accompany them you have a heart of gold. And where, I wonder, is honest Bazin? Strange that he did not come with you.

"I am here, Monsieur d'Artagnan," said a voice. D'Artagnan started. From the floor at the foot of the bed uprose the melancholy figure of Bazin. "I was seeking a physician, and when I came back with him, you were here."

D'Artagnan burst into laughter, which he checked instantly for fear of waking Aramis. He knew very well with what feelings Bazin regarded him, and he made haste to set the lackey's mind at rest.

"Well, my good Bazin, I have not come to drag your master back to a secular life, I can assure you. As a matter of fact, he will be very lucky if he hangs on to any sort of life, for his wound is a bad one; but I imagine he will have the best of care, at Dampierre."

"He will, monsieur," said Bazin, with a sort of groan.

"I have, it appears, appropriated his breeches -- I came with only my shirt," said d'Artagnan. "Can you find me some clothes, any clothes at all? I have no money, but I have an extra horse which seems to be a good one. If you can arrange to sell this horse for me in the morning -- "

"I can arrange everything, monsieur," said Bazin. "Do you go to Dampierre with us?"

"Unluckily, no. I leave you here, and I leave as quickly as I can get clothed."

"Then, monsieur," said Bazin, brightening visibly, "I will

arrange it. As for clothes, my master has a whole portmanteau in the coach, and I recall that his clothes fit you perfectly. Since he will have no use for riding-boots, you might as well take his."

"Good," said d'Artagnan. "Then I will bid you good night."

He returned to the adjoining room; but, upon entering, found it empty. He glanced around in astonishment. At this instant he caught sharp voices from the courtyard. Leaving the room, he came out upon the stone staircase just in time to see two horses dash from the gateway and go into the night at a gallop. The host was ascending the stairs, and held up both hands at sight of d'Artagnan.

"Ah, monsieur, they have gone!" he exclaimed. "The gentleman left his coach and postilion to bring the wounded gentleman in the morning, and said that you were to have his room in his place --"

"The devil!" muttered d'Artagnan. "So she fled on getting that message, did she? My dear M. de Richelieu, I congratulate You on effecting more with a dozen words than I could with my sword-point!"

And, with a sigh, he turned back.

CHAPTER X

THE EXTRAORDINARY ADVENTURE OF THE COMTE DE LA FERE

Left at the Pomme d'Or, Athos and Porthos learned from Grimaud what d'Artagnan had cried out, and how he had departed. They lost no time in following; unluckily, the horses had to be saddled. Upon reaching the bridge, they made inquiries, and a soldier there declared he had seen a horseman answering the description of d'Artagnan take the highway north to Paris.

At the best pace possible, they followed this false scent, but saw nothing of their comrades, naturally enough. When darkness fell, they rode into the Croix de Berny, their horses staggering, and realized that they had come amiss. Inquiries revealed that d'Artagnan had certainly not been seen at the Croix.

"Supper, wine, a bed!" declaimed Porthos, stamping into the main room. "Capons, beef -- ah, what a hearth-spit I see there, and loaded too! Not so bad, Athos! Our lieutenant no doubt took that road bearing to the left from Longjumeau, eh?"

Athos nodded, gestured Grimaud to see to the horses, and followed Porthos inside. Once seated, he emptied two goblets of wine before speaking, then regarded Porthos fixedly.

"Do you know what day this is?" he demanded severely.

"That I do; Tuesday, thanks to the saints, and no fish until Friday!" rejoined Porthos carelessly. "Only, I wish d'Artagnan were sitting here. We must go back to Longjumeau and take that cursed western road, comrade."

"We cannot," said Athos gloomily. "Tomorrow is the thirtieth of July."

"Eh?" Porthos wiped his lips and stared at him inquiringly. "What of it?"

"You forget. Lord de Winter will be expecting us in Paris tomorrow. His errand is of the most supreme importance -- we know this already."

"Pardieu! You are right, Athos. But are we then to abandon poor d'Artagnan? We can find him at Dampierre, certainly -- "

"Our business lies ahead," said Athos, with an air of finality. "D'Artagnan knows the place and date of appointment; he will be there, if he is alive. We, on the contrary, are not yet at Paris."

"Bah!" exclaimed Porthos. "Half a day's ride away, my friend!"

"In six days the entire world was created," rejoined Athos. "In half a day, I assure you, Richelieu can undo a large part of the work of creation."

And he applied himself to the wine and food before him, without further remark, until the meal was finished. Then, regarding Porthos with the noble yet indefinably sad air which told of strange thoughts in his soul:

"My friend, I have a presentiment -- and you know that I am never deceived. I feel that this meeting with Lord de Winter holds for me either a terrible grief, or a great happiness, I cannot tell which."

The eyes of Porthos widened; and before he could reply, Athos had left the table.

Next morning they left the Croix de Berny at an early hour, passed through Chambord without incident, passed Arcueil, and were almost within sight of Chatillon when the huge Norman horse of Porthos suddenly went lame. Inexplicable as it seemed, there was the fact -- the animal had apparently strained a ligament or tendon.

"Ah!" exclaimed Porthos, purpling with abrupt anger. "You recall -- we baited the horses back there at Arcueil? And those grooms crowding around? Pardieu! I'll wager a pistole -- "

Athos made a sign to Grimaud. The latter sighed, dismounted, held his stirrup for Porthos, and himself took the Norman.

"Forward!" said Athos. The two friends rode on, and ere reaching Chatillon had lost poor Grimaud to sight. They were only a short distance from the gates of Chatillon when two men, who had been standing with their horses at the roadside, mounted and rode into the town ahead of them.

"Did you see that?" said Athos. "They were awaiting us. They bear word ahead. Porthos, we must separate here."

"And why, if you please?" demanded Porthos in some wonder.

"One of us must keep that appointment with Lord de Winter," said Athos, and drew rein. "if we go on together, we shall both be stopped -- depend upon it! Therefore, separate here. You ride to the east, enter Paris by the Porte St. Antoine. I will ride west, make Issy, cross the Seine and enter from Passy. You comprehend?"

"I comprehend this," said Porthos, puffing out his cheeks. "if they watched us enter Chatillon, they will certainly watch us leave!"

"Yes, but by separating, we divide their forces, throw their plans awry, and gain greater chance of winning through," said Athos calmly. "Bourg-la-Reine lies ahead; from there it is just two leagues to Paris. It is not yet noon we need not reach the Place Royale until tonight. You know the rendezvous? The Hotel de St. Luc."

"Well, then," said Porthos reluctantly, "I shall wait here for Grimaud."

"Do so,,' said Athos. "Farewell! Until tonight."

And, without looking back, he turned into a side street and was lost to sight.

Athos knew very well that no one wished to prevent any of them meeting Baron de Winter, for this rendezvous was probably known to no one, and would give no suspicion. It was far more likely that d'Artagnan had been seen to leave Grenoble with one friend, and Lyon with two friends and a lackey. Their road had been roundabout; thus Montforge, easily ahead of them, could have made dispositions to kill them all.

"And that is undoubtedly his purpose," reflected Athos. "Why, we do not yet know. He has his orders; that is enough. Ah, Richelieu! You are powerful; but when you turn your power against the honor of a woman, forces of which you know nothing will blunt your weapons! Once before, you pitted yourself against four men who had only heaven to assist them, and you lost. Be careful lest this time you destroy yourself!"

Crossing the Seine at Issy, Athos mounted the heights of Passy and took the Paris road. It was now noon; he had seen no indication of any further danger, and he was hungry. At the Auberge de la Pompe just outside Passy, he turned in and ordered his horse fed, and commanded a meal for himself. He was in funds, since d'Artagnan had shared Richelieu's purse with his friends.

Athos was in the act of mounting, at the gate of the inn, to resume his journey, when a voice arose from a throng of country-folk returning from market at Passy.

"M. le Comte! M. le Comte!"

Athos paused. A man broke from the throng and ran to him -- an elderly man with an air of respectability, who came up to him with an expression of astonished joy.

"Ah, M. le Comte!" he cried out. "To find you here -- "

"I believe you mistake," said Athos coldly. The other halted abruptly.

"Mistake? Monsieur, do you not recognize me -- do you not know Gervais, your father's old steward, now the steward of your uncle? No, no! Monsieur, you are the Count de la

Fere"

Athos glanced quickly around, then he held out his hand to the older man, and his warm smile lighted his face.

"Ah, Gervais!" he said affectionately. "It is indeed you? But you have changed terribly -- "

The steward seized his hand and kissed it, with tears upon his cheeks. Before he could speak, Athos checked him, gave his horse to a groom, and led Gervais into the inn. He demanded a private room, and in two minutes they were alone.

"Ah, monsieur, I have searched all Paris to find you!" cried the old steward in agitation. "What luck, to see you here on the road! No one knew what had became of you. Some say you are with the army, some say you are dead -- "

"Gervais, I am dead," said Athos, with his air of inflexible calm. "Whence come you?"

"From Roussillon, monsieur! I have a message from your uncle. He is very ill, he will not live long; he begs you to come to him. He sent me to find you -- he has no one of his own blood in the world, you alone are left -- "

"I, I only remain!" said Athos, and lowered his head. "Yes, that is true."

"I have been in Paris for a week, searching everywhere," went on Gervais. "Yesterday I came to see a cousin of mine, who lives here near Passy, who has a farm here. Monsieur, you will come home with me! Say you will come "

Athos raised his head. His features were composed; one would have said they were of marble, so cold and bloodless had they become.

"My good Gervais, the Comte de la Fere is dead," he said calmly. "Athos, the Musketeer, alone remains -- "

"Monsieur," pleaded the old man, "you have a duty. Ah, pardon me -- it is true! Your uncle is dying. He begs only to see you. Whether you are dead or alive, I implore you to come and speak with him!"

"Ah!" said Athos. "Yes, one has a certain duty -- " He sighed, and suddenly clasped the withered hand of the steward. "Gervais, look you: I am engaged in a matter not my own. I cannot answer you here and now. You have money?"

The other made a gesture in the affirmative. "Also, monsieur, I have a thousand livres which your uncle sent, thinking you might have need."

"I do not wish his money; keep it," said Athos coldly. "Come to the Hotel of the Musketeers, or rather the Hotel de Treville, in the Rue du Vieux-Colombier, precisely at noon tomorrow. Ask for M. Athos, you comprehend? If I am not there, come the next day at noon, and the next. For the present, I am not my own master. The first day I am free, you will find me."

The faithful steward uttered a cry of joy.

Ten minutes later, Athos was once more riding toward Paris. He rode carelessly, blindly, not looking whither he was going; he was steeped in reflection, and his features wore an expression of gloomy bitterness. He was quite lost to everything around. The country-folk on the road avoided him carefully. His distinguished air, his garb, and above all the magnificent horse he bestrode, the horse which Richelieu had presented to d'Artagnan, showed them that he was some noble best left alone.

At the point where the road dipped down under the hill of La Chaise, to seek the banks of the Seine, his horse suddenly halted of its own accord.

Athos lifted his head. This little glade, enclosed by trees, was empty save for a coach which stood directly ahead of him. A rear wheel was broken. In the coach, thus tilted to one side, sat a young woman, magnificently dressed, and of the most dazzling beauty. She was staring at Athos; by the terror in her eyes, by the pallor of her features, he perceived that she was in great fear. A glance around showed him that she was absolutely alone.

Approaching the coach, Athos doffed his hat and bowed in the saddle, with that absolute grace of which he alone knew the secret.

"Madame," he said, "I see that you are in some distress. If I may have the honor of assisting you, I beg that you will consider me entirely at your service.

At these words, the terror passed from her eyes, and she clasped her hands together.

"Ah, monsieur -- you are a gentleman -- will you have the goodness to remain until my servants return with another coach? Two soldiers just passed by; if they had not discerned your approach, they would have robbed me --"

"Be at rest, madame." Athos dismounted and bowed again. "My name is Athos, of the Musketeers; you are safe. If you will tell me of what regiment those soldiers were, I shall see that they are punished as they deserve."

"I do not know, monsieur -- I was too terrified to observe! I am the niece of M. d'Estrees, who is with the army. Our tiny chateau is close by -- if you will have the goodness to escort me home, I shall be eternally grateful!"

Athos assented with his air of grave courtesy. To himself he thought that never had he seen so beautiful a woman as this girl, for she was little more than a girl. Athos was a person who looked upon women with a jaundiced and critical eye; but this creature delighted him. Her fresh completion, her air of frank innocence, told that she was not of the court; her hair, of a rich golden yellow, was unpowdered; her eyes were of a limpid and serene blue. Above all, she radiated that indescribable charm which is the attribute of one woman in ten thousand, and which not one man in ten thousand ever encounters.

Before he could more than assent, however, a coach appeared, coming from the direction of Paris. The coachman drew up, the postilion opened the door, with bows to Mlle. d'Estrees and glances of curiosity at Athos.

"If mademoiselle will enter -- "

"Good," she said. "This gentleman will escort me -- you will bring his horse, Francois."

Athos handed her into the other coach, followed, and sat by her side. He felt somewhat ill at ease; the closeness of this charming girl, the air of frank abandon with which she turned to him, provoked singular feelings within him.

"You are a gentleman of the Musketeers?" she asked. "Ah, monsieur, how fortunate you came when you did! My father was in your corps -- well, shall I make a confession? When I saw you, I said to myself: 'That is no ordinary man! He is some great prince in disguise.' Confess, monsieur -- I was right? Athos is the name of a mountain, not of a man."

"You are well versed in geography, mademoiselle," said Athos, and turned to her with that noble and singularly charming smile which he rarely showed, and then only when he was with someone who pleased him greatly. "We are all princes in disguise, my child, but too often the disguise -- "

"Tiens! What sort of talk is this?" she broke in with a gay laugh. "My child, indeed! My reverend gray-haired father -- nonsense, monsieur! I am no babe, and you are no philosopher. But there is our chateau ahead; come, confess, is it not a pretty place?"

"It is adorable!" exclaimed Athos.

"Then you will enter with me, drink a glass of wine, allow your horse to be rubbed down, allow my cousin to thank you for your kindness, and if you are polite you may kiss my hand."

"With all my heart, mademoiselle," said Athos, and for once his grave manner was somewhat lightened. Her arch words, her laughing eyes, her youth and innocence, affected him in an extraordinary fashion.

During this brief conversation the horses had been pushed hard, and the coach approached a little chateau set in a small and evidently ancient park, closely crowded by surrounding buildings, yet all having the air of being far in the country. Two enormous oak trees quite shrouded the entrance gates of stone; the chateau itself proved to be a small structure but of very beautiful proportions, in the style of those erected during the reign of Francois I -- that is to say, a century earlier.

Athos alighted, handed Mlle. d'Estrees from the coach, and she spoke to the servant who appeared at the doorway.

"My cousin -- he has not departed yet?"

"I think he has gone to the stables, mademoiselle, to select a horse."

"Good! Tell him I wish to see him, and that we have a guest."

The servant departed. Athos was by this time very curious, and willingly accompanied the young lady into the house. He knew the name of d'Estrees, but he did not know that anyone of the name could be living here; the former mistress of Henry IV had bequeathed her children a title, and not a name.

Athos asked no questions, however. In a day when Chavigny was twitted to his face upon being sired by Richelieu, Athos possessed a singular delicacy and refinement, which was not the least of his virtues.

Having ordered wine, his hostess led him to a small library having only one window, high in the wall, and completely lined with books from floor to ceiling.

"This is our coolest chamber on such a day," she stated. "Also, it is my favorite room. Further, I desire to look up the name of Athos in an atlas."

"Then I may save you the trouble," declared Athos. "It is the name of a mountain in Greece, inhabited solely by anchorites, who admit no woman to their inclosure."

"While you, monsieur, by force of contrast -- "

Athos smiled. "I, mademoiselle, present neither contrast nor conformity. But what an admirable library! When you shall have read all these tomes, I dread to think of how scholarly you will become!"

"Oh, I have read them all," she rejoined. "That is to say, all except the Plato, which I find dull. And apparently I do not look the scholar, to judge by your observation!"

A servant entered with a magnificent salver of massive silver, on which were exquisite Venetian glasses and wine in a beaker of chased gold. Athos glanced at the shelves of books closest to hand; he was astonished to see the most handsome bindings, and among others the works of Rabelais in the superb binding designed by Fevart for Henri II. The Greek, Latin and French authors were mingled indiscriminately; Montaigne nestled cheek by jowl with a royal Book of Hours of the XIV Century encased in a jewel-studded box from the hand of Pierre Lovat.

Mademoiselle d'Estrees poured wine, and extended a glass to Athos, then raised her own.

"To the broken coach," she exclaimed gaily, which led to so fortunate a meeting! Ah -- I hear my cousin -- I pray you to excuse me for one instant, monsieur -- "

And setting down her untouched glass, she left the room

hastily.

Athos held his glass to the light, sniffed the bouquet of the wine, which was his favorite Malaga -- then checked himself as he was on the point of sipping. His eyes had caught a few grains of white powder on the tray at the foot of the beaker; the more singular, as the salver was highly polished.

Setting down his glass, Athos glanced around. A frightful suspicion seized upon him. He turned, went to the door, opened it, looked out into the hall. No one was there. He caught an echo of low voices from a half-closed doorway beyond, and stepped softly toward it. The voice of a man came to him with astonishing words.

"You fool! It's the wrong man -- pardieu, they picked the right horse, though! The pair of them must have exchanged horses."

"Is it my fault, then?" came the tones of Mlle. d'Estrees, but now singularly low and sullen. "We got the message, did our part well -- "

"Finish it, then -- I've no time to waste, Helene!" returned the man. "I must be off at once. You say no admission can be gained without the ring? Well, I must get a ring made, since the one you sent is lost."

"Be sure it bears the arms of Bassompierre!" cautioned the woman. "And remember, they have guards at St. Saforin!"

The other laughed curtly. "Bah! I'll take the child to Grenoble -- no news today?"

"None from London as yet. Marconnet came this morning from Lyon -- it is rumored that the king is ill," said the woman's voice. "If you have trouble, bring the boy here. But have a care! Bassompierre is in Paris -- he will be here today or tomorrow."

"Tonight or tomorrow night, you mean," and the other laughed again. "Here -- I've no more time to waste. I will take a look at our man; if he has not drunk your potion, then we must put a sword into him -- "

Athos, who had listened to this conversation with incredulous horror, made his way back to the library. He caught up his glass and emptied it behind a bookshelf, then replaced it and sank into a chair, closed his eyes, relaxed as though drugged.

The terrible paleness of his features assisted the delusion.

He was as though frozen in a sort of nightmare. What he had just overheard, made it clear to him where he was, who this woman was, and how he had been entrapped. This girl, whose innocence had so appealed to him, was the Helene de Sirle of whom d'Artagnan had spoken; the ring mentioned was the ring on d'Artagnan's hand. The horrible realization left him benumbed, incapable of thinking or acting; for the moment he could only play his part supinely.

"He has it, pardieu!" said the man's voice at the door. "Good; I am off. Marconnet will take care of this one for you. The address of the goldsmith who made the other ring?"

The girl's voice responded, inaudibly. Footsteps receded.

Athos opened his eyes, sat up, sweat starting on his brow. Only now did it occur to him that the man must have been Montforge. He went to the window, and caught sight of a cavalier mounting and knew the man must be departing.

"Just God!" murmured Athos in a sort of desperation, sweeping a terrible look around the room. "Into what sort of hands have I fallen? Well there is only one way out."

He drew his sword. The trembling which had seized upon him passed, and was resolved into a cold and deadly anger. Since meeting the broken-down coach upon the highway, much time had elapsed; the afternoon was beginning to wane.

To gain the entrance, Athos was forced to pass the length of the hall. As he came to the door of the room where he had heard the conversation, a lackey came out, saw him, stopped in astonishment. Athos lifted his rapier.

"Not a sound!" he commanded sternly. "Turn around, lead the way

Instead of complying with this order, the lackey caught a poniard from his belt and at the same instant sent a cry ringing through the house. The rapier of Athos drove into his throat, too late to check that cry of alarm.

"The devil himself," said Athos, freeing his weapon, "has evidently supplied servants for this house!"

He strode hastily to the entrance -- then checked bimself. Helene de Sirle, as he now knew her to be, stood at the foot of the steps. She had doubtless been saying farewell to Montforge, and had heard the lackey's cry; swift, shrill orders were coming from her lips, and Athos caught sight of three men running across the garden, their weapons bared.

"It is he -- kill him!" cried out the young woman in a tone

of indescribable ferocity, and moved as though to lead her three men up the steps to the portal.

Athos perceived that he was trapped. Outside, near where the coach still stood waiting, he saw the horse he had ridden, but he was unable to reach the animal. With a swift motion, he caught hold of the open doors, swung them shut, and dropped a bar into place just as the three men hurled themselves upon the barrier with angry cries. The doors trembled, but did not give way.

Turning, Athos made for the wide staircase winding to the upper floor. He had recognized at a glance that his one hope of leaving this place alive lay in reaching his horse; but the cries of domestics ringing through the lower part of the house showed that he could not seek another entrance or even make use of a window. He dashed up the stairs, and was halfway to the upper floor when a pistolet exploded below.

Athos staggered, lost his balance, fell upon hands and knees. At the same instant a man with bared sword appeared at the head of the stairs. "Marconnet!" came the cry from below. "Monsieur Marconnet -- kill that man!"

"Gladly," responded the man above and, descending a step or two, darted a thrust at Athos.

The latter, however, had realized his peril, had heard the cry, knew that the man above was the courier arrived from Lyon that morning. He still held his own sword; parrying the lunge as he rose, he engaged Marconnet with a ferocity augmented by the sounds of men ascending the stairs behind and below him. Another moment, and he would be taken in rear.

That moment did not arrive.

A terrible cry burst from Marconnet. The rapier of Athos entered his stomach from below, and emerged beneath his shoulder-blade; before the steel could be plucked out, the unfortunate man plunged headlong, as though shot from a catapult, and his body was hurled upon two servants in the act of attacking Athos from behind. They were swept from their feet, carried downward, and came to the floor below with a crash, punctuated by cries of anguish.

Athos, catching up the rapier dropped by Marconnet, darted on to the top of the stairs. He had lost his hat; the pistol-ball had caught it away, ploughing a slight gash across his scalp from which the blood was running freely.

Having already made up his mind exactly what he was to do, Athos started down the upper corridor to gain one of the rooms giving upon the front of the chateau. A door opened, a femme-de-chambre appeared, and uttered a scream at sight of this stranger, sword in hand. Athos pushed her back into the room, slammed the door upon her, darted to a door farther on, and hurling himself into the room, closed and locked the door again.

"The devil!" exclaimed a voice. "What means this, monsieur!"

Athos whirled. He had gained the room which he desired, whose windows opened upon the front balcony of the chateau -- but this room was not empty. It was a magnificent chamber. A massive oak bed, sculptured with passages from the lives of famous women and draped with the most exquisite of brocades and satins, occupied one entire end of the room. At one side was a long dressing table of mahogany, holding perfumes and pomades, linting with jeweled trifles -- that of a lady, beyond question.

Standing before the windows was a pale and half-clothed young man who had apparently just left the bed to draw the curtains when the alarm was sounded. He had caught up a sword, and bared the blade as he addressed Athos. The latter recognized him as a wealthy young noble of the court, one M. Sourens, who was rapidly acquiring a reputation for extreme profligacy.

"Your pardon, monsieur," said Athos, having turned the key in the lock. "I did not know this room was occupied. If you will have the goodness to let me pass --"

"Pass as you came," said Sourens heatedly. "Ventrebleu! To have canaille like you rushing into one's room -- out of here before I chastise you, scullion!"

Athos became very pale, "Monsieur, if your chastisement is as out of date as your oaths," he said with contempt, "it is scarcely to be feared. Stand aside, if you please."

He advanced toward the window, but Sourens flung himself before the glass, angrily.

"Devil take you, I'll teach you how to speak to a gentleman -- " and he attacked the intruder swiftly, viciously.

Athos met the attack with a slight smile of disdain, and for a moment held the infuriated young man in play. Cries and the stamp of feet were resounding through the building.

"Monsieur," said Athos politely, as the blades rasped, "I have no desire to harm you, but it is imperative that I leave this house at once by way of your window. I ask you to give me passage, in default of which I must kill you."

Maddened by the calm contempt in the air of Athos, the other heaped oaths upon him.

"Gallows bird!" he concluded. "Sneak-thief -- I suppose you are some bretteur of the faubourgs, are you? Pass, indeed! You break into the room of Mlle. de Sirle and then -- "

"Ah!" said Athos with an expression of satisfaction. "Since you appear to be occupying her room, monsieur, it is evident that you have no right here. Therefore I must keep my word."

And he ran the young man through the heart, composedly stepped across his body, and wrenched open a window.

The sun was just setting. Before him was a balcony, the gardens some twelve feet below. No one was in sight outside; the coach and horse still stood there, unguarded. Obviously, everyone was searching through the house.

Athos thrust the borrowed sword into his own sheath, lifted the baldric over his head, and cast it into a flower-bed below. Then, bestriding the rail of the balcony, he leaped after it.

Inside, the chateau was filled with confusion, but no one thought to look out in the gardens for the intruder. Athos picked up baldric and sword and mounted. In less than a moment he was riding toward the entrance gates, which stood wide open.

"Decidedly," he observed, "I do not envy d'Artagnan his

errand to that young lady!"

He swayed suddenly, caught himself from falling, and passed a hand across his eyes. Then, settling his feet in the stirrups, he was between the gates and out in the road, where people began to stare at him, bare-headed and hurt as he was.

He forgot that he himself had not yet entered Paris.

CHAPTER XI

THE STILL MORE EXTRAORDINARY ADVENTURE OF M. DU VALLON

Since everyone knew that M. de St. Luc was with the King, and his hotel in the Place Royale was closed for the summer, there was some astonishment in the quarter when, on the thirtieth day of July, servants appeared, the gates were opened, and the shutters flung back. However, in this vicinity of hotels and residences of the nobility, nearly all of which were shut up, there was none to ask questions.

On the morning of this day, a traveling coach entered the courtyard of this hotel. A gentleman of stern features, sober but rich attire, and wearing pistols beneath his cloak, alighted. This gentleman was Lord de Winter, Baron Sheffield. The steward of M. de St. Luc approached and bowed deferentially.

"Milord will find everything ready," he said. "The larder is stocked, the beds are aired; the orders from our master are to obey you as himself. We are at your service, monsieur, and we trust you will have no reason to be dissatisfied with us."

Lord de Winter nodded. "Very well. In the course of today I expect four gentlemen who will ask for me here. They may come together or singly. They may come at noon or midnight. I desire to have ready for them the most sumptuous banquet possible, with the finest wines."

"At what hour, Milord?"

"At whatever hour they come," said Lord de Winter.

"And if they delay until evening, monsieur will dine -- "

"On bread and milk only, in my own chamber."

So saying, he retired to the chamber prepared for him, and rested most of the day.

The afternoon drew on, evening came; lights were put out, the banquet was ready, no guests arrived. At nine o'clock Lord de Winter supped lightly in his own room on bread and milk. He was served by his lackey, who spoke a sort of French, but who only shrugged when the anxious steward questioned him about the expected guests.

"My master has invited them," he said. "They will arrive."

At ten o'clock Lord de Winter, who had been seated by an open window, appeared upon the grand staircase and encountered the steward.

"I hear a horse at the gallop," he said. "Let us descend."

The steward thought him mad. They descended to the courtyard, where cressets had been lighted, and were just in time to see an exhausted horse come through the gates and halt, trembling. The rider alighted; he was bareheaded, but so covered with dust from head to foot as to be unrecognizable. He took two steps, and staggered.

"M. de Winter!" he exclaimed in a croaking voice.

"By the love of the saints!" exclaimed de Winter. "It is M. d'Artagnan!"

And he caught d'Artagnan in his arms, embraced him warmly, then assisted him to enter and ordered a bath prepared and garments laid out from his own wardrobe.

D'Artagnan, who had ridden all day at breakneck speed, had killed his horse; but he had arrived.

He bathed hurriedly, dressed, and was being conducted to the salon where Lord de Winter awaited him, when the steward entered.

"Monsieur, there is a gentleman below -- he came on foot, and he appears to be covered with blood. He asked for you --"

D'Artagnan turned, gained the courtyard at a bound, and clasped Athos in his arms. Athos was, it is true, covered with blood, and he had arrived on foot, for excellent reasons. Upon entering Paris he had suddenly fainted, had fallen from his horse, and for two hours lay in the house of a surgeon whither he was carried. Upon regaining consciousness, he had forced his way from the house and had come to the Place Royale afoot, like a man blind and deaf, answering none who spoke to him.

Athos, in turn bathed and with the wound across his scalp dressed anew, presently joined d'Artagnan and Lord de Winter. The latter was filled with curiosity, but said nothing. Athos paused in the doorway and regarded his friend.

"D'Artagnan, you did not fulfill your errand at Dampierre?"

"I did," said d'Artagnan, "but I did not go to Dampierre. Two men attempted to kill me; I killed them. Unfortunately, one of them hit me a blow between the eyes -- I think it is quite discolored. Peasants, in passing, took me for dead, and stripped us all. However --"

"You did not find Aramis?"

"Yes. All is well. But you, my friend -- you, Athos! I have never seen you in such a state?"

Athos shrugged. "Bah! I fell from my horse and struck my head, that is all. I separated from Porthos, and left Grimaud with him. They have not arrived?"

At that instant Grimaud arrived, alone. He was brought into the salon.

"Speak," said Athos. "Where is M. Porthos?"

The unhappy Grimaud spread out his hands. "God knows, monsieur! We halted at a tavern just inside the gates. Two other gentlemen were there; both were masked. M. Porthos joined them, and I think he is drunk by this time. Half a dozen more gentlemen arrived just before dark, and were ordering supper when their servants forced me to leave."

"How?" exclaimed Athos. "Masked, you say? Were the other arrivals masked also?"

"Two of them were masked, monsieur, besides the first two."

"This is singular!" murmured d'Artagnan. Lord de Winter smiled.

"Good -- we will not await Porthos, then. And Aramis?"

"Is wounded, but in the care of friends. He does not join us."

"Then let us proceed to supper, my friends -- to supper, and to what we have to say. For, to judge from what I have seen and heard," he added, "each of us has a good deal to recount."

"That is true," said Athos in a grave voice. "But not before servants."

The three passed into the stately dining-hall, built by the Gerard de St. Luc who was said to have slain the Duke of Burgundy, Charles the Bold, at the siege of Nancy in '477. Here they were served with a supper, or rather a banquet, composed of the most marvelous dishes that could be concocted by the finest chefs in PariS -- that is to say, in the entire world.

Athos accepted all this as a matter of course; he drank the superb wines as though they were common vin rouge, he left half the delicate foods almost untasted. He was preoccupied, weighed down by one of his dark moods. D'Artagnan, on the contrary, was astonished at each new course, relished each fresh wine with gusto, and could not contain his admiration.

"This is no dinner, my dear baron, but a feast!" he exclaimed. "You are the soul of generosity."

"That, my dear d'Artagnan," said Lord de Winter, "is because I come here to appeal to generosity."

Porthos did not arrive. Presently the table was cleared, save for wine, fruit and nuts, and the baron's English lackey closed the doors and took up his station outside. Lord de Winter passed Athos a carafe of old Xeres wine, and spoke.

"With your permission, my friends, I shall first tell you my story; then, if you will, tell me of your adventures. You received one at least of the letters I sent, and you discovered what was written with secret ink. Therefore, you know that I referred to Her Majesty the Queen."

Athos pushed away the carafe of Xeres, which he had been in the act of lifting.

"It is a brief thing to tell, but not one to write in words," resumed the Englishman. "You gentlemen were friends of the late Duke of Buckingham; you were in his confidence; therefore it was to you I turned. As you may or may not know, I have friends in Nancy -- I am, in fact, distantly related to Duke Charles of Lorraine. One of these friends, who is also a friend of Madame de Chevreuse, recently wrote me of a very serious matter. I at once wrote you.

"Ah! Ah!" exclaimed d'Artagnan, his eyes widening. "You cannot mean -- no, it is impossible! Not the Thounenin will!"

As though by a thunderbolt, the calm of the phlegmatic Englishman was shattered.

"What!" he cried. "You cannot know of it already -- "

"Be silent, my son," said Athos suddenly, to d'Artagnan,"until our host first tells us everything. Then we, in turn, will complement his tale with what we know. Rather, with what we have heard; for we know little."

"Very well," said de Winter, recovering. "A village cure near Versailles, a relative of Madame de Chevreuse, received from her an infant, some four years since -- a newborn child. He was given money and precise directions for the care of the child.

Being in Lorraine about a year ago, knowing himself facing death from an incurable malady, he added a codicil to a will which he had made in 1624. This codicil of two pages, written on vellum, told of the child and its origin; I may say that this cure firmly believed that the infant had been born of Her Majesty, who had been seriously ill at this time, at Versailles, under the care of Madame de Chevreuse."

At these words Athos to whom any slur upon the honor of the queen was a blasphemy, became livid.

"This cure," went on the Englishman, "made incautious statements in his will. They are statements which, if this document came into the wrong hands, might work incalculable harm to Her Majesty. As an Englishman, it was no affair of mine; as a gentleman, it became my affair. Further -- "

"Ah, ah!" cried out d'Artagnan, unable to control himself. "This is the child which is under Bassompierre's care! This is the document which is on the way to Richelieu!"

"On the contrary," said Athos, whose aspect was frightful, "this child is now being taken from St. Saforin by agents of the Cardinal! But stop. Continue, monsieur. It appears that each of us has important contributions to make to this dossier."

Inexpressibly astonished by this knowledge on the part of his guests, Lord de Winter inclined his head and pursued his story.

"Further, gentlemen, I know absolutely that this is not the child of Her Majesty. You will remember that I was in the confidence of the late Buckingham. Also, when M. de Bassompierre was Ambassador to England, I knew him intimately.

There is a secret regarding this child, and I impart this

secret to you upon your honor as gentlemen. This child was not born of the queen, but of Madame de Chevreuse. The fact was so strictly concealed, that the cure in question leaped to the wrong conclusion. However, if his will is obtained by enemies of Her Majesty, there will undoubtedly be a terrible injury done an innocent lady. That is why I wrote you I cannot act in this matter; you can act freely. I know your devotion to Anne of Austria as queen and woman, I know your chivalrous natures, and above all I know of what you are capable."

"Good," said Athos. "But remember, we know very little. Can you tell us where that paper or document is now?"

"I can tell you everything," said Lord de Winter, with a trace of agitation. "That is why I asked you to meet me here. I can tell you who the man is that carries the document, where he is, whither he is going. The agents of Richelieu who extracted the document from the archives were caught, almost in the act. While they escaped, they could not send the paper to France. They sent it to England for security, and to cover their own traces. The man bearing it to Paris left London for Calais the same day I left. At Dover he was arrested on a false charge, search was made for the document. It was not discovered, but he missed his passage to Calais, and I got ahead of him. I have remained ahead of him. Sometime tonight a messenger will arrive to tell us exactly where he now is, what road he is taking to Paris, and how many are with him."

"Excellent!" cried d'Artagnan. "We ask no more depend

upon it, monsieur, that document is as good as destroyed this moment!" Athos looked at the Englishman with a species of admiration.

"And it was to tell us this, monsieur," he said, "that you sent for us, that you came to Paris, that -- "

"No, no!" broke in de Winter. "It was not for this. It was because I, like you, cannot see the honor of a woman whom I revere made a pawn for politics by an unscrupulous prelate!"

There was a moment of silence. Then the Englishman looked at d'Artagnan.

"I have finished, monsieur. It is your turn."

D'Artagnan began to tell with eagerness and vivacity of all that had happened to him since leaving Athos and Porthos at Longjumeau. At last he himself understood everything, or nearly everything, and he kept back only one item -- Richelieu's verbal message to Chevreuse.

"I may say this much," he concluded. "The message spoke of the child, and upon receiving it my masked cavalier first fainted, then fled like a startled rabbit. And here is her diamond, to prove my tale. But you, Athos -- come, tell us about this fall from a horse!"

"With pleasure," said Athos. "More especially as it has a direct bearing upon our entire errand and, I fear, a very terrible bearing!"

He told of his encounter with Helene de Sirle, of what he had heard and done at her house; but he said nothing of meeting his uncle's steward, Gervais. D'Artagnan heard the tale with anxiety; Lord de Winter only nodded from time to time, as though he were no longer to be amazed by anything these extraordinary men might say.

"So, my friends," said Athos in conclusion, "we may be certain of two things in regard to the Comte de Montforge. He has been ordered to destroy us, or at least d'Artagnan; and he has been ordered to carry off this child from the abbey of St. Saforin."

"Very good," observed Lord de Winter calmly. "I believe we may now sum up? The document, then, is on its way to Paris, where it will be handed over -- "

"To Mlle. de Sirle," said Athos, as the other paused. "The child is at St. Saforin. How came he there? Why did Marshal de Bassompierre assume his guardianship?"

"For several reasons," replied Lord de Winter. "Bassompierre is a Lorrainer and friendly with Chevreuse. I myself know this lady well, and she, who might be expected to take most interest in the child, takes none. After its birth, she desired never to look upon its face. True, she makes provision for the child, but she is a selfish woman who cares not who loves her so long as she is not known as the mother of illegitimate children. In such case, you comprehend, the Duc de Chevreuse might very well abandon her, and Richelieu would certainly hold her in his power."

The brow of Athos was dark and gloomy. "Her attitude toward this child is a crime," he said. D'Artagnan stared, for he had seldom heard Athos so speak of a woman. "She denies herself a son. She denies the child a parent. She places others in danger. What a woman! Bah!"

Lord de Winter shrugged. "Well, whoever may have been the father of the child, which is a somewhat vexed question, there are the facts. He was placed in St. Saforin under the name of Raoul d'Aram -- "

Athos started so violently that his arm knocked over the carafe of Xeres wine, which d'Artagnan recovered.

"What is that? What is that?" cried Athos in a low but piercing voice. "Raoul d'Aram! Do you comprehend, d'Artagnan? This explains everything! Aramis is a friend of Bassompierre; he has been a lover of Chevreuse for years; the boy, named Raoul d'Aram -- "

He fell silent, staring at the others. Lord de Winter nodded again. D'Artagnan swore.

"Diantre! And he is helpless, unable to leave his bed, caring nothing for the child -- ah, Aramis, what a pretty mess your gallantry has entangled us in! And this scoundrel Montforge is now on his way to St. Saforin, Athos?"

"Yes, my son; but rest assured -- he cannot proceed there until he has a ring made like the one on your finger. That requires time. He cannot get the ring before tomorrow night at the earliest. We shall be ahead of him."

"Ahead of him?" D'Artagnan looked at Athos inquiringly.

"Certainly," said Athos with his calm air. "Our errand is twofold. We have, first, to meet this messenger from London, kill him, secure the document, and destroy it. Second, we have to carry off this boy from St. Saforin."

D'Artagnan looked at him with incredulity; Lord de Winter with stupefied surprise. Athos met their gaze with his rare smile, whose high nobility was touched with sadness.

"My friends," he said, "I confess to you, I am tempted to perceive the finger of God in all this affair. Our endeavor is first to defeat the schemes of Richelieu, that man whom ambition has blinded to honor; by defeating him, we save Her Majesty. Good! Aramis has abandoned this child to the care of a friend. The boy faces a terrible destiny; he is without a father, he is without a mother, yet his father and his mother are of the noblest blood in France!"

"Bah!" said d'Artagnan uneasily. "It is no hindrance to be a bastard, my friend. Look at Orleans, who drove the English out of France! Look at the Duc de Vendome -- "

"I am looking, at this instant, at the son of Aramis, who is my friend," said Athos, with so noble an air, so lofty and severe a tone, that d'Artagnan fell silent. "In order to accomplish our task, I propose that we first carry off this boy, cause him to vanish utterly from the sight of Richelieu or any other. I will then provide him with a father, with a mother, with a name. In brief, I will myself adopt him."

"You!" cried d'Artagnan in amazement.

"You?" echoed the Englishman, as though not crediting his ears.

"I," said Athos calmly. "My friend," and he turned to d'Artagnan. "I have determined to leave the service and retire to a small estate. Heretofore, I have had nothing to live for; now, it would seem, I have found a son. He will bear the name of my estate of Bragelonne."

There was a knock at the door. The English lackey opened.

"My lord," he said to his master, "Franklin has arrived."

"Bring him," said Lord de Winter, and turned to his guests. "My messenger, gentlemen."

A dust-covered cavalier appeared, saluted, and at a command from Lord de Winter spoke in French.

"Milord, our man stopped at Compiegne for the night. I rode on. He arrives in Paris at noon tomorrow, at the earliest probably not until later, for he is exhausted."

"Good," said de Winter. "You learned nothing about the document we failed to discover?"

"I learned nothing," said Franklin. "But when he came to Compiegne, he removed the pistol from the right-hand side of his saddle, and carried it to his room with him."

"Eureka!" exclaimed d'Artagnan. "The paper is in the barrel of that pistol."

The messenger was dismissed, and the doors closed.

"Well, my friends," said Lord de Winter, "I must depart in two days for Venice -- I have an errand there for the King of England. While I remain here, this house and all I have or can borrow, are at your service."

"Thank you, monsieur," said Athos. "We have need of nothing, except the name of the man who bears that document."

"His name is the Comte de Riberac."

"Ah!"exclaimedd'Artagnan,halfinconsternation."Riberac -- whose brother was killed at La Rochelle -- whose relative is Madame de Combalet, niece of Richelieu -- whose --"

Athos burst into a laugh -- a thing almost unknown for

him.

"Whose pistol carries the honor of Her Majesty!" he intervened. "That is enough for us. You know him by sight, I think?"

"Yes," said d'Artagnan, who perceived that Athos had formulated everything clearly in his own mind. "Proceed, I beg of you! Your judgment is unsurpassed, Athos! Give the orders and I will obey."

"You honor me, my friend. I propose that you deal with this gentleman, secure the document, deliver your letter to Mademoiselle de Sirle. I, on my part, shall take Porthos and Grimaud, and go to St. Saforin -- it is a short half-day's ride from Paris. We shall need your ring."

"Here it is," and d'Artagnan handed the circlet of gold to Athos. "And since I, for one, have some need of repose, when does this program go into effect?"

Athos reflected. "Your share is to you; mine to me. I will ride to St. Saforin tomorrow evening, remove the boy early next morning, and return to the Hotel de Treville to await word from you."

"Very well," said d'Artagnan. "I will sleep until noon tomorrow, then ride out on the Compiegne road and meet M. de Riberac."

And if you miss him?"

"Then I will find the document at the chateau of the lady."

"Be careful, my son!" Athos bent a terrible look upon his friend. "You do not know of what that woman and those around her are capable! She serves the Cardinal, who is probably her lover; Bassompierre is certainly her lover; she would deceive an angel from heaven with her airs of innocence! Be careful!"

"I promise it, Athos," said d'Artagnan, alarmed by these words.

Again there was a knock, and the lackey opened the doors.

"My lord," he said, "a gentleman is here by the name of Monsieur Porthos."

There was a cry of acclaim from all three. A moment later Porthos appeared.

M. du Vallon had this peculiarity; when he was extremely drunk, he was apparently in perfect control of his faculties, but in reality had not the least consciousness of anything except what passed through his brain on the instant. He entered the room, bowed ceremoniously to Lord de Winter, and gazed blankly at Athos and d'Artagnan. He was, if possible, more magnificent than ever in his bearing.

"This is most extraordinary, gentlemen," he declaimed in a loud voice, without noticing the greetings of anyone. "Here I left you on your way to the Hotel de Chevreuse, and I find you awaiting me here! However, I do not try to understand anything. Ah, messieurs, so you have unmasked? Monsieur," and he bowed profoundly to Lord de Winter, "you will, I promise you, have no reason to regret attaching me to the service of Your Highness."

"Heavens!" d'Artagnan broke into a laugh, and pulled at the Englishman's sleeve. "He is drunk -- he takes you for the

Duc d'Orleans!"

Porthos turned to Athos, and bowed again.

"Monsieur le Comte," he declaimed, "it is an honor to have shared your enjoyment of that exquisite Chablis, and your views upon the subject of His Eminence the Cardinal."

"Ah!" said Athos, amused. "It seems that I have become the Comte de Soissons!"

Porthos twirled his mustache magnificently, and bowed to d'Artagnan.

"I did not need a whisper from M. de Bassompierre to penetrate your identity, but be assured, monsieur, it is entirely safe with me!" he said loftily. "None shall know that you are in Paris. If any inquire of me, I shall say: "Certainly! M. le Duc de Guise is spending a few days at my country house.' But I do not see our honest Bassompierre, that dear friend of my comrade d'Herblay -- well, well, let us see if this wine can match the Chablis --"

And coming to the table, he seated himself amid the laughter of the three men, and with a perfectly steady hand poured himself wine, and sipped it.

"Excellent," he exclaimed. "Excellent! Gentlemen, damnation to the Cardinal, happiness to our new king -- and may it prove true that the king is dead!"

And Porthos gravely drank the toast he had proposed.

The laughter of the three listeners froze into a frightful silence, which d'Artagnan was the first to break.

"Porthos!" he said severely, leaning forward.

"Awake -- for the love of heaven guard your tongue,

think of what you say! Do you not know me?"

Porthos set down his glass.

"That is admirable wine -- the bouquet is magnificent," he observed, and regarded d'Artagnan with a blank stare. "Gentlemen, you did well to meet me. You do well, M. le Duc, to appreciate my qualities and ask my advice. Yes, I heard rumors at Grenoble that the king had not been well, but devil take me if I expected such news as this. I presume, Monsieur," and he turned in a stately fashion to Lord de Winter, "I presume your first move will be to arrest Richelieu? Ah, yes -- I believe you mentioned something of the sort. I desired to carry the order of arrest -- you had promised it to my friend M. de Bassompierre, was that it? Yes, yes."

Lord de Winter sat stupefied. Athos, bending his penetrating gaze upon Porthos, had turned pale. D'Artagnan, who sat there staring with his mouth open, suddenly moved as though a fly had stung him.

"Ah!" he said. "Those masked gentlemen -- no, no, it is impossible! He is the victim of some hoax!

He is drunk and -- "

"He is nothing of the sort," said Athos. "You think this news about the king is quite reliable, M. du Vallon?"

"Eh?" said Porthos, transferring his stare to Athos. "You ask me that, M. le Comte? You yourself showed me the despatch, brought from Lyon by your own cousin -- upon my word, monsieur, if you were not the Comte de Soissons I should imagine you to be drunk!"

And he poured himself more wine, very gravely.

"Monsieur," he said to Lord de Winter, applying to that gentleman the title usually accorded the king's brother, the Duc d'Orleans, "it has pleased Your Highness to consult me about your plans. I will even carry my advice a step farther. I advise you to marry Her Majesty the Queen immediately, and thus secure the throne by making peace with Austria. You could not do better than create M. d'Artagnan a Marshal of France, and my friend the Comte de la Fere would make an admirable Minister. For myself, I desire nothing; I believe, however, that a mere barony would quite delight Madame du Vallon. I beg, Monsieur, that you will think over this advice very seriously."

Cold sweat started upon the brow of d'Artagnan, and he saw in the face of Athos something like terror.

There was now no doubt that by some chance Porthos had encountered the greatest enemies of Richelieu, who were supposed to be far from Paris. By what magic of wine or talk he had insinuated himself into their company and penetrated their identities, was impossible to say; ordinarily the most simple fellow in the world, Porthos when in liquor had a certain subtlety.

D'Artagnan could picture that scene at the tavern; unfortunately it was far from being incredible. Gaston of Orleans was a dissolute fool always turning to some new prank or eccentricity, careless what he did or said. Soissons was a popinjay who blew in any wind and was headstrong in the wrong direction. Guise, learning that the king was dying, was capable of anything. That they had amused themselves with Porthos was evident. The very improbability of their discussing such matters with him was the surest proof of it having occurred, particularly where Orleans was concerned.

"If this has happened," murmured d'Artagnan, "it means the Bastille!"

"On the contrary," said Athos, who had recovered himself, "if it has happened, it may mean power and honor! Reflect; it is clear that the Comte de Soissons has news that the king is dying or dead. Therefore, the Duc d'Orleans ascends the throne -- "

"We must sober M. Porthos and drag the truth out of him," said Lord de Winter.

"Impossible!" said d'Artagnan, with a gesture of despair. "I know him, monsieur. One more drink, and he will be asleep. When he wakens, all memory of what has happened will be utterly gone from his mind."

"That is true," said Athos.

In another five minutes, indeed, Porthos dropped his chin on his breast and fell sound asleep.

Porthos, however, had not been deceived, nor had he deceived.

At the exact moment he was creating d'Artagnan a Marshal of France, terrible things were happening in Lyon, where the king had some time since joined the court. Attacked by dysentery and fever, Louis XIII was informed that medical skill could do no more for him, and he could not live another day.

He confessed, and receiving the Viaticum from the

hands of Pere Suffren, bade farewell to his mother, his wife, and Richelieu. The court ordered mourning. Anne of Austria meditated upon the future and at her bidding Countess de Fargis wrote Gaston d'Orleans and mentioned a marriage between them. Marie de Medici sent couriers in every direction and prepared for her triumph over the Cardinal, a triumph which would know neither scruple nor mercy.

As for Richelieu, he saw the abyss opening under his very feet, and was utterly powerless to save himself. "I do not know," he wrote that night to Schomberg, who was in command of the army, "whether I am alive or dead."

Thus did history, in these heroic days, hang upon the life or death of a king.

CHAPTER XII

IN WHICH D'ARTAGNAN ACCOMPLISHES TWO THINGS FOR OTHERS, ONE FOR HIMSELF

When d'Artagnan wakened, at noon the next day, he found at his bedside a magnificent suit of blue and silver-cloth; lying upon it was this note:

"My Friends: I have gone to Chaillot with M. de Bassompierre, and I shall make peace for M. Porthos provided he forgets everything that happened to him last night. Memory would be excessively dangerous for him. The king is believed to be dying. I shall await word from you; go, with God!

WINTER."

D'Artagnan asked after his friends. Grimaud appeared with word that Porthos was snoring, Athos still asleep.

"I have orders to waken them at two o'clock, monsieur."

Obey, then. I shall be gone. One moment -- where is the convent of St. Saforin?"

"Halfway between Paris and Soissons, monsieur."

Obviously, Athos had ordered Grimaud to inform himself on this point.

D'Artagnan bathed and then dressed in the superb habiliments provided, finding that they fitted him to a marvel; and in the courtyard discovered a horse being saddled for him. This horse, presented to him with the compliments of

Lord de Winter, was even finer than the one given him by Richelieu, and now lost somewhere in Paris.

When he had eaten, d'Artagnan examined his sword, inspected the letter for Mlle. de Sirle, and rode for Passy and the Compiegne highway.

He was unhurried, and appreciated to the full the glances of admiration which his magnificent costume and his royal steed drew from every side. He did not fail to note, however, an undercurrent of excitement in the streets, and he knew the reason full well.

"Pardieu! Rumors have spread," he muttered. "And what is this? Bassompierre's liveries!"

He encountered six of the finest horses imaginable, each one caparisoned with real splendor, in charge of two grooms wearing the Marshal's livery. He halted them, curious.

"Will you have the goodness to tell me the reason of this?" he inquired. "I understood your master was at Chaillot today."

The grooms, seeing that this young man, so regally mounted and attired, had recognized their liveries and must be some great noble and friend of Bassompierre, did not hesitate to answer him.

"We are taking them as relays, monsieur. Our master leaves at dawn tomorrow for Lyon, and has wagered a thousand pistoles that he will reach Lyon before midnight tomorrow."

Thanking them, d'Artagnan rode on, stupefied with astonishment at such prodigality. Bassompierre had better reasons than a wager for reaching Lyon, he perceived -- but why, then, was not the marshal leaving today instead of tomorrow?

"If I were M. de Bassompierre," thought d'Artagnan shrewdly, "I would be finishing my journey tomorrow morning instead of beginning it! However, I suppose he has the best of reasons for remaining here; and it is lucky for Porthos that he is! Our friend must have learned some pretty secrets last night, and if he ever breathes one of them, he is a lost man.

He need not have worried, however. When Porthos wakened, he had not the slightest recollection of his last night's adventure.

It was not yet two o'clock when d'Artagnan, past the barrier, was upon the Compiegne road. A word with the guards showed that the Comte de Riberac had not yet entered Paris, but this did not mean that he had not reached Passy, which at that time was well outside Paris. So, at a slightly quicker gait, d'Artagnan rode on. He knew Riberac, and could not miss his man, who would be unsuspecting any danger so close to his journey's end.

With his characteristic curiosity, d'Artagnan sought out the chateau of Mlle. de Sirle, and slowly rode past, admiring the situation of the little park. Then he had reason to curse his imprudence, for as he came opposite the gates they opened and a cavalier rode forth and drew rein in surprise.

"M. d'Artagnan!" he exclaimed. "It Is you, indeed?"

D'Artagnan recognized Sieur de Roquemont, lieutenant

of the Cardinal's guards and a close relative of Chateauneuf, at this period the most able of all Richelieu's supporters. He noted that Roquemont seemed quite disconcerted at the encounter, and wondered what on earth this gentleman could be doing in Paris.

"Good morning, my dear Roquemont, he rejoined with entire aplomb. "A happy meeting, indeed! I fancied you were in Savoy, becoming another Bayard!"

"And I," said Roquemont, opening his eyes at d'Artagnan's horse and equipment, "fancied you were in Lyon with the court!"

"So I was," said d'Artagnan, twirling his mustache, "but at the present moment I am on my way to Calais, and in two days I shall be in London.

What news from the army?"

"Faith, I know not!" and Roquemont shrugged. "I have been in Paris for ten days, and am even now starting for Lyon. Au revoir and bon voyage, monsieur!"

"And to you," rejoined d'Artagnan, and rode on his way. "Ah, liar!" he said to himself. "You lied to me -- even as I lied to you! Now there's something in the wind. You were astonished to see me, therefore you knew nothing about me or my errand. That, it seems, lies in the hand of the Comte de Montforge. But what the devil are you doing at this house?"

He was uneasy. Roquemont, he knew, was a man of savage character; it was Roquemont who had dragged from his bed and killed the unfortunate Villeroy; it was Roquemont who, according to report, had coolly held a pistol to the dying body of Concini and finished the assassination. With such a man, anything was possible.

However, Roquemont lay behind, Riberac ahead; d'Artagnan rode on. The day, which had begun brightly, had now become overcast; rain threatened, and d'Artagnan, who had no cloak to cover his magnificent suit, scowled at the unkind heavens.

At three-thirty, d'Artagnan was in the open, flat country just beyond Bourg-Royale. The fields were empty, no one was in sight along the road; but ahead, a growing spurt of dust indicated a rider spurring to reach Paris before the storm arrived. D'Artagnan drew rein, inspected his pistols, loosened his sword in the sheath, and waited. A single rider was coming toward him. Presently, recognizing his man, d'Artagnan moved his horse into the road.

Riberac, at sight of this impassive figure blocking his way, slowed his pace, and then drew rein a few feet distant, staring at d'Artagnan.

"This is a strange meeting, M. d'Artagnan!" he exclaimed. He was a pleasant young man, rich and handsome, destined for high fortune.

"I regret, monsieur," and d'Artagnan bowed slightly in the saddle, "that the meeting was inevitable."

"Your words are also strange, monsieur," said Riberac, "and so is your tone. You cannot have come on purpose to meet me?"

His hand dropped to the pistol on the left side of his saddle.

"Be careful, monsieur!" said d'Artagnan. "I have two pistols here, you have only one."

"Ah!" Riberac checked himself, regarded d'Artagnan fixedly. "So that is it!"

"That is it, monsieur. It is with the greatest regret in the world, I assure you, that I must ask you for that pistol."

"Your regret is only equalled by mine, monsieur, in refusing it," said Riberac, and then dismounted and drew his sword.

D'Artagnan did likewise, for he was dealing with a very polite gentleman. Riberac, who had great confidence in himself, smiled with assurance.

"I must warn you, monsieur," he stated, "that I have been taking lessons from the Italian fencing-master of the Prince of Wales, in London."

"And I," said d'Artagnan, "have been killing those who give lessons. En garde, monsieur!"

The blades crossed. At the second pass, D'Artagnan's rapier drove through the heart of Rierac, who fell backward and was dead before he struck the ground.

This victory gave d'Artagnan no satisfaction; rather, it filled him with sadness. He went to Riberac's horse, drew the right-hand pistol from its holster, and inspected the weapon. A wooden plug was in the muzzle. Removing this, he presently extracted a tightly-rolled length of vellum.

"In this matter," he reflected, "I cannot afford to make any mistakes."

He unrolled the vellum, and found it to consist of three

sheets, folded in the center and sewed together. A glance at the outer page showed him that this was the will of Francois Thounenin of Dompt. He examined the remainder of the pages. The center sheet proved to be a codicil to the will -- undoubtedly the document of which he was in search. He removed the outer sheet and placed it in his pocket. The other two sheets he rolled again and held in his hand.

"These," he reflected, "must be destroyed. The first sheet, which holds nothing of peril to anyone, must be sent to Madame de Chevreuse as evidence that the work is done. Good."

He mounted and retraced his way along the road toward Paris. In half a mile he came to an inn at a cross-roads. Dismounting, he entered. A fire was burning below the spit in the hearth, and going to it, he placed the rolled sheets of vellum on the flames, watched them writhe and fall into ashes, and then turned to the host of the inn.

"Monsieur," he said, "half a mile from here a gentleman lies in the road, dead. He is a noble, a man of family, and a favorite of Cardinal de Richelieu. I advise you to send for his body, communicate with the authorities, and forget having seen me.

And with this he returned to his horse and mounted.

He had been successful in his mission. The document was destroyed, the queen was saved -- but d'Artagnan felt no exultation. On the contrary, he vowed that upon returning to Paris he would have ten masses said at St. Sulpice for the repose of the soul of Comte de Riberac, who had been a gallant gentleman. Upon reflection, however, he changed this vow to one mass only; for one would undoubtedly be as efficient as ten, and at one-tenth the cost.

At five o'clock that afternoon, with rain still threatening and black clouds massing, d'Artagnan rode into the little park occupied by the chateau of Helene de Sirle. He found the gates standing wide open, as though he were expected. As he entered, the first spattering raindrops began to fall. A groom came to take his horse, and a lackey appeared as he mounted the steps to the entrance.

"Mlle. de Sirle?" he inquired. "I am M. d'Artagnan, Lieutenant of Musketeers."

"Will you have the goodness to enter, monsieur?" said the lackey.

D'Artagnan followed him. Here was the identical house Athos had described -- the curving staircase, the corridor, the dark library of which d'Artagnan had a glimpse in passing. He was ushered into a charming little salon, hung with yellow satin, and filled with the most beautiful furniture and bibelots.

Our Musketeer was distinctly on his guard; he was alert, wary, suspicious. The tale of Athos was vividly in his mind, in each terrible detail. The beauty and peace of this charming place only served to enhance his caution. Yet, when his hostess appeared, he was staggered; susceptible young man that he was there arose within him a cry of protest against such things being possible of this creature.

She was younger than the tale of Athos had led him to

suppose very young, indeed, pale and beautiful, in her delicate features an air of vivacity which was tempered by a frank and openinnocence -- the most charming thing in the world to the eye of d'Artagnan.

"You desired to see me, monsieur?" she asked in a low and musical voice.

"Yes, mademoiselle -- I have the honor to be the bearer of a letter from His Eminence, Cardinal Richelieu -- "

"Ah!" She started, and broke into a smile that dazzled the young man. "Then it is my sister Helene you desired! I am Eugenie de Sirle, monsieur. I regret that my sister went to Paris this morning and has not yet returned. Give me the letter -- I will place it on her escritoire."

Having no instructions restricting the delivery of the letter, d'Artagnan produced it.

"One moment, monsieur, if you please," said she, and departed with a lithe step and so radiant a smile that d'Artagnan remained spellbound where he stood. That smile -- did it promise anything? Instinctively he twirled his mustache, brushed a speck of dust from the silver facing of his coat, and his heart leaped.

Danger was suddenly banished -- the perilous woman was away, his name had created no impression and was evidently not known to this girl. He was, therefore, running no immediate risk.

"Decidedly," he reflected, "I am not a foo1! When a woman looks at me, I can read the message in her eyes -- if there is one there. If I leave this house instantly and ride away, what good? I am in the enemy's country, and it is the first rule of war to profit by the enemy wherever possible! And what delicious -- "

He checked his thoughts, and decided that he must be a fool after all. Yet he could not gainsay the hammering of his pulses, the flame of his imagination, caused by the eyes of this girl. That she was not the lady of Athos' tale, caused him inexpressible happiness.

It must be confessed that Monsieur d'Artagnan had not wasted his time since coming to Paris. It was a period when a young and gallant man was appreciated to the full, and was indeed more sought after than seeking; a period when the privilege of the aristocracy was unlimited, and when impulse was better comprehended than discretion. It is true that the unperfumed feet of Bassompierre cost him the love of a queen; but to atone for this the gallant Lorrainer made more than one conquest at first sight.

Eugenie returned and came up to d'Artagnan.

"Will you not sit down, monsieur?" she said sweetly. "I believe my sister will return soon, and she will not forgive me if I let you depart. Or perhaps you would prefer a turn in the gardens -- the rain ceased almost as it began, and the house is oppressive."

A turn in the gardens was exactly to the mind of d'Artagnan. What could be more attractive than those secluded paths among the lilacs. with this charming creature on his arm! He hoped, his hope became conviction; his conviction became daring. In a word, ambition seized upon him.

At the rear of the gardens, built against a corner of the walls, was an exquisite little pavilion, furnished in the most superb manner imaginable. A patter of rain was heard on the leaves; conducting his companion to the shelter of this pavilion, d'Artagnan was soon left in no doubt whatever as to her feelings for him or her capability of affection. He was transported to the seventh heaven; his heart was bursting with happiness.

Suddenly, an expression of fright crossing her face, she escaped from his arms.

"Oh!" she murmured. "My sister -- I hear the gates opening! If we are discovered here then you are lost, I am lost! You do not know of what she is capable!"

D'Artagnan flung himself at her feet.

"Only tell me where and how our happiness may be completed!" he implored fervently, and seizing her hand, covered it with kisses. She lifted him, gently.

"Come, then -- there is not a moment to lose!" she exclaimed breathlessly. "I hear the coach entering -- you must remain here hidden, wait!"

"With all my heart," cried d'Artagnan, bursting with joy at this prospect of happiness. He followed her to a small room, adjoining the bedroom of the pavilion; this little chamber was built against the corner of the garden walls, had no window, and was furnished as a tiny household chapel -- apparently little used for this purpose, however.

"I will come for you later -- this pavilion is my own

abode," whispered the girl in some agitation. For one brief moment she yielded as d'Artagnan clasped her in his arms; her lips sent the wine of passion leaping through his veins; then she was gone, and the door closed.

Next instant the young man was transfixed -- he heard, outside, a short peal of merry laughter, as the lock of the door clicked.

"A pleasant wait to you, Monsieur d'Artagnan!" came a faintly mocking voice. "You shall have the pleasure of Tantalus in hearing how another enjoys what you desire -- turn the crucifix on its pedestal. A pleasant evening, monsieur! We were expecting you -- "

And with another peal of laughter, the lady departed.

D'Artagnan was absolutely frozen with horror for a moment; he was incapable of movement; he could feel her kisses burning his lips while her words sent ice into his very soul.

Too late, he recalled the warnings of Athos, and a groan burst from him. This was no sister, then, but Helene de Sirle herself; she had caught him in a network, had trapped him like a sturgeon in the fisher's weir! He thought of her beauty, of her innocence, of her half-timid, half-yielding embrace -- and with an oath, he flung himself at the door.

It was massive, locked, unyielding.

CHAPTER XIII

ONE MEANS OF ADMISSION TO THE ORDER OF THE HOLY GHOST

When the first emotion of d'Artagnan had passed, he sat down upon a prie-dieu in the darkness, and, faced by a situation of extreme peril, almost at once regained all his coolness and aplomb.

At this moment d'Artagnan was extremely dangerous. It is the prerogative of youth that it may overlook insults, forget hatred, forgive injury; but when its self-steem is wounded, vengeance is invariably exacted. D'Artagnan had seen himself in possession of the fruits of a superb conquest -- only to find it delusion. He had arrived here fully warned, exercising extreme caution; without the least effort, he had been tricked and duped by the very person he had supposed vanquished. His person was unharmed, but his vanity had received a blow that penetrated to every fibre of his spirit.

"Good!" he said calmly. "At all events, I now know with whom I am dealing. There is a score to settle on behalf of Athos, and a score to settle on my own behalf. Certainly she has not poisoned me; if I am in prison, at least I have my sword."

He set about thinking how he could use this sword.

When he first entered this room, there had been a little light; an opening six inches square, high in one wall, supplied air. Now darkness had completely fallen, and from the little opening he could hear the steady thrum of the beating rain. At this instant a flash of lightning lighted up the chapel. Except for the prie-dieu on which he had been sitting, and a small altar against one wall, the place was bare. Above the altar hung an ivory crucifix.

Catching sight of this crucifix by light of the bolt, d'Artagnan remembered the last words his jailer had flung at him. Plunged once more into intense darkness, he made his way toward the spot. What she had meant by turning the crucifix, by her mocking words, he could not tell.

His groping fingers encountered the ivory image, seemingly fixed in the wall. He found that it turned about, apparently upon a hinge or pivot. Exploring, he discovered that the crucifix opened from the wall like a door, leaving a slot in the stones, an inch wide and three inches high. The meaning of this remained inscrutable, for it was quite dark, contained nothing, and his fingers could not reach through the hole.

"Cadedis! I'm a rat in a trap," he reflected, found his way back to the prie-dieu, and sat down, gloomily. There was only one egress from this chamber, and that was blocked solidly by the massive locked door.

The prisoner was, as has been said, entirely calm. He was even cheerful; for the chief portion of his mission had been accomplished. The essential part of the Thounenin will was destroyed, the plans of Richelieu were checkmated, the queen was saved. Having leisure to consider private affairs, d'Artagnan considered them.

"If I could get out of this place," he murmured, "I would find myself without a horse; for it would be impossible to get my own animal from the stables. On the other hand, I would find no difficulty in getting away, since this storm drowns out everything. But I do not desire to escape, since I have my sword. I cannot kill that woman, since she is a woman; besides, she deserves a very different sort of fate -- "

His reflections were interrupted by a ray of light falling across his prison cell. This ray came from the slot in the wall, which he had left open.

Starting to his feet, he approached the opening, and a sudden trembling seized upon him. He heard the voice of Helene de Sirle, and her voice wakened in him all the emotion he had felt in her presence, at her kisses, at the pressure of her fingers. True, he burned to avenge himself, but when it is a question of a woman, a gentleman has other means of vengeance than a sword.

Putting his eye to the hole in the wall, d'Artagnan repressed an exclamation. This opening pierced through to another chamber in which a tapestry had just been drawn aside, giving him a view of the room, bright with candelabra. This room was a salle-a-manger; directly before d'Artagnan was set a table, with places for two, glittering with gold and silver dishes. At this table, but with her back to him, sat Helene de Sirle; and, facing d'Artagnan, Marshal de Bassompierre.

D'Artagnan stared in utter amazement. He knew

Bassompierre too well to be mistaken; he knew that somewhat stout figure, that powerful, gay countenance with its carefully brushed mustaches, far too well. Bassompierre had laid aside a cloak, and wore a magnificent suit thickly sewn with seed pearls -- similar to the famous suit for which he had paid fourteen thousand crowns, but certainly not the same, since Bassompierre never wore the same suit more than once.

A moment later the tapestry was drawn on the other side of the hole, and d'Artagnan was again in darkness.

Through the aperture d'Artagnan could now hear everything, but he could see nothing.

Biting his nails in fury, he made his way back to his seat. He comprehended now the full extent of the lady's cruelty -- and he comprehended a good deal besides. This, for example, fully explained why Bassompierre had remained for the night in Paris.

"And I -- I must sit here like a snail!" thought d'Artagnan in despair and rage.

His chagrin was complete. From the adjoining room he could hear the voices plainly, now low, now high; he could hear the suave, merry tones of Bassompierre, he could hear the soft laughter of Helene de Sirle, he could even catch the savor of the exquisite viands that were served -- viands which Bassompierre, one of the first epicures of his day, applauded with vehemence.

Further, d'Artagnan could comprehend even more than this. From what he had seen of this pavilion, knowing that his prison-cell lay in a corner of the wall against which the pavilion was built, he understood that its bedroom lay on the opposite side. His cell, in effect, lay between dining-room and bedroom. The cruelty of the fair one was complete.

As the moments passed, d'Artagnan felt his own hunger more acutely, for he had not eaten since leaving the hotel of St. Luc. Evidently Bassompierre was not sparing the wine, for its effects sharpened the tones of both hostess and guest, and gay sallies were interspersed with bursts of laughter. D'Artagnan pricked up his ears, as he heard a well-known name uttered.

"Richelieu? Bah! You have dismissed the servants, I think?"

"We are alone, my love," returned the voice of Helene.

"Listen, then! You have heard rumors today?" said Bassompierre.

"That the king is ill."

"Ill? Ventre de St. Gris!" cried Bassompierre, who affected the favorite oath of Henri IV. "He is better than ill, upon my honor! He is dying -- at this moment he is doubtless dead. That is why I spur to Lyon tomorrow -- that is why I must leave you with dawn, my sweet charmer! Death of my life -- who is king, think you, but Gaston of Orleans? Well, I bear his order to arrest Richelieu. There's a secret for you! A kiss for it -- a kiss!"

D'Artagnan sat transfixed. So the Duc d'Orleans, who would be king the moment Louis XIII was dead, had given Bassompierre an order for Richelieu's arrest! This explained everything; the gathering of the princes, the mad haste in which Bassompierre was riding at dawn.

"Orleans has signed the order?" came the voice of Helene sharply.

"Doubtless. It will be awaiting me at the Hotel de St. Luc, with my horses and gentlemen," said Bassompierre, whose tongue was thickening. "But come! One more glass of this marvelous vintage and then, my charmer -- and then Paradise!"

D'Artagnan almost lost sight of his own chagrin in view of what he had just heard. Chaillot lay outside Paris. Bassompierre had come here to Passy, and at dawn would go to the Hotel de St. Luc -- ah! This meant that the Englishman was concerned in the matter somewhere! Well, so much the worse for Richelieu, at whose door lay the assassination of Buckingham.

Suddenly d'Artagnan started to his feet. He had remembered something -- he had remembered meeting with Sieur de Roquemont outside these gates. And Helene de Sirle was certainly the agent of Richelieu. A dreadful suspicion seized upon the young man; he stood trembling, indecisive, hesitant.

At this moment a cry sounded from the other room -- a cry, the sound of a laughing struggle, the sound of a glass smashing on the floor. A peal of thunder, a vivid lightning-stroke, drowned all else. In the ensuing silence, he heard the laughing voice of the lady.

"No, no -- impatient lover!" Another laugh, and d'Artagnan judged shrewdly that not Bassompierre alone had misused the wine. "I demand five minutes of grace, M. le Marechal, before surrendering my defenses!"

"I demand an unconditional capitulation!" thundered Bassompierre, and roared with laughter. "Good, then -- you have five minutes of grace, no more! But I have no guide to Paradise, my angel -- "

"The door will lie before you, monsieur," came the answer, and then an interval of silence.

D'Artagnan comprehended. Helene de Sirle had preceded her lover. With a muttered oath, the young man came back to his own situation, and cursed his own blind folly.

"Charming creature!" soliloquized Bassompierre's voice. "A charming repast, charming food, a charming end to the evening -- let the tempest howl, and devil take all poor souls who lack the luck of Bassompierre! One more glass -- "

D'Artagnan considered speaking through the aperture, giving the marshal warning -- but of what? Bassompierre was, to put it bluntly, drunk; and when in liquor, was famed for his blind rages. Undoubtedly he would be unable to think or act coherently. Before d'Artagnan could decide, the moment of opportunity had flown. He heard Bassompierre stumbling from the next room into the corridor.

"Fool that I am!" exclaimed d'Artagnan in despair. What mattered the marsbal to him, after all? His own fate was the thing at issue. He ground his teeth at thought of the chagrin Helene de Sirle was heaping upon him --

The key was turned in the lock of his door.

D'Artagnan started to his feet, his rapier bared. Had they come to assassinate him, then? Undoubtedly. He had witnessed the prelude to the comedy; now, in refinement of cruelty, her men were about to put an end to him.

The door opened, showing the corridor dimly lighted. Against this background was a single figure, that of Bassompierre.

"My love, you are devilish modest!" said the marshal, taking a step forward. Then he recoiled, as the rapier of d'Artagnan touched his breast; the cloak fell from his hand, and he stood motionless.

"Not a sound!" said d'Artagnan, confident that he was safe against recognition in the darkness of the oratory. "One word, one call, and you are a dead man. Fool that you were, to prate of your errand at Lyon! Do you not know that my mistress is the chief agent of Richelieu in Paris -- that Richelieu is her lover?"

A choked exclamation broke from Bassompierre.

"So you bear an order to arrest Richelieu!" pursued d'Artagnan. As he spoke, he moved around the intruder. "In with you! Come forward! You are too late, M. de Bassompierre -- my mistress holds an order from Richelieu to arrest you."

"Who are you?" murmured the unhappy Bassompierre, overwhelmed by these words, and realizing that he had fallen into a trap.

Without response, d'Artagnan slipped through the doorway, closed the door, and turned the key in the lock. Bassompierre was imprisoned.

D'Artagnan looked about. There had been no alarm; everything was peaceful. A hanging lamp burned dimly in the corridor. The door to the little dining-room stood open. The door at the end of the corridor was closed, half shadowed by a turn. The mistake of Bassompierre, to one who did not know the situation of the rooms, was entirely natural.

On the floor lay the cloak of Bassompierre, still wet with rain. D'Artagnan picked it up, shook it out, wrapped it around him. Upon it was fastened the cross of the Order du St. Esprit, an order to which only Princes of the Blood and very great nobles belonged.

"Good!" murmured d'Artagnan, and his pulses leaped swiftly. "Cruelty for cruelty -- humiliation for humiliation -- mockery for mockery! That is justice."

And he passed to the door at the end of the corridor, tried it softly, found it unlocked. It opened upon modest darkness, indeed, but not upon complete darkness. Beside the heavily curtained bed, there burned a candle.

Wrapped in his cloak with its splendid insignia, d'Artagnan advanced and extinguished the light A soft laugh sounded in the room, thrilling him to every nerve of his being, inflaming him madly.

In his excitement, in his burning passion for vengeance, d'Artagnan had not thought to lock the door behind him. His dread suspicions were forgotten; his caution was flung to the winds; in the blind ardor of youth, intoxicated by enjoyment of the most delicious vengeance imaginable, he forgot all else.

He even forgot the unfortunate Bassompierre, with whom he had exchanged places.(Since the memoirs of Bassompierre were written under the eye of Richelieu, it is obvious why they contain no mention of this incident.)

Outside, the storm swept past in its fury, the rain lessened and died into the thin drippings of trees. In the dining-room of the pavilion, the candles burned down to their sockets, guttered and died out. The hanging-lamp in the corridor alone shed light in the darkness.

D'Artagnan, who had fallen into a heavy slumber, was suddenly awakened by that unknown sense which so often comes to our rescue in the depths of night. By his side, Helene de Sirle slept with the quiet and regular breathing of a child.

A board in the floor creaked lightly. Someone was in the room.

Startled, wide awake on the instant, d'Artagnan was aware of a dim light showing through the bed-curtains. He did not hesitate; as the curtains, on one side of the bed, were abruptly jerked away, he flung himself to the other side, across the sleeping figure of Helene de Sirle. A sword plunged at him, and another -- two men stood there, a third holding aside the curtains.

There was a cry, a choked scream. D'Artagnan, throwing himself over the far side of the bed, had a frightful vision of Helene de Sirle writhing half upright, pierced by the two blades intended for him -- then he was on the floor, scrambling cat-like to his feet, darting to his clothes and sword at the foot of the bed.

Oaths resounded, shrill curses. One of the three men rushed to the doorway, blocked it, the two others hurled themselves on d'Artagnan. Naked, he bared his rapier as they came upon him, and recognized one of the two as Roquemont.

"Ha, assassin!" he cried, and engaged both blades at once.

From Roquemont burst a cry of dismay, of rage, of consternation. "It is not he -- it is not our man! In upon him finish him quickly!"

For reply, d'Artagnan's rapier pierced the throat of Roquemont's companion. The third bravo, darting forward from the doorway, attacked the young man in the rear. Only a miracle of agility saved him.

D'Artagnan now comprehended everything perfectly. It was Bassompierre these three assassins had sought; they had arranged with Helene de Sirle, had planned to murder him while he slept at her side. The species of horror which had enveloped d'Artagnan, upon seeing those bloody swords torn from her body, passed into a furious rage.

"So you sought Bassompierre, eh?" he exclaimed. "Cadedis! Murderers of women, you have found retribution instead!"

As he spoke, his point touched the third assassin in the groin, and the man sank to the floor, groaning. D'Artagnan faced Roquemont, laughed wildly, and pressed in a furious attack that drove his opponent backwards until he stood against the bed and could retreat no farther.

"Good!" cried d'Artagnan. "You shall die with her whom

your base blade murdered, you dog!"

Roquernont rallied, cursing heartily; the superb attack of d'Artagnan dazzled him, held him mercilessly rooted to the spot. Sweat streamed down his face, his lips drew back from his teeth; d'Artagnan's point touched his breast and blood gushed out. He fought on. At his back, the torn bed-curtains revealed the figure of Helene de Sirle, lying dead in a terrible crimson tide.

Suddenly d'Artagnan lunged, lunged again, uttered a sharp cry of triumph. Roquemont dropped his blade. Pierced through the heart, he flung out his arms and fell backwards and lay half across the bed.

A terrible sound caught the ear of d'Artagnan. He turned, saw the wounded man half rising from the floor, coughing horribly. Without hesitation, as he would have pierced a snake, he drove his rapier through the throat of the assassin.

"Justice!" he exclaimed, and stood leaning on his rapier, until a sudden trembling seized upon him. With a choked cry, he turned to his clothes and dressed, hurriedly. Cold horror of this place of death spurred him, froze his very marrow.

Dressed, he caught up Bassompierre's cloak, seized his bloody rapier, and strode down the corridor to the chapel door. This he unlocked, threw open.

"Are you there, M. de Bassompierre?" he ex-claimed. Quickly, quickly!"

Bassompierre, dagger in hand, stumbled into the doorway. At sight of d'Artagnan standing with dripping blade, he stopped short, blinked, then recoiled a step.

"Ha! It is M. d'Artagnan!" he exclaimed in astonishment.

"Is this your cloak, monsieur?" D'Artagnan extended the garment, which the other took. "I was in time to save you, then -- they came to kill You, monsieur! Go and look in the room yonder -- "

Bassompierre was bewildered, yet comprehended that he was in no immediate danger. He did not comprehend everything; d'Artagnan did not desire that he should comprehend everything, in fact. He went to the door of the bedroom, and took a step inside. A low cry burst from him. He turned, came back to d'Artagnan, and his eyes were starting from his head.

"She -- dead -- who killed her -- "

"How do I know?" D'Artagnan laughed harshly. "Come -- let us get out of here and talk later! Have the goodness to follow me, monsieur -- "

Still holding his sword, he led the way out into the rain-wet gardens, and directed his steps toward the stables, with Bassompierre at his side. Under the lantern in the doorway of the stables was a sleepy groom, three saddled horses waiting at hand. D'Artagnan pointed to them with his crimsoned sword.

"The horses of your assassins, monsieur!" Then, advancing upon the groom, he put his point at the man's throat. "Up! Walk in front of me, see that the gates are open! Assassins have murdered your mistress, but I have avenged her. Forward!"

He drove the groom before him. Bassompierre, mounting

into the saddle, followed with the horses. Reaching the gates, they found these unlocked and unguarded; the terrified groom opened them.

A moment later, the two were away from the chateau, in the darkness of the road. Here Bassompierre drew rein.

"I do not understand this, monsieur -- except that you have saved my life," he exclaimed warmly. "If I can in anyway repay you -- "

D'Artagnan brought the horses stirrup to stirrup.

"You can, monsieur," he said simply. "Madame de Chevreuse desires to send a message of four words to the queen. These four words will inform Her Majesty that she has for the moment no more to fear from her enemies."

"Ah, ah! Chevreuse -- noble creature! Then she sent you?" exclaimed Bassompierre. "Yes, yes, by all means give me the message! I comprehend perfectly. The four words?"

"God loves the brave."

"They shall be delivered."

"Thank you, monsieur. And allow me to say that my friends, one of whom is Lord de Winter, are about to place the child in better security than St. Saforin affords at the moment. He will be taken care of."

"Ah! Death of my life?" cried Bassompierre, who could no longer contain his amazement. "M. d'Artagnan, you overcome me -- "

"We must part, if you are to gain Lyon tonight," and d'Artagnan turned his horse before any further explanations could be made. "Farewell, monsieur!"

"Farewell -- and accept my thanks," came the voice of Bassompierre, already half swallowed up in the dawn-darkness. "I am in your debt -- believe me, I shall not forget it!"

D'Artagnan, who now heard cries of alarm rising within the park of the little chateau, put spurs to his horse.

"And I," he said to himself, "owe you a good deal -- for the loan of your cloak! Our accounts are balanced, my dear Bassompierre."

He rode -- but not toward Paris.

CHAPTER XIV

INSTEAD OF ONE FATHER, TWO APPEAR

There were at this period two Saints Saforin -- the village of the name, lying close to the highway, and the royal abbey which owned the village and many other fiefs. The abbey, however, lay a league distant, and was gained by an indirect road.

On May 3, 1542, Francois I rode out of Paris with a single companion, on one of those pleasant excursions so beloved of that amorous monarch. He had a rendezvous at the village of St. Saforin with a lady of the vicinity who had promised to entertain him fittingly in the absence of her lord.

Unluckily, the king was misdirected, took the road to the abbey, was recognized, and was that night entertained by the worthy prior instead of by the charitable lady.

Athos and Porthos, on the contrary, asked directions from a country lout who knew much of village wenches and little of monasteries or abbeys.

Toward midnight they found themselves in the village of St. Saforin, with rain pouring down and thunder rolling across the hills. To gain the abbey that night was an impossibility.

"Very well," said Athos calmly, and looked at Grimaud. "Sunrise!"

At sunrise, they were breaking their fast and the horses were ready. An hour later they were dismounting before the entrance of the abbey.

Some years previously the abbacy had been conferred upon a gentleman of Picardy, who drew his revenues and did not trouble his head about the place whence they came. The direct rule of the abbey was in the hands of the prior, Dom Lawrence, a distant connection of the Luynes family and in earlier years a boon companion of Bassompierre in the campaign of Hungary against the Turks.

Athos and Porthos were conducted into a reception room by a black-clad lay brother upon whom the rule of silence had not yet been imposed.

"Dom Lawrence will be with you in a few moments," he said, and left them.

Porthos was vastly impressed by the well-ordered place, with its massive walls and its air of indomitable strength. Wine was brought them, and he tasted it with appreciation.

"This is excellent!" he observed. "I perceive that these monks know how to live. Athos, my friend, drink! You are pale. Does the fact that you are about to become a father so weigh upon your spirit?"

"I was thinking of d'Artagnan," said Athos. "Ah! Here is Dom Lawrence."

Dom Lawrence Was a very spare and vigorous man of sixty. He gravely inclined his head to the bow of his visitors, dismissed Porthos with a glance, and then gazed fixedly at Athos.

"I am at Your service, gentlemen," he said. "But, if I am not mistaken, I have met one of you at least -- a long time ago."

The pallor of Athos became accentuated.

"This, Dom Lawrence, is M. du Vallon," he replied. "As for me, I am named Athos, formerly of the company of M. de Treville, now of the company of M. Rambures."

"Eh? Eh?" Dom Lawrence frowned slightly. The lofty countenance of Athos seemed to bring other memories before him. "Of the Musketeers? But, my dear monsieur, I am quite certain that I have had the honor of meeting you, not recently, but in the past."

"It is entirely Possible," said Athos. "Louis XIII married Anne of Austria at Bordeaux on Nov.28, 1615 -- that is to say, fifteen years ago. Upon that occasion I was a page of the Duc d'Orleans; and you, if I mistake not, were the father confessor of -- "

He paused. Across the face of Dom Lawrence flashed a look, almost of terror, as though some frightful scene had suddenly recurred to his mind. His eyes widened upon Athos.

"I remember now, M. le Comte," be said in a low voice, and he bowed as though he were silently saluting a person whom he reverenced. "You desired to see me, you and your friend?"

Athos took from his finger the gold ring with the arms of Bassompierre.

"You recognize this ring, undoubtedly? I have come to take away the boy."

The prior started. "Ah! Monsieur, as to his departure I have no orders. I can allow you to see him, certainly -- "

"Pardon me, intervened Athos. "Dom Lawrence, I come to take the boy as my own son; he is the son of one of my oldest friends."

"Unfortunately, monsieur, the gentleman who placed him here gave strict orders -- "

Again Athos intervened. "Within a short time, perhaps within a few minutes, other men will arrive on this errand. They will bear a forged ring; but they will bear the orders of Cardinal Richelieu as well. As for M. de Bassompierre, you need not worry. We act on his behalf and would bear a letter from him had he been given time to write one."

At the name of Richelieu, a look of alarm flashed into the eyes of Dom Lawrence.

"The Cardinal -- knows the boy is here?" he ejaculated.

"Worse; he he has sent to get him," said Athos calmly.

There was a moment of silence; struggle was depicted in the face of Dom Lawrence, who knew that he would not dare refuse the child to an order of the Cardinal. As for Porthos, to whom the veiled past of Athos was ever revealing new surprises, he stood staring, yet wise enough not to open his mouth.

"Monsieur," said the prior suddenly, "I remember certain events in the past; I can read your face as you stand before me. Do you swear upon your honor that all you say is true?"

"Upon my honor, and upon the Christ, it is the truth," said Athos firmly, and so lofty and serene was his clear gaze that it would have removed doubt from St. Thomas himself.

"It is your purpose to adopt this child, then?"

"No; it is my purpose to make him my own son," said Athos.

Dom Lawrence summoned a lay brother, gave him certain instructions, and motioned to chairs.

"We shall not keep you long, gentlemen. As to the boy, I can only say, M. le Comte, that I have studied his character well, and I believe him worthy to become your son."

"Then keep the confidence as sacred," said Athos solemnly. "No one must know this, no one must suspect where the child has gone! M de Bassompierre alone will know. As to the child I already know already what his character is, since I know his parents."

"Ah!" said the prior, and regarded him searchingly.

The next moment, a lay brother led in a child of four years. Porthos could not repress an exclamation of surprise and admiration; Athos rose to his feet ceremoniously. The boy, young as he was betrayed in his features a singular beauty and loftiness of character. He wore a miniature cavalier's suit, and bore at his side a tiny Sword. He bowed to the prior -- a bow of such grace and dignity that the eyes of Athos lighted up.

"M. d'Aram, said the Prior, "I wish to present M. Porthos, and the Comte -- "

He checked himself; with a glance at Athos, who concluded the sentence.

'The Comte de la Fere."

The boy bowed to Porthos, then to Athos -- his gaze remained fastened upon the latter.

"Ah!" he exclaimed curiously. "Now I know something I have long desired -- "

He checked himself; and flushed.

"Yes, my Son?" said the prior, with a smile.

"I was about to say," said the boy, still looking at Athos,"that I now know what a gentleman looks like."

"Eh? Eh?" exclaimed Porthos, puffing out his cheeks in mock anger. "And I, then -- am I not a gentleman, eh? And honest Dom Lawrence, here?"

The boy turned and regarded him with perfect composure.

"Monsieur, you are a soldier," he answered. "Dom Lawrence is a monk. That is not the same thing."

"The thought is to the mark, if not the words!" cried Athos in delight, and kneeling, held out his arms. "My son, my son -- embrace me!"

The boy looked at him, turned very pale, and his eyes widened.

"What, monsieur!" he stammered. "You -- you are not the father I have prayed for -- "

"My son," said Athos, in a grave and solemn voice, "I am the father you have prayed for; you are the son I thought never to hold in my arms! Dom Lawrence, I ask you to give this union the blessing of God; and I swear before Him that from this day forward I will be such a father to this boy that he may all his life remember me with love, respect, and reverence."

And as he spoke, tears came from his eyes and bedewed his cheeks. With a short, sharp cry the boy was in his arms, and they embraced warmly. Dom Lawrence, himself visibly moved at this singular emotion, lifted his arm above the two, and his fingers made the gesture of benecdiction. As for honest Porthos, he was also dabbing eyes, but of a sudden he fell upon his knees and held out his arms to the boy.

"Name of the devil, I say the same thing!" he thundered terribly. "Embrace me! If everyou stand in need of a father, if ever you need money, strength, help -- devil fly away with me if I don't supply all this and more! My son, I am your second father!"

And he, too, folded the boy in his arms. Dom Lawrence, who had looked stern at these resounding oaths, perceived that they went, as it were, by contraries; and a smile came to his lips.

Athos rose. "We must be off," he said.

"May I saddle a horse or mule for -- "

"No." Athos shook his head, and took the hand of the boy. A smile came to his lips -- a smile of ineffable sweetness and serenity. "My son, you will ride in my arms, for we may have to ride fast. If I cannot carry you, my faithful Grimaud will -- "

"Ha!" cried Porthos. "He is a flea, this little one! I could carry him on my hand -- here, my son, step to my hand!"

And in a moment he held Raoul, who stood upright, on the palm of his hand; and then he extended the hand and held the boy at arm's length, with scarcely an effort. Laughing, Athos caught up the boy and set him on the floor.

"Come, Raoul!" he said. "Say adieu to Dom Lawrence.

You have clothes, perhaps, toys, things you would fetch?"

Raoul looked up at him, smiled, pressed his hand.

"There is nothing in the world I lack, my father, now that I have found you!" he said, with an expression of such heartfelt affection that Athos turned pale from very emotion.

The farewells said, Dom Lawrence went with them to the courtyard. Athos signed to Grimaud to bring up the horses. As he did so, there was a sudden commotion at the gate, a shout, and into the courtyard came a horse covered with mud and lather, staggering with exhaustion; from the saddle slipped d'Artagnan, his blue-and-silver garments splashed with mud from neck to boots.

"Ah! I rode hard to find you here!" he exclaimed. "All is well."

"Good." Athos presented him to Dom Lawrence, then looked at the foundered horse. "You cannot ride that poor beast a rod farther -- "

"Let that be my care," broke in the prior. "A moment, gentlemen -- I will myself select a fitting horse from the stable -- "

He hurried away. Athos turned, pointed to d'Artagnan. "My son, let me present a man whom I am proud to call my friend, and whom you may ever call your friend with the same pride. M. d'Artagnan, this is my son Raoul, Vicomte de Bragelonne."

D'Artagnan dropped to one knee, his face beaming, and embraced the boy. As he rose, Athos gave him a swift look of interrogation.

"And your errand?"

"Accomplished," said d'Artagnan. Then his face changed, as he looked from man to boy. He suddenly realized that never again would Athos address him with the title which had so charmed and warmed him with its affection -- the title of my son.

"You met no one on the way here -- Montforge, for example?"

"No," said d'Artagnan. He put hand to pocket, and drew forth the outer sheet of the Thounenin will. Silently, he held it before the eyes of Athos, who changed countenance.

"What? You have not preserved that document -- "

"The outer sheet alone; the remainder I destroyed."

"And the bearer -- Riberac?"

D'Artagnan made the sign of the cross. Dom Lawrence was approaching; behind him came a lay brother, leading a beautiful horse, saddled and bridled.

"With my compliments, M. d'Artagnan," said the prior. Then, as the four mounted, he handed up Raoul to the arms of Athos; he lifted his hand, and they bared their heads to his benediction.

Another moment, and with Grimaud following they were out of the courtyard of St. Saforin and riding Parisward.

"Athos, my friend, you appear like a new man," said d'Artagnan.

"I am a new man," said Athos gravely. "Did I not predict that from this meeting with Lord de Winter would come either a great happiness or a great sorrow? Well, it has come, as you can see for yourself. But tell us all, d'Artagnan! What happened at that house last night? Why did you ride to join us here, instead of keeping the rendezvous in the Vieux Colombier?"

"Merely to join you, I think. Terrible things have happened, Athos." And, while Porthos crowded close to hear them better, d'Artagnan began to recount his adventures since leaving the Hotel de St. Luc.

As the tale proceeded, Porthos uttered admiring ejaculations; Athos listened in silence. D'Artagnan concealed nothing, but poured forth his story as it had happened.

"Ah, my friend," said Athos, when it was finished, "I fear you did wrong, very wrong -- "

Raoul twisted about in his arms, and looked up at him with an expression of childish surprise.

"Mon pere, you told me you were proud to call this gentleman your friend. How, then, can you say that he did wrong? I think he was another Bayard!"

Athos, usually pale, flushed deeply; d'Artagnan was frankly embarrassed, then both of them broke into a laugh as their eyes met.

"And," said d'Artagnan, "since I saved the life of a Marshal of France -- "

"My dear d'Artagnan," cried Porthos in admiration, "I always said you yourself deserved a marshal's baton! This proves it. Then we have succeeded to perfection! The document burned, everything as we would have it! Yet there is one thing we have forgotten." "And what is that?"

demanded d'Artagnan.

"We ride to Paris. Montforge rides from Paris. Ergo, we are fairly certain to meet."

This was true, and the fact had been entirely overlooked. While thus conversing, they had drawn into the highway, from the road leading to the abbey, and now Athos turned and beckoned Grimaud. He made a gesture to ride in advance, touched his pistols, and Grimaud comprehended. The faithful fellow, who was staring with all his eyes at Raoul, put in his spurs and rode on as a vanguard.

"Let us suppose," said d'Artagnan, a trifle uncomfortably, "that the king is not dead. My dear Athos, do you imagine that our activity in this little matter will be remembered by His Eminence? Or, more specifically, my activity?"

Athos shrugged. "Remembered, yes; by Montforge, with whom you must some day settle accounts, also. Punished -- no. Should the king live, Richelieu will be engulfed in a terrific struggle with the Queen Mother and the princes. He knows you are not his enemy, but a servant of the Queen. Since his agents failed to destroy you, he is apt to leave you alone. If he loses the fight, you have nothing to fear. If he wins, he will be so busy sending the Bassompierres and Marillacs to the scaffold or the Bastille, that he will not think of lesser folk."

D'Artagnan nodded, and felt some assurance that Athos spoke the truth.

Grimaud remained half a mile in advance, far enough to give them plenty of warning in case he encountered trouble. No danger appeared, however. Noon was drawing on when before them appeared the inn of Le Moine Qui Keude -- an ancient wayside tavern occupying the triangle between forks of the road.

"Faith!" exclaimed d'Artagnan, staring at the swinging sign. "Is this French or English?"

Athos smiled. "In Champagne, my friend, they say keude for cueille. This is the famous auberge where Henry V of England halted on his way to Paris; it was here that Henri III of France first met the charming Lais; and it is here that we shall stop for a bite if you will ride on and bring Grimaud back."

D'Artagnan touched up his horse and rode past the curious old tavern, which stood apparently to itself between the two roads, the adjacent buildings being at some distance.

He caught up with Grimaud, recalled him, and turned back. This required some little time, for Grimaud had been well in the lead. When they rode into the courtyard of the Plucking Monk, the others had entered the auberge and a groom was baiting the horses; also, a cavalier was in the act of mounting and riding. He saluted d'Artagnan as he passed, and rode forth, but not for Paris; instead, he headed north, and spurred as though in haste to reach Soissons before night.

"Who was that man?" d'Artagnan asked the groom who took his horse.

"I do not know, monsieur. He stayed the night here."

D'Artagnan turned to the inn entrance. He heard the voice of Porthos inside, and was on the point of entering when Grimaud halted him. To his surprise, he saw that

Grimaud was in some agitation.

"Well? Name of the devil, you need not be dumb with me! What is it?"

"That -- that man, monsieur!" said Grimaud, in a sort of croak, and pointed after the lately departed rider.

"What about him?"

"Nevers, Arceuil, Paris!" said Grimaud, with an expression of alarm.

Athos had appeared at the doorway and was listening.

"Eh?" said d'Artagnan, perceiving him. "You heard, Athos? Grimaud says that he saw this same man, who had just departed after spending the night here, at Nevers, Arceuil, and Paris! And I remember now, he rode away at a gallop."

Athos motioned him inside. To Grimaud he made a gesture which the lackey perfectly understood; Grimaud went to eat and drink hurriedly.

D'Artagnan, following his friend, was astonished by the perfect composure of Athos, who betrayed not the least alarm or haste.

CHAPTER XV

TWO DEPART, THREE REMAIN

The interior of the Plucking Monk was astonishing. The structure had originally been built during the English wars; the doors were of iron-bound oak, at least a span thick, and the interior had at some time been nearly gutted by fire.

It was one large room reaching to the roof, and lighted only by two small, high-placed windows. To the right of the hearth was a narrow doorway, the only means of egress to the kitchens and upper buildings; for here was a sharp slant of the ground, so that the front of the auberge was lower than the rear, and there were two steps in the floor.

This hearth was of enormous size. Across its front ran a spit of iron, seven feet in length, which fitted into sockets at each end; these sockets were supplied with chains and weights, and when the weights were raised the spit would turn for an hour at a time of itself. At one side, leaning against the chimney, stood a spare spit, a sharpened bar of iron which would have served Goliath for a bodkin.

In this dark, gloomy, ancient room, whose stones were blackened by the smoke of centuries, Porthos sat at a massive oaken table before the fireplace -- a table eight feet in length and carven magnificently. At the head of the table Raoul was placed, avidly watching while the fat host inspected the fowls browning on the spit and basted them.

"Fetch bread and wine, instantly," said Athos to the host.

Porthos looked at him, surprised, and glanced at d'Artagnan. The latter, comprehending that Athos did not wish to speak before the boy, made a gesture which Porthos understood.

"My son," and Athos held out his hand to that of Raoul, "I am about to make a request of you. Some important business detains me and these gentlemen here. Therefore, I am going to ask that you go on to Paris with Grimaud. I will follow you soon, rejoin you, and together we will go to our future home."

"A little thing to ask, mon pere," replied the boy, smiling. "But I do not like to leave you so soon after finding you!"

"It will not be for long, I promise you," said Athos.

Porthos gaped in astonishment at all this. Grimaud stumbled in, wiping his lips, and came to the table. Athos regarded him sternly, and for once did not spare words.

"Grimaud, you have served me faithfully; upon your service today depends your entire future. Succeed, and you shall never lack. Fail, and I myself will kill you. Do you comprehend?"

"Perfectly, monsieur," said Grimaud, with a bow.

"Very well. You will take my son, here, to Paris. Proceed to the Hotel of the Musketeers. At noon tomorrow, or at noon of whatever day you reach there, Gervais will arrive."

This was altogether too much for the taciturnity of Grimaud. "Monsieur!" he exclaimed. "Not -- not Gervais your father's steward -- "

"The same," said Athos. "If I do not arrive within three days, you and Gervais will take the Vicomte de Bragelonne home to my uncle, and he will become the Comte de la Fere. However, I will arrive. That is all."

He turned to the boy. "My son, you have heard. Eat quickly; you must depart at once."

Raoul began to eat the bread which had been placed on the table. Grimaud departed; in five minutes he reappeared at the entrance with a sign signifying the horse was ready. Athos took Raoul by the hand and conducted him to the doorway. There the boy looked back, and bowed.

"Au revoir, messieurs!" came his sweet, boyish voice. The others bowed. Then they looked at each other as they removed their seats.

"What the devil does this mean?" demanded Porthos.

"The devil," said d'Artagnan.

Athos came back into the room. "There is no one coming as yet," he observed, and advancing to the table, sat down calmly as though nothing remained to be said.

"Well, well!" said d'Artagnan testily. "I confess that I do not comprehend all this, my dear Athos. We see a gentleman departing; we find that he stopped here for the night; Grimaud had seen this man at Nevers, at Arceuil, and at Paris.

Athos smiled at him gently. "So, my son, I take warning! Why was that man here? We do not know -- not to watch us, certainly. Since Grimaud has thrice encountered him, he was obviously watching us upon those occasions, however.

Therefore, he is a Cardinalist. Where Montforge is, we do not know. You did not meet him on your way from Paris; but his errand is certainly to get hold of Raoul. Good! Where the danger is unseen, it is omnipresent."

"Eh? Eh?" Porthos opened his eyes wide. "So that is it -- that man! I thought I had seen him somewhere, myself. But, Athos -- regard! Why do we not all of us ride with the child?"

"They want him, not us," explained Athos. "That man was stationed here for some purpose; I think, to take the child and ride on, in case Montforge and his companions were pursued after getting the boy. You comprehend? Ile recognized us, he knew we had got ahead of them. Therefore Montforge must have been ahead of us after all, perhaps was delayed or caught by the storm. At all events, that man must have ridden to bring him up."

"And," added d'Artagnan, "we would have to do some hard riding to reach Paris ahead, eh?"

"Exactly," affirmed Athos. "I chose to place Raoul in safety. In case Montforge comes, he will think Raoul is here. I do not care to be pursued all my life, my friends; I must meet this man and kill him. It is no longer your affair. Mount, I counsel you, and ride."

"Bah!" said d'Artagnan. "You forget I have my own account with him. Porthos, leave us! Ride after Grimaud -- "

"Will you have the goodness to go to the devil?" roared Porthos angrily. "One for all -- all for one! Am I a fool, a coward, a poltroon? Devil fly away with me if I leave you!

Besides," he added thoughtfully, "there is nothing to show your fine theories are right, Athos."

Athos shrugged. "Granted. We shall wait an hour; if no one arrives, we go on our way."

"And if they do come, then?"

Athos only shrugged again, and said nothing.

D'Artagnan could very well imagine that the man who had spent the night here knew exactly whither he was riding. He eyed the huge room, and laughed shortly.

"Athos," he said, "we could hold this fortress against an army! Here are the capons, the wine is good; what more do we lack?"

"Pistols," said Athos laconically. "All our powder was wet in that accursed rain last night."

So saying, he applied himself to the meal set before them. He was entirely composed; but in his composure was something terrible.

D'Artagnan was by no means composed. He knew that in Montforge they had an adversary as crafty as he was determined; a man no doubt armed with powers from the Cardinal, who would stop at nothing to accomplish his end. As he ate and drank, d'Artagnan thought; and the result was a sudden exclamation which made the others look up.

"Vivadiou! I forgot something. Host!" At his call, the fat host came hurriedly. D'Artagnan laid a gold piece on the table. "Come, my friend! Another like this if your memory is good. The gentleman who was here last night did not give his name?"

"No, monsieur. He arrived just before the storm and went to his room, and remained there."

"Then you have rooms? Where?"

"There, monsieur." The host pointed to the rear door. "Two good ones."

"Ah! And this man said nothing about any companions?"

"Nothing, monsieur. True, he expected a company of gentlemen this afternoon and inquired if I had plenty of fowl ready. As you can see, monsieur, we were making the extra spit -- "

"Gentlemen? How many?"

"A score or more, monsieur."

"Ma foi! From Paris?"

"No, monsieur. I think he said they would be riding for Paris."

D'Artagnan, in consternation, looked at Athos. The latter, however, calmly took out his purse and put it in the hand of the host.

"There is payment in advance, my good man."

"In advance, monsieur!"

"Exactly. For the damage that will be done here. You may leave us."

The host was so astonished that he quite forgot to ask after the other gold piece promised by d'Artagnan.

"You see?" said Athos. "A score of men at least, perhaps more. Montforge could not get the ring made, or would not wait for it. He went to seize the boy, took plenty of men, and depended on his authority from Richelieu. We may yet have to hold your army in check, d'Artagnan."

"Good. We are at your orders, my dear Athos."

"Then I propose that as soon as we appease our hunger, we inspect our defenses."

Porthos was already raising an entrenchment of bones and empty bottles.

In twenty minutes the three friends quitted the table and began their examination. As Athos pointed out, they could hope to hold only this main room of the inn; therefore they looked first at the small doorway by the fireplace. This was regrettably weak, being a makeshift door without bar or bolt. Porthos remedied the lack by overturning the oak table and placing it against the door, whereupon the host appeared with loud wails.

"Be off," d'Artagnan said to him. "Be off, or you will be lucky to escape with your hide!"

"But send us more wine first," added Porthos.

"Alas, monsieur, 1 cannot reach the cellar -- you have blocked the door!"

"Then go around, dolt!" cried d'Artagnan angrily. "You have been well paid in advance; get the wine and set it in the courtyard."

They examined the main entrance, and here found that the double doors, iron-mounted, were almost fitted to withstand grenades. The courtyard was small. Along one side were stables, a high pile of manure before them. On the other flank were the pump and troughs. At the apex of the triangle were the gates, solid barriers on well-oiled hinges. The inn entrance occupied the base of this triangle.

"The walls can be climbed," said Athos, sweeping a glance around. "D'Artagnan, you will open the pourparlers, while we stand ready to shut the gates. We will defend the courtyard first, since our aim is to gain time. When we can no longer hold this position, we will retreat to the inn."

"That is," added Porthos, "if the enemy appears!"

"They have appeared," said d'Artagnan, and pointed to a large body of men just sweeping around a bend in the road, a quarter-mile distant. Applying themselves to the gates, the three friends closed one, leaving the other slightly ajar; beside this, Porthos stood in readiness with the beam of wood which served to hold both closed.

Seeing these preparations, and sighting the horsemen approaching at a gallop, the host and hostlers were no longer in doubt as to what portended; they vanished hastily. Athos eyed the enemy.

"Twenty-three or four," he said. "Good! When the attack opens, gentlemen, I will retire and hold the rear entrenchment; for they will certainly surround the place and attempt entrance from the rear."

"And I," said Porthos, indicating the pile of manure, which lay close to the wall, "will hold this side. The other to you, d'Artagnan."

D'Artagnan advanced to the half-open gate. The enemy were now at close quarters; sighting d'Artagnan, they drew rein, perhaps expecting to be greeted by pistol-shots. At their head d'Artagnan recognized the Comte de Montforge, with the cavalier who had lately departed from the tavern. The others, he perceived, were neither gentlemen nor soldiers, but hastily gathered riffraff of Paris -- lackeys, bretteurs, anyone who could ride and use sword.

While his men dismounted, Montforge rode on alone and halted a few paces from the gateway.

"Good morning, M. d'Artagnan," he said.

"And to you, monsieur," responded d'Artagnan politely. "You have come, no doubt, to finish our interrupted conversation?"

"Unfortunately, monsieur, that is not the case. I am engaged in an errand for His Eminence, and until it is finished, am not my own master."

"In that case, monsieur," said d'Artagnan, "pray do not let me detain you."

Montforge became very angry.

"Monsieur," he exclaimed sharply, "let me warn you that I am acting by the express orders of His Eminence."

"Who is not the ruler of France," said d'Artagnan calmly. "As you may know, monsieur, I am an officer of Musketeers, whose officers take rank over those of other corps. However, I must confess that your words cause me extreme astonishment. One would imagine that I am obstructing or hindering you, when I am doing nothing of the sort. In fact, monsieur, I shall be only too glad to further you in every way possible, since I have only the liveliest good feeling toward His Eminence."

Montforge listened to this speech with suppressed rage, but managed to control himself. He was about to speak when the bellow of Porthos broke forth from the wall to their right.

"Far enough, gentlemen! Halt, or I fire!"

In effect, several of Montforge's companions had come close. D'Artagnan was astonished to see the figure of Porthos looming up above the wall, in his hands a huge old-fashioned arquebus. This weapon had been hanging above the fireplace in the tavern, and besides being at present empty, had certainly not been used since the time of the League; the enemy, however, were not aware of this, and promptly halted.

"You were about to say, monsieur -- ?" prompted d'Artagnan.

"That you have misunderstood me," returned Montforge. "Or rather, you know very well what I want. I have an order from His Eminence to arrest the person of a boy named Raoul d'Aram."

Monsieur," said d'Artagnan, "that is interesting information; but do you expect me to believe the word of an assassin?"

A tide of red suffused the face of Montforge. Then, taking a paper from his pocket, he came close to the gate and handed it to d'Artagnan.

"Let us cease this byplay, monsieur," he said acidly. "You took this child from St. Saforin; he was seen to arrive here with you; he is inside this place. There is my authority, and I demand in the name of the Cardinal that you deliver him to me."

D'Artagnan opened the document and found that Montforge spoke the truth.

"Very well, monsieur," he said, with a bow, as he returned the paper. "I have every respect for the orders of His Eminence, I assure you."

"Good. You will deliver the child at once?"

"Eh?" D'Artagnan assumed an expression of surprise. "I? But, my dear M. de Montforge, this order has nothing to do with me! The boy is not here, I assure you! He is now on the way to Paris; if you hurry after him, you have every chance in the world of catching him!"

"Bah!" said the other, with a gesture of contempt. "I am astonished, monsieur, that a gentleman of your reputation would stoop to lies!"

"No less astonished, monsieur," returned D'Artagnan, "than I am that a gentleman of your name would acquire the reputation which you possess.

The angry features of Montforge went livid at this thrust. "Then you refuse to obey the orders of the Cardinal?" he cried.

"No, monsieur," said d'Artagnan. "I refuse to obey the dictates of a dishonored assassin."

With the rapidity of light, Montforge drew a pistol from its saddle-holster and fired.

Artagnan, however, had glided into the opening behind him; the bullet struck the planks and was deflected. At the same instant the gate swung shut and Porthos hurried from his perch to help with the beam. It fell into place.

Athos departed to the interior, Porthos to his pile of manure. From outside, sounded shouts and orders. The assailants crowded close about the gates, found them solid, and being unable to force an entrance, sought to create one.

The first man to reach the top of the wall did so, unluckily for himself, opposite Porthos. The giant, whirling the heavy arquebus about his head like a feather, loosed it suddenly; the missile struck the unfortunate man, knocked him from the wall, and when his comrades ran to him, they found his body a crushed and lifeless mass.

The battle of Le Moine Qui Keude was open.

CHAPTER XVI

THE ASTONISHING EFFECT OF A KICK UPON A DEAD MAN

The wall of the courtyard was ten feet in height. Within two minutes, the head and shoulders of a man appeared on the side of Porthos; another appeared opposite d'Artagnan. They then remained stationary, without attempting to scale the wall.

"Come, descend!" roared Porthos, who had drawn his sword. "Over with you, rascals!"

"We are too polite, monsieur," said the man on his side, and he turned to look back at his comrades who supported him. "They have no pistols," he said. "Quickly!"

The man opposite d'Artagnan said nothing, but took a pistol handed to him, leveled it at d'Artagnan, and fired.

The bullet pierced the musketeer's hat.

"Another!" exclaimed the man.

D'Artagnan ground his teeth with rage. He perceived instantly that without powder they could not defend the courtyard. The enemy had no intention of risking a hand-to-hand combat when these two men on the wall could shoot down the defenders without peril to themselves.

"Back, Porthos!" he exclaimed sharply. "Take shelter!"

Am I a crab to run backward? Name of the devil!" cried Porthos furiously. "We held the Bastion St. Gervais against an army -- cannot we hold this fortress against a rabble?"

His adversary on the wall grinned at him and raised a pistol upon the parapet.

"Here is a flea too large to miss!" he observed. "Vive le Cardinal!"

The explosion of the weapon drowned his words. Porthos, as though buffeted by an invisible hand, was knocked backward and rolled to the bottom of the manure pile. D'Artagnan ran to him, but Porthos rose, holding the hilt of his sword. The bullet had struck the blade and shattered it.

"Vive le Roi!" bellowed Porthos."Cowards! Traitors! Murderers --"

At this instant the man on the right flank fired again.

Porthos spun around, took two or three steps, and then fell headlong at the inn entrance. Dropping his weapon, d'Artagnan caught him by the shoulders and dragged him inside. The face of Porthos was covered with blood.

"Athos! To the doors!"

"Impossible," came the calm response of Athos. "I am --"

There was a crash. The massive table, blocking the small door beside the hearth, flew backward and fell to one side. The door behind it was carried off its hinges. D'Artagnan saw the end of a beam forced into the room, carried by several men, who stumbled along with it.

Athos, standing beside the opening, lunged as coolly as though he were in a salle d'armes. The first man fell forward on his face. The second plunged across him, clutching at his throat. Above and across them fell the beam.

"Hail, Mary!" screamed the third man, as Athos' sword transfixed him.

Fascinated by this spectacle, d'Artagnan suddenly turned to his own flank. In the courtyard, two men had dropped over the walls and were unfastening the gates. Pulling Porthos farther inside, d'Artagnan closed the massive doors of the inn, dropped the bar in place, and caught at his sword as the voice of Athos reached him.

"D'Artagnan! They are preparing to fire -- "

Two or three pistols were discharged together, the balls whistling through the chamber and flattening on the stone walls. After them, a man came rushing through the opening, sword in hand; he hesitated before the obscurity of the place, and Athos ran him through the heart. This made the fourth body upon the heap.

"Good!" said Athos coolly. "They burst down our door, and replace it with their own bodies. That is fair. Porthos -- he is dead?"

"I do not know," confessed d'Artagnan. "I think he is."

A tremendous clang resounded through the room. The enemy were battering at the closed doors.

"Inside, there!" As the summons came to them through the half-closed passage, d'Artagnan trembled with fury; he recognized the voice of Montforge. "Surrender at once, or I will give no quarter!"

"It is we who make offers; we do not receive them," returned Athos imperturbably.

"Fire!" shouted Montforge.

A number of pistols were discharged. Athos staggered, turned half round, then took two steps and dropped into a chair by a table against the side wall.

"Athos!" With a terrible cry of grief, d'Artagnan ran to his friend. Athos, lifting his head, pushed him away.

"Quick, to your post!" he cried. "I am not yet dead -- "

And laying down his sword upon the table, he tore open his shirt and calmly began to bandage two wounds, one in his thigh, the other in his left shoulder. A thunderous sound re-echoed through the room; the massive doors were beginning to bend beneath the battering of the men outside.

D'Artagnan darted to the rear entrance. He was barely in time; two men were scrambling over the pile of bodies, and with a cry of joy d'Artagnan recognized one of them as Montforge.

"This time you will not escape me, assassin!" he cried.

For response, Montforge lifted a pistol and fired; but the powder flashed in the pan. His comrade flung himself upon D'Artagnan, slipped in a pool of blood, and spitted himself upon the rapier of the musketeer as he fell. He lay upon the floor, coughing terribly in the fumes of powder, and presently coughed no more.

No others came through the rear entrance.

Dropping his pistol, Montforge attacked d'Artagnan, sword inhand.

"Now for your comb, my cockerel!" he exclaimed mockingly. Then he staggered -- the rapier of d'Artagnan struck him exactly over the heart, but it did not pierce.

"So!" cried d'Artagnan furiously. "I forgot that you were a coward and wore mail beneath your shirt -- "

"In the throat, my son!" came the voice of Athos, who was watching them. "In the throat!"

Montforge turned his head for an instant, and saw Athos sitting at the table.

"Your turn next, my friend," he cried.

For an instant, d'Artagnan despaired of his life, so deadly was the attack of Montforge that now overwhelmed him. For all his skill, he could scarce parry those incredible lunges, those ripostes which rippled from a wrist of steel. He was driven back, was forced to remain upon the defensive; and all the while there thundered a louder and louder clamor as the doors began to yield, their ancient iron hinges bending and breaking.

Suddenly the foot of d'Artagnan slipped. He fell heavily upon hands and knees; the rapier was dashed from his hand by the force of his fall. Montforge drew back a pace. Then, as d'Artagnan was in the act of rising, he leaned forward and plunged his sword into the young man's breast.

A terrible cry burst from Athos, as he saw d'Artagnan fall prostrate.

Next instant, Montforge found himself confronted by a frightful spectacle -- a man, half naked, blood upon shoulder and leg, whose eyes blazed from a livid countenance. So awful was the aspect of Athos in this instant that Montforge recoiled a step.

"Assassin!" cried Athos, and engaged that sword, wet

with the blood of d'Artagnan.

In this moment Athos, ever a magnificent swordsman, was swept to superhuman heights by his grief and fury. Thrice his blade swept about the blade of Montforge, thrust it aside, lunged for the throat; thrice Montforge evaded those inimitable attacks. Suddenly the arm of Athos moved. His blade seemed to curl about that of Montforge, then tore it from the latter's hand and sent it flying across the room.

"Life for life!" said Athos in a hollow voice, and drove his point into the throat of Montforge.

He drew the blade clear of the falling man. For an instant he looked down at Montforge, then he threw the weapon aside.

"I have dishonored my sword for the first time," he murmured, "but I have avenged my friend."

And quietly, with a smile upon his lips, he came to his knees, drooped, fell forward.

At this instant the doors at the entrance sagged down. The cross-bar held, but the hinges of one door burst, and those of the other cracked. The enormous mass of wood and iron swung inward at one side; it checked, caught, hung there by the cracked hinges of the other door, giving access to those without by the one open side. They attempted to shove it down, but it resisted. They gave up the effort and flooded into the room.

"Ah! ah!" cried the first man in, as he stumbled across the figure of Porthos. "Here is the big rascal I purged with a leaden pill!"

And he kicked the body of Porthos heavily. At this kick, Porthos opened his eyes, but no one perceived him, for the scene before them had now drawn the attention of all those men, and with confused oaths and cries they hastened across the room.

The scene was frightful; it appeared that no living person remained to greet them.

D'Artagnan lay upon his face, a trickle of blood coming from beneath his arm. Athos lay across the legs of Montforge. Behind them, the dead men and the fallen beam were piled in the rear entrance.

"The captain is dead!" cried one of the throng in consternation.

"They are all dead!" cried another.

"Name of the devil, then who pays us?" shouted a third. "Get the captain's purse, take what we find!"

And all of them with one accord clustered about the body of Montforge, to plunder the dead.

Near the entrance, Porthos came to one knee, then gained his feet. He was almost unhurt; the ball that stunned him had barely cut the scalp, letting blood but doing no worse damage. As now, among those struggling, plundering figures, he saw the half-naked form of Athos and the fallen body of d'Artagnan, his eyes distended, a flood of color rushed into his face, and from his lips burst a wild and horrible cry.

"Murderers -- you shall pay for this!"

Unarmed as he was, he rushed forward.

Next instant, even through the madness of his despair

and rage he could perceive his folly, for they heard his cry and swung about, snarling like wolves. Swords glittered; a pistol crashed out, but the ball went wild. Porthos, evading the lunge of a rapier, caught sight of the huge spit leaning against the fireplace. He hurled himself toward it, reached it, and grasped it in both hands.

This pointed bar of steel, which one man could scarce lift, whirled about his head like a sliver of wood. The nearest bravo, rushing upon Porthos with sword extended, was struck full across the face by this terrific weapon.

A fearful scream burst from the others. Instead of crowding forward, they crowded back, away from this giant who flung himself upon them, face empurpled, foam slavering his lips. Porthos was in the grip of one of those convulsive rages in which he was no longer a man but a destroying angel.

He leaped among them, striking.

Now in the obscurity of this room, through the fumes of powder, ascended fearful and hideous sounds; the revolting reek of fresh blood stank in the nostrils of men. Amid the rising cloud of dust might be discerned frantic shapes rushing to and fro. The piercing sharpness of cries and screams followed swift upon thudding crunches as that grisly weapon fell, now here, now there, crushing out life and human shape.

Panic fell upon these men; they crowded about the entrance, and there Porthos fell upon them and scattered them, and slew two as they fought madly together at the narrow opening. At this, their blind panic was changed into the instinct of the wild beast to destroy that which is destroying him. Their weapons had been flung away or dropped. None the less, they came crowding upon the dim and terrible figure of Porthos gripping at him before and behind; he thrust the pointed bar and transfixed one man so that he screamed and writhed like some helpless beetle dying upon a pin, but there the steel spit was torn out of his hand and lost.

In this chamber of dust and blood and death, the one uprose among the dozen that tore at him, a giant among pigmies. Suddenly something was seen to move in the air above their heads, and there sounded a rushing as it were of wings, and the pitiful terrified wail of a man sharply rising. Then they fell back from around him in mad horror, for Porthos, stooping, had plucked up a man by the ankles and was swinging him about his head, and beating with this flail of flesh and bone upon those before him, and crushing them down. Upon this, they fled.

And now, abruptly, the madness went out of Porthos. He dropped the broken body from his hands, wiped the blood and sweat out of his eyes, and stood peering around him in a sort of half-comprehending abhorrence. A trembling seized upon him. A dying man was shrieking at his feet, and he turned away, crossing himself with shaking hand.

"Mon Dieu, what have I done!" he groaned.

He went to the doors, wrenched at them. In a spasmodic effort he put forth his strength and tore them from the remaining hinges; the mass of iron and wood swung at him, he checked and turned it, and with a heave of his shoulders sent it over with a resounding crash. He stumbled out into the sunlight, wiping his streaming face.

Upon his benumbed brain broke sharply the remembrance of Athos and d'Artagnan. He turned, went back into that place of death, and presently bore forth the body of Athos in his arms; the body breathed, and with a sob of relief Porthos laid it down and went back inside. He paid no heed to the remaining assailants, nor cared that these were escaping by the rear entrance. He searched until he found d'Artagnan, picked him up, and carried him outside, where he set him down beside Athos.

Panting, he stood and gazed around with blood-shot eyes. From the interior of the inn came a low groaning of stricken men. From outside the wall of the courtyard lifted the sound of men running; five figures came into sight through the shattered gates, making for the clump of grazing horses. There were five survivors of Montforge's party.

Porthos paid no heed to these things. He went to the pump, plunged his head into the trough, and, dripping, brought back water which he dashed over Athos and d'Artagnan. The latter stirred, moved, and suddenly sat up, blinking around.

"Ma foi! Where am I?" he exclaimed. "Is that you, Porthos?"

Porthos, seeing that d'Artagnan was not greatly hurt, was kneeling over Athos and bandaging the two wounds of the latter.

"Yes, it is I," said Porthos gloomily. "I thought you were dead, my friend."

"Evidently I am not," said d'Artagnan, and surveyed himself. "Ah! There's a scrape along my ribs at least -- "

He opened his clothes, to disclose a wound, alarming in appearance but not at all dangerous, where the sword of Montforge had glided along his ribs.

"My new suit is certainly ruined," he observed. "Well, I must obey the example of M. de Bassompierre, who never wears a suit more than once or twice!"

He drew from his pocket the folded vellum sheet of the Thounenin will. It was disfigured by a cut where the sword had passed through, and was stained with blood, but was none the less readable.

"Good!" said d'Artagn an. "And Montforge where is he? What has happened?"

"He is dead," said Porthos. He suddenly desisted from his work, and began a frantic search of his person. He explored pockets, looked everywhere; at length he stared at d'Artagnan with an expression of such terror that d'Artagnan, despite his wound, struggled to his feet.

"What is the matter, Porthos?" he exclaimed in alarm. "What has happened?"

"Ah!" Porthos uttered a groan. "I am lost!"

"Why, in heaven's name? You are hurt?"

"I am lost," repeated Porthos in a sepulchral voice, and showed a broken silver chain which he had taken from beneath his shirt. "The portrait of Madame du Valon, which

I swore never to remove from about my neck -- well, it is gone!"

D'Artagnan gaped at him, then suddenly broke into a laugh.

"It is no laughing matter, I assure you," said Porthos. "You do not understand these things -- "

D'Artagnan laughed the harder. At this instant he perceived that Athos had opened his eyes; and kneeling, he clasped the bandaged figure in his arms.

Porthos departed to search for his lost portrait, but he did not find it.

EPILOGUE

The three friends reached the Hotel de Treville late the following afternoon, for it was necessary to obtain a coach before Athos could be transported. Thanks to the miraculous balsam of d'Artagnan, his wounds promised to be in no way serious, but they effectually prevented him from keeping the saddle for some days. At the hotel of the Musketeers, they learned that Grimaud and Raoul had arrived, had met Gervais at noon, and had departed with him. Since Athos did not know the whereabouts of his uncle's steward, it was necessary to await his return on the following day.

They discovered, further, that Mousqueton had thrice arrived in search of Porthos, and on the third occasion the former Madame Coquenard had come also, promising to return very shortly. At this news Porthos was in some consternation.

D'Artagnan had his wound dressed anew, and immediately after dinner that night prepared two missives. The first contained no writing; it held only the outer sheet of the Thounenin will, and was addressed to Mme. la Duchesse de Chevreuse, at her chateau of Dampierre. As Athos rightly said, the sword-thrust and the blood staining the document told their own story.

The second epistle was a letter addressed to His Eminence Cardinal de Richelieu. In it d'Artagnan wrote:

"Monseigneur: I have the honor to report that the two errands which you had the goodness to confide to me, have been performed.

The verbal message was delivered. There was apparently no response, since the person to to whom it was addressed was subject to fainting spells. The letter to a person in Paris was also delivered. As Your Eminence said nothing of any answer, I did not await one but departed immediately.

I regret that I have not the honor to deliver this report in person, owing to a wound received at the hands of certain bretteurs who attacked me. I await your orders, Monseigneur, being your very humble and very obedient servant,

Artagnan."

D'Artagnan showed this letter to Athos, who read it attentively.

"You must rewrite it."

"How?" said d'Artagnan. "What have I misspelled?"

"Nothing. You must change the wording to read 'a severe wound . . . which confines me to my bed.' It will make an excellent impression upon His Eminence. No one knows exactly what happened among you, Bassompierre, and Mile. de Sirle -- except Bassompierre, who does not know all. Richelieu will probably deem you sufficiently punished. If he discovers that Raoul was not the son of Her Majesty, but of Chevreuse well, you may be entirely safe!"

"But I am not confined to my bed "

"Confine yourself for the night. Our complaisant surgeon will gladly add a notation to this effect."

"But you, Athos -- "

"I leave the service, my son. As soon as I am able to write, my resignation goes in. There is nothing to fear, believe me! If the king dies, Richelieu is lost. If the king lives -- then greater men than you and I are lost, and in the stench of their blood we are forgotten, I promise you!"

D'Artagnan did not entirely agree with this reasoning, but he perceived the force of the advice, and promptly followed it.

Neither he nor Athos saw Porthos again at this time, for when they arose next morning, it was to learn that a coach had arrived very early, a lady had alighted and asked for Porthos, and that Porthos, summoned from his bed, had mounted into the coach with the lady and departed. He did not leave so much as a note for his friends, but Grimaud, who witnessed the scene, said that Porthos had flung both arms toward heaven as though in supplication, and had then meekly obeyed the orders of the lady.

A week later, Athos departed for his estates, d'Artagnan for his duty.

Upon the day Louis XIII was expected to die at Lyon, at almost the very hour predicted for his death by the physicians, he unexpectedly recovered; but he made his mother a secret promise that as soon as peace was concluded with the Empire, he would dismiss Richelieu.

The court returned to Paris, the king going to Versailles, the queen-mother to her palace of the Luxembourg. She dissembled, and pretended great friendship for the Cardinal. Alarmed by this, Richelieu investigated, heard of the promise made by Louis XIII, and despatched a courier to Ratisbon ordering Pere Joseph not to sign the treaty.

It had already been signed. Marie de Medici sent imperatively for her son.

On the morning of November tenth, the king arrived quietly at the Luxembourg, accompanied only by Bassompierre. Richelieu, already warned, made haste to be present at this interview, but when he reached the Luxembourg, it was too late. The doors of the ante-chamber were locked. The king and Marie de Medici were alone in the latter's cabinet; orders were given that no one was to be allowed entrance.

Here in the heart of this vast palace, secure from the disturbing influence of Richelieu or others, Marie de Medici indicated the desk beside the window, and commanded her son to sit down and write the dismissal of the Minister. Louis, who feared the tongue of his mother above all things, yielded and took his seat.

At this instant a small door opened in the wall. The door led by a private passage into the chapel of the Luxembourg, and had not been locked. In the opening was framed the scarlet-clad figure of Richelieu.

"He is here -- all is lost!" exclaimed the king.

Pretending not to hear these words, Richelieu smiled and came forward.

"Your Majesties, I believe, were speaking of me?" he observed.

Marie de Medici was infuriated by the audacity of this man whom she had raised to power. The intrusion upon her privacy outraged her pride; the upsetting of her plans kindled her virulence; she flew into a paroxysm of rage and unloosed upon Richelieu all the floodgates of her hatred and wrath.

She berated him, reproached him, accused him, in a storm of the most violent passion imaginable. Her storm of fury could not be checked nor averted. Richelieu fell upon his knees before her; his excuses, even his tears, only added fire to her rage. Perceiving himself lost, he rose and demanded permission to retire.

The king dared not reply. The queen-mother loosed a fresh storm of passion. His features livid, Richelieu bowed and quitted the room.

Upon the following day, the king signed an order placing Louis de Marillac in command of the army, as Marie de Medici had demanded; this order recalled Schomberg and La Force, who were Richelieu's adherents. Louis XIII then departed for Versailles; he was followed by Michel de Marillac, named by Marie de Medici as Minister in the place of Richelieu. The great Cardinal had fallen.

That day, the hotel of Richelieu was deserted. The entire court thronged to the Luxembourg, paying their addresses to Marie de Medici, complimenting her, surrounding her with adulation. The Spanish Ambassador was overjoyed. Anne of Austria smiled for the first time in months. Couriers were sent forth to carry the news to Madrid, Vienna, London. All Paris rejoiced at the ruin of the hated Cardinal.

Richelieu perceived that he was lost. He prepared to take refuge at Le Havre; his mules, laden with his most valuable effects, set forth upon the Pontoise road. He gave orders to prepare his coach. He was on the point of departure, when St. Simon arrived from Versailles ordering him to the presence of the king.

When Richelieu arrived, Louis XIII ordered that they be left alone together.

Marie de Medici was holding triumphant court at the Luxembourg, surrounded by the nobles of the realm and throngs of sycophant courtiers; she was intoxicated by victory, and paused at nothing inventing her hatred of the fallen Minister. And at the same moment, the king was signing orders at Versailles which were being dictated by Richelieu; unknown to any, not only was the Cardinal reinstated in power, but this power was made absolute. Marshal de Marillac was arrested and sent to Paris a prisoner. Michel de Marillac was deprived of the seals and banished. This eleventh of November, 1630, was named by Bassompierre "The Day of Dupes"; unfortunately for himself, he was one of the dupes.

Richelieu had turned disaster into triumph; and those who had caused his disaster, now paid. The Duc de Guise fled into exile. Marie de Medici was arrested, to die in exile. Those about her were struck down right and left. Bassompierre, warned, might have fled; he preferred to go home and destroy the six thousand love-letters he bad received from ladies. He spent the next twelve years writing his Memoirs in a room of the Bastille, of which he had at one time been the Governor.

On the morning after the arrest of Bassompierre,

d'Artagnan was summoned to the cabinet of the Cardinal. He first destroyed all his letters and papers, then obeyed the summons.

"Good morning, M. d'Artagnan," said Richelieu affably. "I understand that you escorted M. de Bassompierre to the Bastille yesterday?"

The young man bowed."I had the honor, Your Eminence, though it was Sieur de Launay who executed the order of arrest."

"I sent for you, monsieur, hoping you might enlighten me upon a certain subject. You have, I perceive, quite recovered from your recent wound?"

"Your Eminence does me too much honor in remembering such trifles," returned d'Artagnan, feeling a cold chill.

"Not at all, not at all," said Richelieu, smoothly. "It has been brought to my attention, monsieur, that a Musketeer of your company has left the service and assumed the title of the Comte de la Fere. Is not this the gentleman known as Athos?"

"Yes, Monseigneur," replied d'Artagnan, whose brow was now beaded with perspiration.

"Ah!" said Richelieu musingly. "He has, it appears, adopted a son, the Vicomte de Bragelonne."

In these words, d'Artagnan perceived that the Cardinal knew everything.

"Your Eminence," he said, in a sort of desperation, "only those who are truly great can know the meaning of generosity. My friend Athos is the noblest man alive; he is incapable of the least deceit, pettiness or dishonor; he is even incapable of ambition, which is the most petty of all things in his eyes. If Your Eminence would have the graciousness to grant Athos a recompense for his years of service, I believe he would appreciate it above all things."

"How?" asked Richelieu, with a slight frown. "A recompense? A pension, you mean?"

"Not at all, Monseigneur," said d'Artagnan. "Your Eminence is a statesman, a minister, a great man; but before these things, a cardinal. If Your Eminence would but send the son of Athos your benediction, I am certain that Athos would esteem it above all other things!"

Richelieu looked truly astonished. His gaze rested upon the features of d'Artagnan, and then, with one of his rare impulses, he smiled and held out his hand to the young man.

"Monsieur," he said, "there are less charming things in the world than the frank audacity of youth. I shall accept your advice in this matter. Have you nothing to ask for yourself?"

"Faith, Monseigneur," said the astonished d'Artagnan, "there is nothing I need, since you do me the honor of commending me!"

This interview cost d'Artagnan above three hundred crowns. Among the papers he had destroyed was a receipt from his tailor; two weeks later, the tailor claimed his bill for the second time, and having burned the receipt, d'Artagnan was forced to pay again. However, he did not regret the loss.

THE END

www.ingramcontent.com/pod-product-compliance
Lightning Source LLC
Chambersburg PA
CBHW031940010726
47493CB00007B/2003
* 9 7 8 1 4 7 3 3 2 6 5 8 3 *